The Ride of Her Life

Also by Jennifer Dugan

Love at First Set

The Ride of Her Life

A Novel

JENNIFER DUGAN

AVON

An Imprint of HarperCollins*Publishers*

THE RIDE OF HER LIFE. Copyright © 2024 by Jennifer Lynn Dugan. All rights reserved. Printed in the United States of America. No part of this book may be used or reproduced in any manner whatsoever without written permission except in the case of brief quotations embodied in critical articles and reviews. For information, address HarperCollins Publishers, 195 Broadway, New York, NY 10007.

HarperCollins books may be purchased for educational, business, or sales promotional use. For information, please email the Special Markets Department at SPsales@harpercollins.com.

FIRST EDITION

Interior design by Diahann Sturge-Campbell
Barn illustration © Brad/The Noun Project
Horse illustration © Semilla Solar/The Noun Project

Library of Congress Cataloging-in-Publication Data has been applied for.

ISBN 978-0-06-330751-3

24 25 26 27 28 LBC 5 4 3 2 1

To anyone chasing their happily ever after with hay in their hair

The Ride of Her Life

Chapter One

Is it still illegal to murder people?"

"It depends on who you ask and how much money you have," answers my best friend Nat, who's also working the morning rush at The Grind coffee bar with me. "Why?"

"Look at him," I say, gesturing to the man by the creamer— the man who is very obviously overfilling his to-go cup and spilling it *everywhere*. "I literally just asked him if he wanted me to leave room for creamer, and he said no." I sigh, reaching for the rag we keep stashed under the counter for this very reason.

"I personally don't think it should ever be illegal to murder a man who spills coffee," Nat says quietly from her place beside the milk frother.

Ah yes, I knew there was a reason I asked her. It turns out, lesbians *do* tend to give the best life advice, something I learned a few years back as a baby gay, just figuring out how to handle life after realizing women were significantly hotter than dudes.

Nat took it upon herself to introduce me around, and explain the politics of living in a city with a small enough queer population that everyone is already someone else's ex—she's only four years older than me, twenty-eight to my twenty-four, but she's been out since she could talk and loves to joke that queer years are like dog years and in that case, she's old enough to be my cranky lesbian grandma . . . even though she's really more of a big sister to me.

We met my freshman year of college, when she was auditing an acting class that I was forced to take as an elective, despite majoring in event and hospitality management. *She* was using it to fatten up her résumé and con the photography students into giving her free headshots.

We're opposite in almost every way—sure, we're both white and queer, but she has chestnut hair to my blond, her brown eyes could only be called striking and dark, while mine are a muddy hazel as if they couldn't pick a color so decided to just be all of them. Nat's also got a Hollywood body and teeth whiter than snow, while I'm a little softer, less flashy. "The perfect girl next door," my mom always says, which always just feels like a nicer way to say "plain."

But most importantly, Nat has her shit together, and I definitely don't. She says it's a confidence thing, but I don't know.

Nat's got the kind of attitude that makes you believe it when she says she's going to be a film star someday, even if she does have to keep changing her date of birth on her acting résumés to make her perpetually twenty-three, while I've been telling everyone that I hope, maybe, sort of, if the stars align, to pursue my dream of running my own event planning company.

I'm lucky to have her holding my hand through this whole figuring myself out phase I've been in since I kissed a girl on my twentieth birthday . . . and through the multitude of moving-too-fast relationships and subsequent breakups that have ensued since. I can't help it; I get excited.

Someone flashes me love eyes and I'm renting a U-Haul faster than Nat can hold me back . . . or remind me that while my taste in women is still developing, my taste in men is decidedly shitty.

That's another big difference between us: I don't fully rule out any other genders. I'm happily bi, no matter who I'm dating. A couple years ago, I had a lovely three-month relationship with a beekeeper with a talented tongue. When she said she wanted to spend our whole lives planting flowers and going down on each other, I believed her. Unfortunately, one expensive bee suit and three beekeeping classes later, I discovered that just because *I* had assumed that meant we were exclusive didn't mean that was actually the case.

After that, came Ashton, a motorcyclist who called me *baby*. Nat was convinced I was going to end up an organ donor the way Ashton rode, which didn't help my nerves any. That one ended when they realized that I had, in fact, significantly oversold my interest and experience with motorcycles. It turns out they were looking for a "backpack" type of motorcycle girlfriend, and I was more of a shrieking, clawing, please-don't-go-over-fifteen-mph kind of girlfriend.

Most recently—as in just a couple weeks ago—I got out of an eight-month live-in relationship with an unfortunate man named Blake who believed his fantasy football team was essentially a legitimate full-time job—like he would literally tweet the players feedback after their games and warn them he would bench them if they didn't shape up. Yeah. Investment banker by day, NFL coach from the couch by night.

I cannot even begin to tell you how fully I tried to immerse myself into that sport. I could tell you the difference between PPR and standard scoring. I could talk about the pros and cons of draft leagues, deep leagues, and dynasty leagues. I could work the waiver wire like the best of them.

I thought Blake was really the one. I thought he was going to stick. He was even nice to my mother, agreeing to join me at her house for dinner a couple nights a week to ease her stress when I finally moved out to live with him.

It didn't stick though—of course not. Worst of all, he was the one who dumped me—well, sort of. He told me he didn't think it was fair to leave me a "football widow" for the several months of the year the games were played, to which I replied that I thought the fact that he was fucking his "work wife" was maybe the real problem here.

He was shocked. He had no idea I knew. It could have been a real boss babe moment. Except instead, like the mess I am, I promptly burst into tears and locked myself in the bedroom while he panicked on the other side of the door. Nat rushed right over, and before I knew it, we were gathering up as much of my stuff as we could and heading back to my mom's.

She says technically my retort—and the fact that I left that night—makes the breakup mutual, but it certainly didn't *feel* mutual, not when he kept the condo and the cat, and I was back living in my childhood bedroom with garbage bags full of clothes. So yeah, lately I've been feeling like the antithesis of adulthood. *Failure to launch, thy name is Molly.*

My mom was thrilled to have me back. No surprise there. If breaking up with Blake didn't already make me want to die, then moving back home definitely did.

Maybe I'm being mean. My mom is great. She wants me to be happy, of course she does. But also, she would love it if I lived at home forever. I can't decide if she just doesn't want to be alone—I've kind of been her de facto partner in life for the last decade plus—or if she's still trying to make up for the fact that she had to liquidate my college savings account after she divorced my dad . . . who coincidentally was also fucking his work wife. That six-figure student loan hanging around my neck isn't doing either one of us any favors.

It turns out entry level jobs in the wedding industry, even with a fancy degree and multiple unpaid internships, pay way worse than the tips I make at the coffee shop. Like *can't pay my student loans* kind of low, and with my mom as a cosigner on them that couldn't fly. The real secret to making it as a wedding planner in this city is money—a lot of it—and connections. I'm not saying all the big planners are nepo babies, but I'm not *not* saying it. They have trust funds and gala connections; I have Pinterest boards, and debt . . . and now a coffee-covered condiment station.

Nat pushes past me to hand a customer their vanilla latte (with nonfat milk and eleven Splendas) wearing the fakest smile I've ever seen. "Kill him or clean up his mess, I don't care, but do something. It's dripping all over the floor and we're getting a line."

I don't miss the way she whispers, "kill kill kill" as I step out from behind the counter with my rag and head toward the tall red-haired man, who is still frantically trying to corral his epic coffee mistake—with his bare hands—before more of it falls on the floor. *The napkins are right there, dude, what are you doing?*

"I got it!" I say cheerfully, pushing him out of the way and catching the river of steaming hot liquid that has just soaked into our sugar. We've lost at least a dozen packets to this atrocity, and not even the generic ones either, the expensive brown ones. Randy, my boss, is going to scream at me when he does inventory. "Sugar doesn't grow on trees," he always grumbles. I wonder if he knows that it *does* basically grow on plants though.

"Thank you," the man says, relieved, but I shoot him a glare anyway. His coffee says *Erik* in big, bold Sharpie letters and suddenly that is my least favorite name on earth.

"I did offer to leave you room for cream, *Erik*," I remind him, the coffee scalding my palms as I finish cleaning up.

"I just wanted a splash! I didn't need room!" He holds his chin up defiantly, even though his tone is somewhat apologetic.

"And how'd that work out for you?" I ask, tossing the damp sugar packets in the trash and slinging the dish towel over my shoulder, remembering too late that it's absolutely soaked. *Shit.* Erik raises his eyebrows at my now irrevocably stained white T-shirt before taking what's left of his coffee and slinking away into a dark corner with his laptop.

I bet he thinks he's going to write the next great American novel. I bet he thinks that even exists. He's about as likely to get a publishing deal as I am to hit the lotto and become a wedding planner. He has his laptop. I have daydreams and too many bridal magazine subscriptions.

And a twenty-nine-point-five-hour-a-week barista job (carefully scheduled so that none of us qualify for health insurance).

And another twenty-plus-hour-a-week virtual job doing customer service calls for a local heating and cooling company.

When you subtract sleep and commute time, that leaves me about fifteen hours a week give or take to eat, shower, and live. I wonder how many hours Mr. I-didn't-need-room gets.

"You're aware your shift ended like twelve minutes ago, right?" Nat asks, wincing at the sight of my shirt when I walk over.

No! That means I'm already down to about fourteen hours and forty-eight minutes of free time this week, and it's only Monday. "Going, going," I call, even though we haven't split our tips yet.

"Hey, KiKi and I were going to go check out that new brew pub up the street tonight for dinner. You wanna come?"

I blow out a breath because of course I want to come out with her and her ridiculously talented contractor girlfriend—they're two of my favorite people in the world—but we both know I can't. "I have to log in for the furnace place pretty soon," I remind her, and she groans.

"What happened to all those 'big city dreams' we had when we were in college," she teases, snapping her towel at me. "Would it kill you to come out once in a while? For old times? I'm starting to get a complex here."

I melt a little at her puppy-dog eyes. "Yeah, well, it was easier to have those dreams when I was living off student loans instead of paying them," I say, slipping my apron over my head and clocking out. "Next time I have a day I don't have to work back-to-back, I promise I'll come out and, hey, if you pick up the tab, I'll even give KiKi a front row seat to how well I can drink you under the table."

"As if," she snorts. "Here, take this," Nat says, handing me the paper cup labeled *Dateline*—today's tip cup battle was *Dateline* vs *48 Hours*, and *Dateline* was ahead by a mile. This isn't fair to her. "No, that's . . . no. There was like one *48 Hours* dollar for every ten *Datelines*. Come on, just split it even. I'll grab my half tomorrow."

"It's fine, Molly," she groans, already walking away. "KiKi moving in freed up a lot of cash. I can swing it this week. Plus, I have that callback. By this time next week, I might be filming in Outer Banks."

"Nat."

"This is where you say thank you, bitch," she says, flipping her hair back dramatically.

"Thank you, bitch," I laugh, doing my best imitation of her.

"Now get out of here before I change my mind."

* * *

"I GOT US a movie from Redbox for later," my mother calls in a singsong voice before I've even gotten my shoes off. "And I'm making meat loaf."

I'm in the front foyer, holding a coffee I brought home for her in one hand, and my *Dateline* tips in the other. I trip and almost drop them both, catching myself at the last minute. Even staring down the barrel of yet another "mother daughter date night," the billionth since I've moved back in, I will not end up like tall cream splash man. I refuse.

"Great," I say, mustering whatever cheer I can. I had been looking forward to a quiet night in my room after my customer service shift. I was going to chip away at my free WordPress website I'm building for Immaculate Events Inc. and study the latest in bridal gown trends, but it looks like my mom found a replacement Blu-ray player after all.

I do not understand that woman's aversion to streaming.

"It's a rom-com about a wedding planner who falls in love with a groom!" she chirps, sticking her head out of the kitchen. "It's right up your alley. I thought we could watch with a late dinner. You're done with the call center at eight, right?"

"Yep," I say quietly, and then add a thumbs-up when she frowns. She's trying, I know she is, but the last thing I want to do is watch a fictionalized version of the life I can't have.

"Is something wrong?" she asks, her frown deepening.

"No, just a long day already," I say. *And now I have to spend the night feeling suffocated and guilty about wanting to move out after spending the next four hours asking homeowners how their recent furnace repair went.*

"We can skip the movie," Mom says, studying my face. "I'll have dinner ready when you're done and then you can just rest. You look tired, honey."

"Okay, thanks," I say. She looks a little crestfallen at how eagerly I agree, and the guilt rises up. "We'll watch the movie another day, it sounds so good. Sorry, I just had a really annoying last customer and I need a minute to reset."

Hey, at least it's only half a lie. Mr. Coffee Spiller *was* annoying, and I do need a reset . . . just more like a total life one.

"Good thing I know just what will cheer you up." Mom grins. "Go look at your bed. There's a surprise for you."

I raise my eyebrows and head down the hall, utterly confused until I push open my door and see my old American Girl doll sitting on the bed, complete with her fancy wedding dress that my mom made for me herself. I had been so desperate to plan a wedding for her when I was nine, I never stopped to consider that I had just made poor little Kaia a child bride.

"Thanks, Mom. I love her!" I call out before I shut my door, because I know she's waiting for me to say it and will be hurt if I don't. She must have been digging around the old boxes upstairs again.

I shove Kaia to the side, throwing my arm over my eyes and pinching them shut as I settle onto my bed. As much as I wish I could sleep, I only have a half hour before I have to start my call center work.

What I need right now isn't an old childhood doll or to be reminded that I used to have big dreams. It's not even extra tips or to revise my business plan for the fiftieth time. No, what I need right now is a fucking miracle.

Chapter Two

"Oh good, you're up. Your aunt Christina died. Sounds like she left you something in the will."

"Good morning to you too, Mom, Jesus." And okay, when I prayed for a miracle, I didn't mean, like, kill off my mother's estranged sister so I could finally afford first, last, and security with the inheritance. I meant like . . . you know, let Randy give me overtime or health insurance or sublet the empty apartment over the coffee bar for a reasonable non-price-gouging amount. Something along those lines.

My mother probably feels like Aunt Christina's death *was* a miracle—other than the occasional passive-aggressive postcard, they haven't spoken in well over a decade since they had a falling-out over something I was too young to really understand. Their last meeting is mostly a blur in my head, an epic argument which somehow devolved into a shouting match. But no matter how blurry the rest of it is, I'll never forget how fierce my tiny mother looked as she accused Aunt Christina of sleeping with half the cowboys in the country instead of dealing with her Daddy issues, or how fast she wilted when Aunt Christina replied "At least I can keep a man interested."

I didn't understand half of what they were screaming about, but I understood pain and recognized it on both their faces as they fell silent. When my mom told her to get out, Aunt Christina did. For good.

"Sorry," my mom says, loading some French toast onto a plate for me. "Good morning, sweetie. Your aunt Christina died. Was that better?"

"What? No, not really. Just, what happened?" I mumble out, because while I'm still half-asleep, I'm also extremely curious why someone I haven't seen since I was a kid would apparently put me in her will.

"I don't know," she says, and waves me off. I look for signs she's secretly upset but don't see any. Then again, Mom always does keep her cards close to her vest when it comes to Aunt Christina. "She probably just left you some old boots or something, don't get too excited."

"I guess," I say, digging into my food.

"Anyway, the executor of her estate wants you to call her back. Apparently, Christina passed a week ago and they're just now getting around to letting us know because they legally have to! Typical. She probably told them not to even tell me," Mom stage-whispers, but I can't help but think this outrage is just an act to cover for any hurt she might be feeling. "I'll grab you the number after we eat, but they're doing a remembrance and reading of the will at the barn this weekend, if you want to go. I think I still have that address if you need it."

"Do *you* want to go?"

Mom looks thoughtful for a moment. "I don't think so, hon.

I made my peace that I didn't have a sister anymore a long time ago. You should though; find out what this is all about. Meet her friends and tell me about them."

I study her face. That's an interesting request for someone who *isn't* sad about her sister.

* * *

THE DRIVE TO the barn isn't horrendously long, just over two hours or so, but still, I'm happy to have Nat with me for company. Randy was nice enough to give me the day off, and I called out from the call center. It was just luck that Nat was already scheduled off . . . *and* that she dodged Randy's call asking her to cover for me.

"This isn't one of those *Hills Have Eyes* things, is it?" Nat asks as we pull back on the road after our first Starbucks stop of the day. "Luring us out into some kind of trap with the promise of vintage cowboy boots?"

"I don't think that's what that movie was about. Plus, we don't know for sure that it's boots," I say, greedily gulping down my caramel frappe. I know, I know, we're both baristas. Shouldn't we avoid the corporate overlords threatening constantly to put Randy out of business? Yes. Do we care in the face of this caramelly goodness? Not one single bit.

"Okay but either way, have you actually *seen* this hillbilly horse Holiday Inn? Like do we know for a fact that it even exists?"

I smile. "I spent a summer here when I was nine, it definitely exists."

"Mm-hmm, but that was a long time ago," she says, putting

on some music. Unfortunately, this also turns off my GPS, and I almost miss the turnoff—if not for the giant rickety sign that says *Christina's Corrals, this way.* It hangs at the end of a dusty, unpaved dirt driveway, and I nearly knock it over as I bank hard to make up for overshooting the drive.

"Holy shit," Nat says, holding the lids on both our coffees.

"Well, if somebody wasn't pulling up the latest Justin Bieber instead of letting me look at the map then—"

"No, I meant *that.*" She points out the window.

And yeah. That. Holy shit.

We crest the hill of the long driveway to see sprawling acres of grass; there are even a few horses dotted throughout. A large barn that looks like it's seen better days is plopped straight in the center, surrounded by various paddocks and mini pastures. Behind it looks to be an auxiliary barn, maybe for storage? Finally, off to the left, is a farmhouse that looks like it's held together solely by some duct tape and a prayer. Half of the siding has blown off, exposing angry, weathered plywood, and the roof curves in a way that looks unnatural.

What. The. Hell.

There are people everywhere and a lot of cars parked all over, so I have to pull onto the grass in front of the house just to find a spot. A few people look at me from the barn, their expressions a mixture of curiosity and disappointment as I put the car in park. I realize belatedly that I have stopped on what looks to be a garden of some sort, and I unintentionally whack a ceramic gnome over with my car door as I open it. Things are off to a great start, as usual.

I also begin to realize that the ultra-high heels I have selected for this occasion—a gift from my mother that she's still paying off from when I graduated and accepted an internship with the hottest wedding planner in the city—were a massive mistake. They sink deeply into the soft ground, forcing me to hobble on my tiptoes until I reach the rickety steps of the porch. Nat, in her much more sensible Nike Blazers, tries and fails to stifle a laugh as she follows behind me.

I freeze in front of the door. I don't know what to do in this situation. Do I knock? Do I walk right in? I'm supposed to find someone named Shani first, according to the half-hearted message my mom took, but I have no idea if they're inside or out in the barn with the others. I wish she had written down that number.

I take a deep breath and decide to head inside, only to be instantly met with a half-dozen curious faces staring at me.

"Just walk right in and make yourself at home," a woman says, and I can't tell if she's joking or not.

I snap my eyes to her, but my apology dies on my lips. She's hot. And not just kind of hot. Like really, really, fucking hot. Her piercing green eyes are framed by dark, shaggy, brown hair sliced over the perfect undercut. Her skin is peppered with just a hint of freckles and enough of a tan to let me know she probably spends some time outside. She has this kind of sun-kissed KStew vibe that's definitely working for her.

And for me.

The woman, who still hasn't introduced herself, is dressed in black, which I guess I should have anticipated. She's paired a mens dress shirt and fitted slacks with honest-to-god midnight-black cowboy boots. It's a look I immediately want to pin to my "western wedding" Pinterest board, and a body that I want to pin other places.

My mouth snaps shut, more to prevent drool than anything else, but she seems to take it as a challenge, her eyes flashing as she crosses her arms.

"Hi, this is Molly," Nat says helpfully, putting her arm on my shoulder, taking control like the best pseudo–big sister, always. "This was her aunt's farm."

"Oh, Molly!" an older Black woman says, standing up from her place on the well-worn sofa. She's maybe in her fifties, plump, with beautiful brown eyes and a kind face that instantly puts me at ease. She pushes past everyone to wrap me in a hug. "I'm Lita, one of the people who board their horse here. Your aunt Christina and I were great friends. She told me so much about you! She always said how much you loved this place."

"Yeah, nice of you to finally visit," the still nameless woman grumbles behind her.

"Oh hush, Shani," Lita says.

And this is Shani? This KStew wannabe is the maybe-executor of my aunt's estate? Wonderful. I'm sure she's downgrading my inheritance from vintage boots to dirty hay as we speak.

I sigh and take in the rest of the people. Everyone around me is dressed either in smart black clothes, or some variation of flannel and jeans. I feel overdressed in my dark green cocktail dress—the nicest thing I own, in an attempt to pay respect— which I just had to top off with the aforementioned Louboutin heels that I should have sold off long ago.

No wonder Shani isn't my biggest fan. Not only did I walk right in, but I'm also dressed for drinks at an upscale restaurant instead of a memorial followed by a probable barn tour. I'd hate me too.

"Come on, hon, let's get you a drink," Lita says, leading me into the kitchen.

"What's that woman's problem?" Nat whispers, following closely behind us.

"Oh don't worry about Shani," Lita says. "She's just a little stressed sorting so much of the business side. Losing your aunt was very hard for her and I think she's trying to stay busy."

"Were they close?"

Lita gives me a funny look. "You and Christina really didn't talk much, did you?"

I shake my head. "Not since her and my mom had a falling-out. There's a reason I haven't been here since I was little. I wasn't allowed."

"Interesting," Lita says, but doesn't elaborate. I have to bite my tongue to keep from asking what's so interesting about it. Families have fallings-out all the time, this one doesn't seem especially remarkable, even now that half of the equation is dead. It's just how things go sometimes.

"Coffee?" Lita asks, pouring herself a cup. I can hear people talking in the other room and the insecure part of me worries they're talking about me. The logical part of me . . . is also sure they're talking about me. I didn't exactly make a good first impression.

"I'd love one," Nat says, graciously accepting the next mug.

"No thanks," I say. "I had some on the way. But back to Shani, for a second? Is she another of Christina's horse boarders? My mom thought she was the executor of—"

Lita laughs. "Technically, she's our farrier, but she was also like a daughter to Christina."

"Oh, right, a farrier." I look at Nat, having no idea what that even is.

Lita takes pity on me. "Farriers shoe the horses. They take care of their hooves, and all that. Shani's also usually first on the scene when any of them are sick. She can get here way faster than any of the vets—not that we have much in the way of vets out here, but still. She's good people and a hard worker. You'll get along just fine."

"Will we?" I mumble to myself, but if Lita hears me, she doesn't let on, keeping the same knowing smile on her face the whole time. Besides, who cares if we get along? It's not like we'll ever have the occasion to hang out again after today. She'll just be another angry crush I'll think about in the event I'm ever alone in the house long enough to change the batteries in my vibrator.

"Come on," Lita says, "let me introduce you to everyone *properly*."

Nat and I dutifully follow her back into the living room, where Shani and her green eyes are still watching me like they're trying to figure me out. Her eyes narrow, just a smidge, and I look away.

Lita, blatantly ignoring any tension, starts introducing me to the others in the room. There's Shani, of course, but also the boarders, including JJ, a tall, fit, white kid with sandy blond hair who looks to be nineteen or twenty at most; CoCo, a very Italian woman complete with Brooklyn accent and a face that says *try me*; and Aiyana, a tall woman in her midtwenties, with warm, olive skin and black hair so straight my heat tools could literally only dream.

"And this is Michael, coming up the steps," she says, pulling open the door to show a white middle-aged man with a briefcase. "He's the actual executor, Molly."

"Oh, we're doing that now?" I blurt out before I can help myself.

"Well, that's all that's left, dear," Lita says, confused. "You came a little late."

"I thought there was a memorial thing first."

"That was this morning," Aiyana says, shifting in her seat. "Most of your aunt's friends are all saddling up for a ride in her honor already. Christina would have loved that. We just hung back because Shani said we were in the will, which I'm guessing is why you're here too."

"Oh, I thought . . . I mean the call said that it started at two, not ended."

"Oops." Shani smirks. "Guess I mixed up the times."

Right. Something tells me that wasn't a mix-up at all.

Chapter Three

*N*at and I hang back awkwardly, fidgeting in the corner feeling a little like a ping-pong ball as we look back and forth between everyone gathered in the kitchen with us. Most people, including Shani, are pressed against the farmhouse kitchen table where Michael is setting up, but it just doesn't feel right for me to take the front row. I'm the outsider here, clearly, and even though I was called to come, I still feel like I'm intruding.

"Are you sure we need to be here?" Nat whispers, clearly catching the same vibe I am. I shift my weight from foot to foot. Technically she doesn't need to be here at all, but as my emotional support friend, I'm hesitant to let her out of my sight.

"If you want to go outside and wait while I do this . . ." I trail off.

Nat looks at me. I can tell she wants to go, but I can also tell by her expression that she's picking up the nervousness that's got my shoulders all bunched up. "Nah, I'm good," she says finally. "Least I can do since you sprang me from getting called in."

I huff out a heavy breath, relieved. "Thanks."

Michael clears his throat, the unmistakable signal that we should shut up, and Shani glances at me over her shoulder just in case I somehow missed the message. I tilt my chin up defiantly, glaring at the back of her head. I know I just said I felt like I was intruding, but technically I have every right to be here as much as she does.

"As you know," Michael begins, shuffling some papers around in front of him before taking a seat on one of the creaky kitchen table chairs. "You were all called here today because our beloved Christina has left each of you something in her will. As her appointed executor, personal lawyer, and longtime friend, it is both my responsibility and honor to make sure that her wishes are carried out to the best of my ability."

Even with the stilted semi-legal jargon, that was kind of sweet. Then he starts in with the full-on legal jargon, and my eyes start to glaze over. I do my best to pay attention, but there's a lot of people here, and it's stuffy. I'm not proud of it, but as he drones on, doling out what I can only assume are sentimental saddles and gear, and occasionally an entire-ass horse, my attention gets pulled more to the window behind him.

It's a large bay window, slightly out of place in the cramped and otherwise run-down kitchen, but as I watch the sunlight glinting off the grass, and the way the late summer leaves are starting to turn already, I can see why she had it installed. I could stare out of it forever.

It makes sense now, why she wouldn't leave even as the house fell into apparent disrepair; I think I wouldn't, either, for the view. Mountains cut up the sky in the distance, but closer, in the small pasture full of trees nearest to the house, two horses approach the fence, with the leisurely walk of an animal that knows even though it's prey, it's safe.

One of the horses steps gently, the unmistakable movement

of age. Beside him, a strong brown horse shakes its head. It looks young and wild next to its ancient companion, but when the old horse bends his head to sip from the small stream cutting through the edge of the property, the younger one carefully remains alert, its gaze flicking over the fields and even in the direction of the house like a little guard horse.

Nat elbows me, snapping my focus back to the room; my own human guard horse. I turn my head, trying to see what she elbowed me for, but the sound of the lawyer saying my name clues me in.

"Molly," he says again, in a tone that makes me wonder exactly how many times he's said it already. My cheeks heat when I realize everyone in the room is staring at me, no doubt realizing that instead of listening to my aunt's dying wishes, I've been watching two horses on their quest to rehydrate. I glance out the window one last time, but they're gone, just the tiniest splash of color still visible as they retreat into the small patch of trees in the center of the enclosure.

"Hmm?" I ask, and hope that he didn't ask me a question yet. Judging by the frown on his face, I suspect he did. Or that I missed something. Something big.

"I said that this next part is especially relevant to you and asked you to come join me up here to sign some papers."

Oh boy. Here we go. Vintage boot time. I mean it's not like she's really going to leave something valuable to someone she hasn't seen in over a decade.

JJ and Aiyana helpfully step back from the table, leaving me an empty seat right beside Shani. Perfect. I drop down next to her and glance back at Nat, who's biting her lip nervously. JJ has taken my place against the wall, and I would give anything, all of the saddles Christina's possibly left me, to trade places. No, not just that, to be out of here, in my car, driving back home, away from Shani's withering stare.

I don't actually register what Michael says next. At least not at first. But I do register the gasps around me, the whispered "what the fuck" coming from the woman beside me, followed by her snatching the papers out of Michael's hands with a curt "let me see."

I sit in my chair, stunned into super inappropriate laughter that doesn't help *anything*. Because I'm sure that I had to have misheard. There is no way. I mean literally no way that Aunt Christina actually left me her entire house, her entire barn, her entire goddamn property. Why would she?

"Am I being pranked?" I ask, looking around the room at everyone's faces. Even Nat looks concerned.

"I'm sorry, Shani," Michael says, taking on a tone more like a comforting father figure than a brusque lawyer doing his due diligence. I'm just about to point out that *I'm* the one he should be talking to right now, but then he adds, "I know this is a shock." And that, that shuts me up. He's being serious. This isn't a joke or a trap, and it doesn't even sound like there's a catch. What is happening right now? Seriously?

"Um, excuse me, Michael?" I say, not wanting to interrupt him and Shani but needing to hear this again. "Did you just say—"

"That you get everything?" Shani says, slamming the paper back down on the table so hard it shakes. "Yeah, he did. Congratu-fucking-lations, stranger."

Shani slides her chair back so hard that it first smacks into my arm, and then drops to the ground as she storms past us. Aiyana picks it up with a reassuring smile and asks me if I'm okay.

I don't answer. I don't know how to. It was one thing to sit here and wish the view was mine (while expecting a bale of hay or something), but it's another to find out that it actually *is*. I'm not a horse girl . . . I'm in freaking Louboutins for god's sake. Secondhand Louboutins that are still being paid off, but still.

I can't run a stable. I can't own a farmhouse, especially not one that looks like it should be condemned. I don't know the first thing about horses *or* homeownership. I'm an event planner. No, who am I kidding? I'm not even that. I'm a barista! A barista who melts down when a customer spills. A barista who uses garbage bags instead of luggage. I don't even own boots, let alone cowboy boots. I—

"Why don't I give you some time to process this," Michael says, standing up from the table. "We can handle the paperwork another time. Here, take my card." He hands me a bone-colored, perfectly printed business card that would make Patrick Bateman weep. When I don't move, Nat steps forward and takes it instead.

"I'll walk you out," Aiyana says to him, looking worriedly out the window to where we can all see Shani storming across the property. She wrenches open the pasture gate and slams it behind her, raging her way through the field.

I stay seated in my chair as the rest of the people filter out, leaving me and Nat alone. She sits down beside me and rests her hand on my arm. I flinch because it's exactly where Shani's chair hit me, but I appreciate the comfort nonetheless.

"Well, you did *want* a new place to live," she says with a wince. I know she's just trying to lighten the mood, but now is not the time.

I lower my head into my hands. "I can't do this. This house is falling apart, and I can't afford to fix it. I can't afford any of this. I can't even afford the gas to get to the coffee shop from here every day. What am I going to do?" And there, finally, is the catch. This place isn't a gift, it's a chain around my ankle to add to my already insurmountable debt.

"Well, you can do the call center from everywhere, technically." But when she sees my face, she switches gears. "I'm kidding, obviously. You should sell," Nat helpfully supplies and Jesus, yes. Why hadn't I thought of that yet?

Maybe there is a silver lining here after all.

"Oh my god, I could," I say quietly. I don't know if the house is worth much, but I'm sure the land is. I don't know anything about horses, but someone out there probably wants a stable, right? Or hell, even a developer looking for a new place to put houses would work.

"Yeah, and this could really set you up!" Nat says, buying into the plan.

A smile crosses my face. "I could use the money to seed my business. Pay off my student loans maybe, depending on how much. I might even be able to put some money down on an apartment in the city if there's anything left. Oh my god. Oh my god! This could be really good."

The sound of a throat clearing behind me snaps my attention to the living room, where Aiyana has returned. "I just wondered if you wanted a quick tour before I left, since I guess it's all yours now?"

I look at Nat and she grins even wider. "Yes," I say, ready to see exactly how large this inheritance really is. What minutes ago felt like an overwhelming burden is more and more starting to feel more like hitting the lottery.

* * *

AIYANA LOANS ME some rubber boots, and takes her time walking me around, showing me the feed room, the office where Christina kept the books and ledgers—the numbers in which I definitely need to check out—followed by the main barn and auxiliary barn, the indoor ring and the massive outdoor rings. She even draws me a quick map of the fields and explains that some horses can't be left alone together, so Christina had some of the land subdivided with fences for safety and just kind of threw up paddocks and pastures wherever they fit—I guess that explains why some of them are full of trees.

None of the amenities here are in the best shape, and everything smells like horses, hay, and manure—but I don't even care. This place is amazing. I'll be damned if this pile of horseshit isn't going to help me take Immaculate Events Inc. from internet daydreaming to the real world.

What do they say? Never look a gift horse in the mouth? I don't really know what that means aside from don't be an ungrateful asshole, and I won't be. I'm all in on this, with bells on.

It turns out eight animals are full-time in the barn. There used to be way, way more horse boarders apparently but people started pulling out when Christina got sick. Aiyana still doesn't mention what she died of, and asking feels weird since she definitely seems to think I already know.

Christina had about ten horses of her own, plus a donkey named Edward Cullen, but they had to be sold off when she got too sick to care for them, except for the donkey and the old horse I saw earlier, who is apparently named Otis and used to be her favorite.

"Who took care of stuff when she was in bed for so long? Is there a barn manager or something?" I ask, as the tour starts to wind down.

"Shani sorta took that over when Christina got real sick, but we all kinda chipped in," Aiyana says. "She cut our fees way down and changed it to self-turnout. We made a schedule to pick up the slack for each other. Shani helped the most though, since she lives on the property."

"She what?" I yelp, and Nat laughs.

"Yeah." Aiyana walks us toward the pasture where I had seen the horses earlier and points to a roof barely visible over some of the trees. "She's on the other side of pasture three. In the staff house. Well, that's what Christina always called it, but it's more of a guesthouse or a rental these days. Although I guess she *is* a farrier so, half credit on the staff thing."

"Yeah, Lita was saying that. That's hooves, right?"

"Hooves and shoeing and all that good stuff." Aiyana laughs. "Christina seriously left you all this and you don't even know basic horsecare?"

I shake my head.

"Can you even ride?"

"I mean I used to be able to," I mumble.

"How long ago was *used to?*"

"Like . . . sixteen years ago, for a summer and someone always held the lead."

Aiyana tries not to laugh in my face again, which I appreciate. Behind me a horse snorts and I jump when the hot air of its breath hits my neck. I'm shocked to see that it's the old horse from earlier. He must have snuck up on me while I was focused on Aiyana.

This time, Aiyana's laugh cannot be contained. "Speak of the devil. Hi, Otis." She rubs his velvety nose gently, like she's not concerned that her entire hand could fit in his mouth if he wanted it to. "He was a slaughter pen rescue she took in a few years ago. He looks grumpy but he's got a heart of gold. He favors Shani though, so if she's around, don't even bother trying to get his attention. You can pet him you know. And that's Gideon over there by the trees, Shani's horse. He doesn't really like anybody new."

"Sounds like his owner," I grumble, but Aiyana politely ignores me. Gideon's ears flick forward, watching from a distance, as I reach out a tentative hand to place on Otis. I jump a little when he jerks his head before settling it against my palm. The hair on his face is scratchier than I imagined, but his gray muzzle is softer than anything I've ever felt before. Gideon whinnies after a moment, calling the other horse back. I feel almost sad when Otis turns to leave, nostalgic. Eight-year-old me would have flipped out to have a chance to live here.

"So, what, then?" Nat ask, breaking the moment. "Does that Shani girl pay rent or . . ."

"She used to," Aiyana says, "but once she became Christina's main caretaker, they called it even."

"She took care of my aunt?" I ask, my eyes fixed on Shani's roof in the distance. I was low-key excited about the idea of kicking her out until I heard she was Florence Nightingale. What am I even supposed to do with that?

"Oh yeah, they were super close, even more so after the cancer diagnosis."

"Cancer?"

"Yeah, pancreatic. You didn't know?"

I shake my head. "Her and my mom had a big falling-out so . . ." I trail off. "I didn't even know Christina was sick until my mom got the call that she had passed. I'm glad that she had Shani here, looking out for her at least."

"Yeah, of course. There was no question. Shani was by her side through it the whole time, which is why we all expected . . ."

"What?"

"Nothing, never mind," Aiyana says guiltily. She reaches in her pocket and pulls out a key ring. "Michael said I could give you these now, even though everything's not really final till you sign. These keys will open the house, the barn, anything you want."

"Thank you, but honestly, what were you going to say? You thought Shani would get everything? Please. I need to know what I'm walking into here. I thought I was just going to pick up, like, old photos or a letter to my mom trying to make amends or sentimental boots or something. I was just here as a family representative. I didn't actually think she was going to leave me *all this.*"

"I bet," Aiyana says. "Not to be rude, but your reaction made it pretty obvious you didn't see this coming, and this tour made it twice as obvious that you're not really prepared either."

"Molly has the worst poker face," Nat helpfully interjects.

"Right," Aiyana says. "But regardless, it's yours. And yeah, we all kinda thought Shani was getting everything. I'm pretty sure she did too. So, don't hold her attitude today against her. Okay? She comes off like an asshole but . . . she's lived here a long time and Christina is the closest thing to a parent she ever had. Keep that in mind, all right? This place is her home, and now it belongs to somebody who doesn't know a thing about it."

"Got it," I say, acknowledging this little hitch in my plan. I hadn't counted on evicting someone from their long-term home, immediately after losing their almost-parent, in my excitement to sell.

Maybe I jumped the gun in saying there was no catch, because it looks like Shani just might be a big one.

Chapter Four

It takes me five days, and multiple phone calls with Michael, to get things straightened out to the point where I feel comfortable dragging a garbage bag of clothes and a box of my "emotional support" belongings—as Nat calls my collection of Taylor Swift memorabilia and old stuffies I never leave home without—over to Christina's.

My mom, of course, is devastated that I'm leaving again so soon, but I reassure her that it's only temporary. Living on-site will make it easier to get things patched up and ready to sell, and I promise her that I'll move back as soon as it does. I leave out the part where I might get an apartment of my own soon too.

Mom's overly enthusiastic about the idea that I'll be launching Immaculate Events from her kitchen table, and I don't have the heart to tell her otherwise . . . or the energy. It's just been me and her for so long, that I think she forgets that's not how it's supposed to be. Still, it's nice to at least have someone believing in me, since I know I'm going to be surrounded by people who don't for the foreseeable future.

Michael reminds me that I still need to sit down in his office and go over all the nitty-gritty details with him, but he's assured me the place is all set for now, and that I should feel free to move in and start fixing it up. I let him know that I'll be selling as soon as possible, and while I expected him to be upset by that, he seems to agree that it's the best case in this scenario.

Nonetheless, it's mine for now and I have the garbage bag of clothes in my back seat to prove it.

Nat was supposed to come with me, and we were gonna push through this whole first day as a barn owner thing together, but Randy wouldn't give her the time off. I can't really be mad at him though, because he *is* letting me take a sabbatical from the coffee shop—not that he's paying me or anything, just that he's saying I can have my job back when the time comes. Before we go jumping up and down singing his praises, it's important to note that he's *always* strapped for workers. So, it's not so much that he's holding my job as he's probably not going to be able to fill it in the short time I hope to be gone.

But still, knowing that I'll have something to come back to in a month or so—which is about how long Michael thinks it's going to take me to get this place organized to sell—is comforting. I'm using most of my meager savings to live off of for this time period—yes, it was earmarked for my business, but it's the only way to make this work—plus whatever I rake in with my call center job once I get the internet all hooked back up. Still, I think it will all be worth it. Once the sale of this place goes through, I'll have my savings replenished and then some.

So yeah, consider this an addendum to my business plan. A prequel if you will.

I run through the plan as I drive, trying not to obsess over how weird it's going to feel when I get there. Step one was to get a sabbatical from my job and put my student loans in forbearance—which has been fully checked off. Step two: crash at the main farmhouse and get the ball rolling with real estate agents, assessors, and maybe find a contractor to fix up anything I can't. Step three, to run concurrently with step two: figure out if Christina's boarding business is even profitable. Randy made some offhand comment that I might be able to get more money out of the deal if I sell the business *with* the property, versus closing up shop. I don't know if that's true, but worth researching. Step four: ??? (Hopefully, that one will come to me once I'm all moved in.) Step five: ride off into the sunset with a bunch of cash and a hard life reset. (Ha, get it? *Ride* off into the . . . never mind.)

Ready or not, I'm pulling into that old dirt driveway before I know it. There are several horses out grazing as I maneuver myself into a safe place to park, and thankfully the fences—while badly in need of repair—seem to be holding them in well enough. I spy Gideon off to the side in the front pasture, with Edward Cullen the donkey nearby, grazing at a respectful distance. The rest of the animals are just a blur of mostly identical browns as they chase each other around or tear up the grass.

Aiyana and Lita have been taking over care of them for me until I could get back. They're supposed to meet me now to walk me through the whole routine so I can help too, but when I finally get out of my car, they don't seem to be around anywhere.

I toss my keys into my bag and start wandering around the property trying to find them. I doubt they're in the house—as far as I know I'm the only one with keys at this point, and I locked it up before I left last time.

I head to the main barn first, assuming that if they're anywhere, it'll be there. Both doors are wide open when I get there though, so I can see that it's empty. I proceed to the smaller barn—the "auxiliary barn for events" I think is what Aiyana had called it, whatever that means—but they're not there either. Instead, I see a figure hunched over in the shadows next to a horse.

They're facing away from me, but the horse isn't, and I immediately recognize that it's Otis, and it looks like his leg is being wrenched off or stabbed or something. A million thoughts flit through my head. *Is that person trying to hurt him? Is this some kind of revenge somebody is trying to get on my dead aunt? Or on me for inheriting things? Is this sabotage? Animal cruelty? Who do I call for this? Oh god, I think this is my responsibility now.*

Otis looks at me with what seem to be big, terrified eyes and—while I've never been an animal person—in this moment I would die for this giant grass puppy. Or at least, attack someone for him.

I pull the pepper spray out of my bag, take a deep breath, and rush down the center of the barn. "Get away from him!" I shout, rushing Otis's attacker.

I shove them away hard, and luckily they lose their balance entirely. Otis gets his leg back and promptly tries to rear up, but he's trapped, tethered to a ring on the wall. I pull the cord free and let him race out, breathing heavy as I turn my attention back to the mysterious figure. Finger on the trigger of the pepper spray, I say, "Get up. I've called the cops." I haven't, but they don't need to know this. They also don't need to know that this pepper spray is at least six years old, and that a little do-nothing fizzle is probably all we're likely to get from it.

"What the fuck is the matter with you?" says a familiar voice.

Shani pushes herself up, dusting off the pine shavings I just threw her down into. She yanks her AirPods out of her ears and stalks toward me. I take a step back, but it's no use. Shani rips the pepper spray out of my hands and throws it across the barn, her furious face just inches away from mine.

I realize two things as she stands in front of me, her chest heaving with rage. One is that I was *definitely* right before, she's HOT. Like all caps, unexpired pepper spray hot, blister on the sun hot, makes me almost forget every celebrity crush I've ever had kind of hot.

It makes me want to kiss her, want to bite her, want to—her nostrils flare as if she senses my distraction and right, yeah, the second thing I realized. The second thing is that her question? It doesn't seem as rhetorical as I first thought.

"What. The. *Fuck* is wrong with you?" she asks again, enunciating each word.

"I—" I start, but she raises her eyebrows at me, waiting. "I thought you were an attacker! I was trying to save Otis!"

Her eyebrows scrunch together in disbelief. "An attacker? An attacker that what? Decided to give you free farrier services before they beat you up? What the hell are you even talking about?"

"I . . ." I trail off. Free farrier services? What? "Wait, what were you doing to him?"

"I was repacking Otis's abscess but now it looks like I'll need to spend the next half hour catching him just so that I can start all over." She runs her hands through her hair. "Please tell me you at least shut the double gates when you pulled in."

"Um . . ."

Shani storms past me, knocking my shoulder as she does.

"Ooh, tension," someone says from the stall behind me, and I jump. "I ship it."

I turn to find the boy from the will reading—JJ, I think he said—dangling off the side of a giant white horse that I didn't even realize was there. He slides to the ground in one lithe movement and walks over to where his cellphone is propped up at the edge of the stall.

"Did I ruin your day too? Were you *also* packing an abscess, whatever that means?"

"Desensitizing my horse, technically—but making a TikTok actually."

"You make horse TikToks?" I ask. Damn, I didn't know that was even a thing. Mine is mostly weddings and flowers and, okay, a lot of attractive actresses and a little bit of exotic dancers, but hey, I'm only human.

"Sort of," he says, sliding his phone into his pocket and draping his arms over the stall doors. "We post some of my competitions and stuff, but mostly I make dancing TikToks that happen to have my horse in them. I'm JJ," he says, holding out his hand.

"I remember," I say, shaking it. "I'm Molly."

"I remember too," he says with a smile. "The new owner."

Not for long, I think, but instead I say, "That's me," and try to sound cheerful about it.

"Is this your stall?" I ask, because it looks kind of . . . empty. I couldn't imagine having to live in it, even as a horse. All the horses in the other barn have sawdust and blankets and toys and stuff.

"No, but this barn has a better lighting system than the main barn for some reason. I film here, and Shani uses it for any farrier stuff she really needs to focus on."

"Oh." I look out into the yard, where I definitely did *not* remember to shut the secondary gate after I pulled in, and where Shani is now chasing after Otis—who is surprisingly spry for a horse that looks to be a million years old.

She's currently trying to coax him away from the end of the driveway and back into our lot. He snorts at her, but eventually relents, probably mostly due to the cookie she's magically pulled out of her pocket—but still. The second she gets him back inside, she rushes to close the heavy metal gate at the end of the driveway. It clanks so loud and angry that I feel it in my bones. Otis skitters away back toward the farmhouse, and Shani stalks after him with one last nasty glance in my direction.

JJ laughs. "I can't believe you tried to pepper spray her. What a great meet-cute. We should all be so lucky."

"What?"

"You know, I used to have this nightmare when I was little. I'd be breaking into a house and then I'd get the door open and there'd be a boy on the other side with a gun. My therapist says it's a metaphor for trying to protect my inner child or some shit, but it isn't. It's because I had a crush on the kid from the *Walking Dead* when I was little, Carl. You ever see that show? My parents were obsessed with it, and I used to sneak out of my room and watch it from the hall. Anyway, somewhere along the line the dreams, uh, changed and I started thinking 'wow what a great meet-cute that would be.' And then Carl would lower his gun and we—"

"Sorry, what are you talking about?" I ask, utterly lost.

"I was just saying, I didn't think super agro meet-cutes were a *real* thing . . . until I saw you toss Shani like a bag of bricks and assault her with pepper spray. Be still my heart."

"I didn't assault her! I was trying to save Otis!"

"Sure, sure," JJ says, giving his horse a quick nuzzle and then slipping out of the stall. "I'm sure Marlowe here would love it if somebody saved her from getting her pedicure too, even though she prances around like a beauty queen as soon as Shani's done."

"She had his leg all yanked around. It looked like it hurt. I—"

JJ bursts out laughing. Again. "Wow, you really don't know anything about horses, do you? This is going to be so fun."

"What is?"

"Teaching you, messing with you, watching you step in horse-crap with those blinding white Nikes you got on—only slightly more appropriate than those red bottoms you had on last time." He snorts.

I huff out a laugh. "You're real nice."

"Thank you for noticing. Now, come on, let's get you out of here before Shani comes back. Marlowe will be fine for a minute. You need help carrying in some boxes or something?"

"There's just a few. I can handle it," I say, but he shakes his head.

"Around here, we look out for each other. It was Christina's one rule for every boarder. Everybody pitches in, everybody steps up. 'We might live in a barn, but we're a civilized family,' she used to say. Just 'cause she died, doesn't mean the sentiment did. So are you gonna let me help you with your stuff or are you gonna make me beg?"

* * *

It only takes us a little while to carry in my stuff, along with the piles of cleaning supplies my mom insisted I bring. During which, I count three different glares from Shani: one when I step out of the barn as she chased Otis toward it, a second when she realized JJ was definitely going to help me unpack, and last but definitely not least, when the box I was carrying broke—its contents spilling all over the muddy driveway in a cacophony that spooked Otis right as she was about to catch his lead.

She did get him a few moments later, while I was still crawling through the mud trying to salvage all the Taylor Swift stuff I brought with me for good luck. I don't know why Shani is so pissed. Horses can be caught, but my loss of dignity? Crawling through mud crying over a pop singer that would never date me? That's forever.

JJ leaves right after we finish, but not before shoving a breakfast bar in my hand when he realized that I hadn't brought any actual groceries with me. I told him I was probably going to DoorDash something later, but apparently that's not how it works out here. He belly laughed, like actually roared with tears, and then left me the name of the closest grocery store . . . which is apparently forty minutes away.

I scrounge through the kitchen to see what's lying around, eating the breakfast bar, but there isn't much left in the way of food. I find an old bag of egg noodles and a pot. I hesitate at using tap water; is it even safe out here? But then decide the boiling will take care of that. At least I hope it will.

While the water's heating up, I wander around the house

taking stock of where everything is—something I definitely didn't have time to do in my shock during the will reading.

There are two bathrooms—one upstairs, one down—a sizable living room, a decent kitchen, and a weird sort of triangular dining room area off to the side that looks like the walls were just kind of thrown up haphazardly. Currently, it just seems to house a bunch of horse gear and old boots. Upstairs, along with the second bathroom, I find three bedrooms. I open the first one and realize it must have been Christina's. There are still random pill bottles lying around, a portable commode I don't want to think about, and various chairs like people had been congregating around the center of the room. It takes a second to sink in that it was probably the horse boarders, Shani, Aiyana, maybe even JJ and the others, and that they were probably sitting around a hospital bed in here once she reached the end.

There's no bed there now. But there is a bag of clothes and sleeping bag—my bag of clothes and sleeping bag. I didn't give a lot of thought to where JJ was hauling them when he carried them in for me, but I wish I did.

I already feel like I'm intruding; there's no way I'm taking over the room Christina probably died in. I back out, shutting the door quietly, like I might disturb her ghost or something. That thought instantly creeps me out, given that I'm alone in this big house, miles from the closest town, with only some apparently abscess-hoofed horses for company and a tenant across the pasture that is more like to kill me than save me.

I push those thoughts out of my head and move to the next bedroom. At first, I think the door to the second room is stuck.

No, not stuck, I realize: it's locked. And I left the keys that Aiyana gave me downstairs. Great. A ghost in one room, a mysterious locked door on the other. I push into the third and final room and flick on the light, hoping for something better, or at least less unnerving.

This room is full of boxes. And I mean *full* of boxes. There's a dresser off to one side and more stuff than I know what to do with piled up all around it. It takes me a second to put it together that this is probably her stuff. The dresser, the nightstands, the disassembled bed. This is probably what they took out to make room for . . . well, to make room for the supplies they needed as she passed. An unexpected sadness fills me.

I thought this would just be business—I hadn't seen her in almost sixteen years, for god's sakes. This was supposed to be a get in and get out kind of thing—but seeing her belongings shoved aside like this, seeing them packed up haphazardly and thrown in a dark room until some stranger like me comes and picks through them? It hurts. It's depressing.

I wonder if this will be my fate too, my whole life packed up into a random bedroom at the end of the hall. The desperate urge to unpack hits me. To get my stuff, what little of it I brought to get me through the next few weeks, as far away from cardboard and plastic bags as possible.

To be as different from the stuff in this room as possible.

I rush downstairs and rip the lid off the first box, just as a movement outside the big kitchen window catches my eye. I pause and look up to see Shani out in the yard, gently petting Otis as she leads him back out to his pasture. His hoof is now wrapped in something blue, which she checks one last time before sliding the lead and halter off him and setting him loose with a happy scritch behind the ears.

I swear she looks back at the kitchen before she heads off toward her house. I realize that with it being dusk outside and light inside, she can definitely, definitely see me staring at her.

So, I do what any self-respecting woman would do in my situation. I flip her off.

Chapter Five

I spend most of the next day settling in . . . or at least trying to.

I still can't bring myself to move into Christina's room, or to throw out her boxes in the spare room, and none of the keys on my ring work on the locked door. I'm going to have to get a locksmith out here or something. In the meantime, the couch seems comfortable enough, and it's not like anybody is coming to visit, so I make up my bed in the living room, put my retainer case on the end table, and use the downstairs bathroom shower curtain rod as a closet rack. It's good enough, and it's not like I'll be here that long anyway.

Michael comes bright and early Monday morning with papers for me to sign. We discuss selling a little more and a timeline for that to happen—not that I really know the state of horse-related realty, but I agree with him that sixty days or so to get it listed feels sufficient, and I'm grateful when he gives me the name of a good real estate agent in town. He also turns over everything I need to take over the bank accounts for the boarding business, although he doesn't have any passwords so that's going to be a headache.

Lita comes around that afternoon with two giant iced coffees—when I ask her how she knew, she laughs and said she could tell I was an iced coffee queer a mile away, and then taps hers against mine with a loud "cheers, baby" that makes me laugh. She apologizes for not being here last night, and says she got tied up at work. She was just glad JJ could be here to step in and take care of the horses.

I don't mention the fact that I tried to pepper spray Shani, but I wonder if JJ did, because she smirks and adds a bit about how safe we are out here and makes it a point to say there are no "attackers" around.

After some teasing, she walks me through what I'm supposed to be doing around the barn every morning. She's going to stop coming before work now that I'm here, and gently reminds me that I'm going to need to pitch in if I expect to keep collecting rent long-term. If she suspects I'm planning to sell, she doesn't mention it, so neither do I.

No matter how much I tell her I shouldn't be "turning out" horses or "giving them grain" she doesn't believe me. She walks me through the schedule anyway, handing me a sheet of paper full of information that she helpfully laminated—well, okay, really she just coated both sides with packing tape—and calls it my "barn life cheat sheet."

It lists which horse goes in which stall, what color they are (I'm grateful she didn't expect me to know breeds), what horses they can and can't be turned out with, and what pasture everybody goes in.

"How is Otis's foot?" I ask.

"Hoof, Molly, hoof, and it's fine. Shani's on it. She's the best at what she does." Lita leads me over to the room we store all the feeds in and reintroduces me to a couple boarders who still pay for full service—Ben and CoCo, who I vaguely remember from the reading of the will. Ben got left a saddle, which he's currently shining up, and CoCo got left a pair of riding boots that made her tear up when Michael handed them to her.

Apparently, they both have wildly busy jobs, so they only come occasionally after work. The rest of the time, their horses are the barn's responsibility, or mine now, I guess. Lita explains that she's been handling most of their care, but now the mornings are going to be up to me.

CoCo hands me a check, and I stare at it, unsure how I will even cash it since it's made out to Christina's Corrals. I'm going to need to take all those papers Michael gave me to the bank and figure it out soon . . . just as soon as I figure out where the bank actually even *is*.

I thank them and shove the check into my pocket before Lita hands me a lead and has me practice taking her horse, Happy, out to the field. It's scary at first, having this giant animal clomping along behind me, but after a few tries, I almost get used to it. In fact, Lita lets me bring out all the horses that need to be turned out, one by one, and I feel weirdly proud of pulling it off. Even if she does have to remind me *several* times that the halters don't stay on in the fields. She tells me that's "rule number one" and I'm still worried I'm going to forget it . . . until she says she's heard of a horse that got hung up by its halter dying before.

Okay, scratch that. I will definitely never, ever forget rule number one.

The tour ultimately ends at the barn office, where Lita pats me on the back—more like shoves me into the room—with a laughing "good luck figuring this stuff out." She tells me to set an alarm for two hours, which I do without asking, and then leaves to clean out her stall—something I apparently am also going to learn how to do soon.

I stare down at the desk, covered in papers and dirt and bits of hay, and realize I'm definitely going to need all the luck I can get. I dig around and try to find something that's remotely like a ledger—it seems Christina didn't have Wi-Fi, so something tells me most of the business information is going to be via old school paper and pencil—but it's no use. I *do* manage to find a rubber stamp (the words "for deposit only" etched into it) in the top drawer with the name of a bank and an account number. I stamp it onto the back of the check CoCo gave me, mainly in an effort to read the stamp more clearly.

At least now I can look up the bank.

* * *

I'm still buried in piles of old receipts and appointment books when the alarm that Lita made me set on my phone goes off. She peeks her head in and tells me it's time to switch the horses in the paddock and give Otis another dose of antibiotics before turning him out in the side pasture with Gideon.

Lita says when I get more comfortable, I can grind Otis's meds up and syringe it in his mouth like a pro, but in the meantime, I can shove it inside a piece of apple or banana while we're making friends. Apparently, if you add it to his food, he'll snub the whole thing for the night, and at his age Otis is not a guy who can miss a meal.

She offers to bring the other horses in for me while I grab the medication out of the little office fridge and the bag of apples that she brought me. I pick the shiniest, reddest apple of the bunch in an effort to win Otis over, and carefully slice it, carving out a little hole and stuffing it full of his medicine. I guess it's sort of hidden, but I'm not sure how smart Otis is. I know I wouldn't fall for it. Let's hope I'm the cleverer one in this relationship.

When I can't delay anymore, I shove the meds, pocketknife, and apple in the front pocket of my hoodie. It might take me a hundred tries, and he might eat this entire bag of apples in the process, but I'm determined to get that medicine into him on my own.

Otis snickers softly and nudges at the air around me as I approach with the apple. His ears are pricked forward in a way that Lita says means he's feeling curious and open to being approached. Apparently, ears back means bad, and so are white eyes. She also terrified me by telling me how horses can't stop midbite so I should make sure my fingers stay out of the way when I offer him snacks. This sounds fake, but I'm not willing to test the theory.

Instead, I place the medicated apple in the flat palm of my hand and extend my fingers so far it hurts, in an effort to keep them clear of his giant teeth. He sniffs it, blowing it off of my hand on the exhale and then stares at me. I pick it up and nudge it toward him again, but he keeps staring. He whinnies and stomps his hoof and it sort of feels like he's laughing *at me*.

"Eat the damn apple," I say, flexing my palm a little harder and faster toward his mouth. He pins his ears back when I do. And shit. Ears back equals bad. I glance over at Lita, who's now busily pretending to be cleaning out her stall. I don't miss how she's angled my way though, so she can watch, or how slow she's moving that pitchfork. She's probably about to call the whole thing off and medicate him herself.

Okay. No. I can do this. I have to do this. Lita is busy, and even though I know she would jump in and help, I also know she won't be here tomorrow morning. Otis is counting on me. Another horse across the way sticks his head out—Uggo, his stall says. He belongs to Ben and seems to be extremely interested in the remaining apples in my hoodie pocket, reaching forward to nip at the fabric, his lips flapping at me like something out of a horror movie. My heart rate picks up, my whole body going rigid, as I realize I've found myself trapped between two horse heads . . . and their very giant teeth.

"You okay over there?" Lita calls.

"Not really."

She stops mucking out her stall, watching me more closely. "You want some help?"

Do I want help? That's a loaded question because yes, of course I want help . . . but also I'm going to feel like the biggest baby in the world if I can't even feed a horse an apple without crying for someone to save me.

"I'm good," I say eventually. A definite lie, but we *are* going to figure this out. Me, Otis, and Uggo. How hard can it be to pill a horse?

I think about my childhood dog, Paulie, and how we used to be able to trick him to take his medicine by switching his treats or hiding stuff in it—same principle, just a bigger beast on the other end. I reach into my pocket and fish another apple slice out, laying it on top of the other one. Still Otis doesn't take it.

Uggo on the other hand leans forward as far as he can, his hot breath making my hair fly around my neck. And oh, oh! The *other* thing about Paulie was that he was extremely jealous. He didn't care why someone else was getting a treat, just if he *wasn't*. Maybe I can turn this giant toothed demon behind me into an asset instead.

"Hey, Lita, can Uggo have some apple?" I ask.

"Not the medicated one," she says, scrunching up her forehead. And wow, I know I'm not coming off *real great* at the barn, but I'm not gonna go all evil stepmother and feed one of my charges a poisoned apple he doesn't need.

"No, I know. I just have an idea," I add.

"Go for it then," she says, still watching.

I turn around, giving all my attention to Uggo, rubbing his soft velvety nose and then offering him some of the leftover apple chunks in my pocket. Behind me, Otis snorts and stomps, clearly not liking this turn of events. I give it a few more seconds, and then I turn back around and offer Otis my palm with the medicated apple still in it.

This time Otis sucks it up in big, giant, gulps, his lips wet and heavy against my hand, leaving little trails of slime in their wake. I take a step back, utterly grossed out, only for Uggo to smack his nose against my back and try to sneak into my hoodie pocket, which makes me yelp and jump forward into Otis again.

I turn around, laughing, and offer both of them more slices of apple. I wonder if having extra apples makes me the cool barn owner, you know, like the cool aunt who lets you drink Mountain Dew and eat Twizzlers for dinner, like Aunt Christina did that one summer.

Aunt Christina was the epitome of cool aunt.

I swallow hard, surprised again by the tug in my chest, the feeling that I lost out on something by not reconnecting with her when there was still time. It's silly; you can't mourn someone you barely knew. You can't—

I turn to grab Otis's lead off the side of his stall door and realize someone else has joined us in the barn. Shani is standing (leaning, really), casually scratching the ear of a horse at the end of the aisle, watching me. I fight the urge to wave—*she hates you, remember, and you hate her; have some self-respect*—but the way she's looking at me right now doesn't seem hateful. If she were a horse, her ears would be up and forward maybe—curious, open—but I can't be sure. And I'm still on a high from getting Otis to take his meds, so I'm not about to let her ruin it with a smart remark if I'm wrong.

I clip the lead onto his halter, careful not to wrap it around my wrist like I would a dog leash—if a horse wants to drag you, he's going to, and you want to be able to let go quickly, Lita warned—and walk him back out to the pasture. By the time I come back to hang up the lead and halter, Shani's gone, but her business card is tucked into the wood where she was standing. I flip it over and find a note.

You can call me if he gives you any trouble with the meds in the morning. —S

It's not exactly an olive branch, but it's the closest thing I think I'm going to get. I shove it in my pocket with a smile, determined not to ever need it.

* * *

I MAKE IT another day before I tap out on my noodles-for-breakfast, -lunch, and -dinner menu, and also, I'm just about out of noodles anyway. I can't put off figuring out the bank stuff and the selling-the-barn stuff anymore either, even though it is way more fun to just play cowgirl every morning, walking out the horses and ignoring the fact that there is *a lot* of work to be done.

I bring the check with me when I go into town, along with the paperwork that Michael gave me, and stop at the bank first, deciding getting groceries afterward will be my reward for acting like an actual responsible adult. The bank people look over everything and help me to get my name on the business accounts, which have about six thousand dollars in them altogether.

This seems like an enormous sum of money to me, especially combined with the two thousand dollars I have on my own—so I don't understand when the banker has his manager come over, who looks nervous and asks me all kinds of questions about deposits and when I will expect more to come in. I give him CoCo's check and explain I'm still figuring that stuff out.

He doesn't seem reassured, but lets me go, nonetheless. I'll have to ask Michael about this next time I see him. Do business accounts have minimums? And are they higher than 6K? Maybe I'm not as ready for Immaculate Events as I thought.

Especially after I call the cable company and find out that literally no one will run internet to my house—apparently, they all stop at the town limits. They suggest I use my cell as a mobile hot spot, like I even have enough bars for that way out at the barn. So helpful. I guess this explains Christina's ancient landline and lack of TVs.

I call my boss at the call center and explain the situation right away. I can tell she's pissed I'm not logging in tonight, and her "we'll see" when I ask about getting hours once I'm back in the city gives me a pit in my stomach. I practically break out in hives at the thought of not even having that meager amount of income coming in, but what can I do? I'll just have to live off cheap ramen packs and cross everything this farm sells fast enough, and for enough money, that I'll come out of this okay.

Which, speaking of, I leave a message for the real estate agent while I'm driving around town, doing my best to get a feel for it. There doesn't seem to be much of anything around here. A post office, a bank, an Applebee's, and a Wendy's, and two bars—Maxon's and The Whiskey Boot—seem to make up the main drag. I finally find the grocery store down a side street with only some mild trouble, tucked behind the biggest Tractor Supply Company store I've ever seen, and load up on my favorite snacks and foods. I have eight thousand dollars in the bank (sort of) and an appointment with a real estate agent, and I know how to lead a horse to pasture. That calls for the party-size bag of chips.

JJ and Aiyana are there when I get back, filming TikToks together while washing their horses. I get out of my car in time to see Aiyana spraying JJ and Marlowe with a hose, while he dances around singing an off-key rendition of some SZA song.

They stop when they see me and insist on helping me carry the bags into the house. They politely do not comment on the bed on the couch or the clothes hanging in the bathroom, and I politely do not comment on the fact that they are both dripping water all over my floor.

I make some oversized chocolate chip cookies from the recipe we use at the coffee shop as a thank-you for everyone helping me get used to things around here, and hand them out around the barn. Everybody seems to really enjoy them, even sharing tiny nibbles with some of the horses. I make it a point to slip a little to Edward Cullen, who brays at me in what I can't tell is a good or bad way. He eventually accepts some scritches behind his ear though, so I'd like to think we're becoming friends.

I could have done without how shocked Lita is that I can "actually bake" when she shows up after work to head out on a ride with the other two, but still.

Shani even grabs a cookie herself when she swings by to check on Gideon—the big brown guy she was petting the other day. I can tell she thinks the cookie is good . . . but once she realizes I made them, she frowns and tells everyone they were a little dry and that it isn't sanitary to leave plates of food all over the barn, as if I had set up a giant buffet instead of bringing out a metal tin that was nearly already empty by the time she found it.

But still, there was a gleam in her eye even as she insulted me, a gleam that no matter how much she scowls she can't seem to shake, and I realize there's a chance that scowl maybe started as a smile that just got twisted as it made its escape.

* * *

THE FIRST TIME I use Shani's number it's because Otis is acting weird—stomping his feet and pinning his ears like he's possessed, when I go to turn him out. She rushes right over before declaring that he's just being grumpier than usual but is otherwise fine. I'm embarrassed I dragged her out of bed for that, but she tells me I did the right thing by calling, and even gives me this weird sort of half pat on my shoulder as she leaves, which feels kind of . . . nice.

The second time is when I find a horseshoe in one of the stalls of the full board horses and panic that someone's foot is falling off or something. This time Shani did say it needed to be fixed, but that it's not an emergency when a horse throws a shoe, so I don't need to be so worked up about it.

Sure enough, she comes around later that same afternoon to take care of it—and if I stare too long at her biceps while she heats the shoe in the little setup she has in the back of her pickup, and then hammers away to reshape it, cooling it before affixing it back to the little gray gelding's foot, oh well.

The third time I call her out though, it's because I finally found Christina's books for the business, and it looks like Shani is overdue five hundred dollars from before Christina got sick. Shani says Christina had bartered free room and board for Gideon, but I insist on paying her anyway.

Shani refuses at first, until I point out that she isn't taking Christina's money—she's technically taking mine now. She grins in a way I haven't ever seen and says, "Well when you put it like that." She rips the check out of my hand so fast I almost regret it.

Two days later, I'm calling her out again. This time I leave her a quick message to say it's not an emergency, but to come when she can and bring her farrier stuff. I'm grinning when I hang up.

See, Lita mentioned last night that Happy was almost due for a trim, and I want to spring for it myself as a thank-you for all of her help. I wouldn't even be able to limp along through the morning routine without the cheat sheet she made me, or all her early-morning check-in texts to make sure things were going smoothly and to remind me people—and hungry horses—were counting on me.

No good deed goes unpunished though, and by the time Shani pulls up just after dusk, looking exhausted and overworked, she rips into me that Happy is apparently on a regular schedule and wasn't due for another week. I let her rant at me about ruining her Friday night plans, and about how I don't know anything about horses, so why did I think I could decide when one needed a trim, let alone one under Shani's regular care.

When she finally stops complaining, I apologize—sincerely for once—and explain that I must have misunderstood, and that I was just trying to repay Lita. Shani's expression softens at that.

"All right," she finally says, rubbing a hand over her face. "No harm in me cleaning them out for her at least, since you were *trying* to be nice."

I question Lita about it the next day when I tell her what happened, and she laughs. Actually laughs at me. "Oh, you're not blaming me for this one!" she says. "You just keep looking for excuses to call her and we're all caught in the crosshairs."

"I do not," I insist, even though okay, maybe in this *one particular* case, I kind of did.

"If you're not careful, you're going to find yourself wifed up and buying horses of your own," she teases.

And that, that's like a bucket of ice water, because no I will not.

I'm the founder and CEO and, okay, only employee of Immaculate Events and the daughter of a woman with a growing stack of rom-com Blu-rays who needs me back home to watch them. I cannot afford, literally, to get distracted by a grumpy-ass horseshoer or her stupid biceps. Screw. That.

Chapter Six

The real estate agent, a woman named Ashley, finally calls me back and agrees to come over later the same morning. She sounds knowledgeable and experienced, although her initial exclamation of "You want to sell that old place?" doesn't instill me with as much confidence.

I call Nat, who manages to talk me through an absolute meltdown over the amount of shit I need to get done before I can sell this place, even though I don't even know what that is yet. Judging by Ashley's tone, I'm expecting it to be one step above burn it down and start over. At best.

"It's going to be okay," Nat says. "You'll find out what you need to do when the real estate agent gets there, and we'll take it step by step. Me and KiKi can come up on our days off to do any odd jobs and help out. The first thing you need to do is get a dumpster delivered. There was a lot of stuff in there that needs to go."

"You can just grab one at the store. They sell them at Home Depot and stuff," KiKi helpfully calls out. And, great, I guess I'm on speakerphone. I hate when she does that and doesn't tell me. One time, I was whining in great detail about the food poisoning

I got and how I hadn't left the toilet all day, only for me to realize I was on speaker. While she was at the grocery store. On Super Bowl Sunday.

"They sell dumpsters at Home Depot?" I ask doing my best to tamp down the weirdness I feel about a) being on speakerphone and b) throwing out Christina's stuff.

"Not real ones. They're like green, fabric-y ones," KiKi says, and I can practically hear her rolling her eyes. I fight the growing urge to remind her that she's not dealing with one of her many subcontractors right now. I'm a barista, and not even that, currently.

"Fabric-y?" I sigh instead, already overwhelmed. "I don't even know what that means. I'll just find a hardware store or something and pray they take pity on me. I'll figure it out." Then, desperate to change the subject, I add, "Hey, did you get that callback?"

I hear KiKi blow out a breath, and I know what's coming before Nat even answers. "No," she says, trying to play it off, but I can hear the hurt in her voice. "My agent said they wanted to go in a different direction. It's a freaking toilet paper commercial! How am I not even good enough for *that*?!"

"You are. You *are*," I say. "Their loss."

"Yeah, well, there's been too many people taking that loss lately," she says. "I haven't booked anything in weeks."

My heart breaks for her. I know how bad she wanted this one—*any* one really. She hasn't read for anything besides student films or random commercials in the last year. I know it's getting to her. I know what it feels like to have Zendaya dreams and a toilet paper reality.

"You will. I can feel it," I say, trying to cheer her up the way she did when Blake and I broke up. The way she *always* does.

"Yeah," she mumbles. "I gotta go. My shift starts in a half hour and I'm not even in my uniform."

"Okay, love you," I say, worry in my voice.

"Love you too," she says, before hanging up.

I check the clock, trying to decide what to do next. I don't really have time to go into town before Real Estate Agent Ashley arrives, but maybe I can start smaller. I dig out some garbage bags from under the sink in the kitchen and head into the basement to see what I can part with.

Aiyana eyes me curiously when she walks by to get her horse as I drag a garbage bag full of paint cans out onto the lawn—which promptly rips wide open—but if she has any opinion on my decision to start tossing stuff, she doesn't say anything. I resist the urge to say that I'll get a dumpster soon, like that will somehow prove I have things under control, but I decide not to, since the claim that I have anything under control is so obviously false.

The real estate agent shows up around eleven A.M. just as I'm carrying a box of old Christmas ornaments out to set beside the now strewn-about paint cans, and I wave to greet her. Ashley is a short Latinx woman, dressed in a smart purple business suit with a bright orange flower on her lapel and a leather notebook that she flips open as she carefully navigates the grass in her cute kitten heels.

I instantly like her, although her raised eyebrow as I wipe the sweat off my hand and hold it out to shake hers tells me she might not be sold as much on me. Perhaps my ratty "On Wednesdays we wear pink" T-shirt I'm wearing isn't making the best first impression. But hey, we all have our favorite cleaning day shirts, right? It couldn't be helped.

"It's been years since I've been over this way," Ashley says, reluctantly shaking my hand and then pulling out a pen from her notebook.

I fight the urge to say "same" and instead ask, "Did you know Christina?"

"A little. Everyone sort of knows everyone in a town this small. She was nice, your aunt, quiet mostly. Kept to herself on this property." She takes a few papers out of a folder as she follows me up the porch steps and into the house. "I pulled some possible comps, but it's a little tricky with the business part of it. Are you hoping to sell the business along with it or are you just looking to offload the property or land?"

"I'm not sure yet. I'm still looking into things."

"Well, I don't know how far you've gotten—or what its current state is—but I know this place was pretty popular for a while. One of the few places around here where everybody felt welcome," she says, giving me a look like I should know what that means. When I don't say anything, she continues, "On one hand, selling it with the business could limit potential buyers, but on the other hand, if we find the right one, it could add quite a bit of money onto the deal."

"I like the sound of that second part," I laugh.

She smiles politely and starts walking around the house, eyeing my couch bed/sleeping bag combo warily. "You're going to need to make this place a little less . . . lived in . . . before I take pictures to list it," she says. "I can already see quite a few repairs and recommendations."

"A few?" I ask, raising my eyebrows at the scratched-up floor, the torn wallpaper on the walls, and cracking popcorn ceiling. Not to mention the creaky porch steps and the fact that part of the outside wall on the second floor is just insulation without any siding over it. And that's just the main house. The barns and fences are twice as rough.

"Your message said you wanted to get it listed as soon as possible. If you want to be fast, we're going to target the things that will have the biggest impact, but unfortunately, even then I think it could sell for a much lower amount than you may be expecting."

I don't bother telling her that anything greater than zero will be a huge help.

"Did you have a number in mind?" I ask.

"I need to walk around the property a little bit more, but if it's sixty-three acres with a house and a barn—"

"Two houses."

"Excuse me?"

"Technically two houses. I guess Christina had a tenant." I point to the roof just visible on the other side of the pasture.

"Is it possible for me to get in there?"

Oh god, I should have seen this coming.

"There's somebody living there," I say. "I'll need to give them some notice."

Ashley nods. "Okay then, I'm going to take a little while to walk around the property if that's all right with you. We can schedule a tour of the other house as soon as you can get ahold of them. Once I have the list of repairs drawn up, and you tell me realistically if you're going to be able to pull them off, then I can give you a better estimate of what it might go for."

"Would you be able to give me a ballpark today?" I ask, anxious to have some clue what I'm dealing with. "A non-binding one, of course."

"Hmm, I'll have a better idea later," she says, leaning around me to scan the property. "But I'd say with a few improvements we could probably get around $250,000, depending on the condition of the other house. In a perfect world with updates, it'd probably go for well over four hundred, but I know you're on a time crunch. Our most likely offer is going to come from a flipper or an investor. They tend to lowball, but it's usually a cash offer, which means a fast closing with no hitches. We might be able to get a developer on board who wants to make this a cute little neighborhood or something." She shrugs. "We'll just have to wait and see."

I nod, every word falling out of my head at the idea of being handed hundreds of thousands of dollars. That would pay off my student loans and still leave me enough to get Immaculate Events going—and to find a new place to live near Mom so she could stop freaking out about me being so far away. She's been calling me so often to "check in" that I've had to start letting her go to voicemail to get anything done—which just makes her call more.

Ashley starts walking around making notes in her notebook and I go make myself busy in the barn before I can annoy her. JJ taught me how to clean out a stall the other night, and right now, while Otis is out in the main field with Gideon, seems like the perfect time.

The barn is empty, all the horses in various paddocks or pastures, so I don't hesitate to grab the little Bluetooth speaker I found in the office and connect it to my phone. Before I know it,

I'm ankle deep in shitty pine shavings, literally, belting out the newest Taylor Swift album—yes, I *am* using the rakes and shovels as microphones, why do you ask?

"You might actually suck a little less than I thought." Shani's voice cuts through the music and I jump, dropping my shovel and slamming my elbow into the wall with a yelp. Shani laughs, because of course she does, and she ambles toward me looking more relaxed than she has any right to.

"Easy, girl," she says, holding up her hands all calm, the way she did that time Otis escaped. "You spook easier than Uggo and he's a goddamn failed show pony."

"You shouldn't sneak up on people," I snap, my good mood ruined by my throbbing funny bone. If I wasn't already wishing she'd step in horseshit for scaring me, I definitely would be now that she's treating me like another one of her freaked-out pets.

"I called your name twice," Shani says, the little smirk back on her face as I hit pause on the music. And damn. I love that smirk. I want to kiss that smirk. I want to smack that smirk right off her face.

She's dressed in faded jeans today, her brown leather farrier apron still on from when she saw her last client. She's even wearing a beat-up cowboy hat, a look that I haven't seen yet. It makes her seem like she just stepped out of one of those spicy cowboy romances that I may or may not have downloaded onto my Kindle upon hearing I was inheriting a horse farm.

As if that wasn't enough to bring the swoons, she's also got the softest-looking light blue flannel layered over a white tank top so sheer I can see her navy-blue sports bra through the fabric and—I'm staring. Jesus, fuck, I should not be staring.

I can*not* be staring. I force my eyes back up just to find that her satisfied smirk has turned to a grin.

She comes closer, leaning lazily against the stall door, blocking me in. "So, what, you adding mucking out stalls to your résumé?"

I scoop up another pile of pine shavings and push past her to dump it into the wheelbarrow I've parked in the aisle.

"Maybe. Are you adding generic cowboy to yours?" I flick the brim of her hat as I walk back. She blushes, clearly embarrassed, so I add, "It suits you, I guess" and then go back to shoveling.

"Oh yeah?" There's a playful look in her eye I don't quite trust as she adjusts the hat back on her head. "And I think shoveling shit suits you."

"Nice," I say. "Such a charmer."

"I always aim to please," she laughs. "You know, speaking of charming, JJ and the others seem to really like you."

"Mm-hmm," I say, half listening while I wait for her next little barb.

Instead, she says, "They think I should ease up on you."

That gets my attention. I turn to face her, resting my arm on the shovel. "What do you think?"

She shrugs. "I think I didn't expect you to start pitching in around here and I may need to reassess my deep hatred. Though considering you charming remains a stretch."

"Deep hatred," I snort. "I didn't sense any of that deep hatred the other night when you snuck back to the office to steal more cookies." She protests but I hold up a hand. "I know, I know, they were very dry . . . that's why you needed to come back for more. Four different times."

"Maybe I was just hungry and hoping eventually I'd get one that wasn't stale."

"Mmm, I bet." I make another trip to the wheelbarrow, but this time when I walk past her, she holds out her hand.

"Shani Thomas," she says, and I look at her, surprised.

"We've met."

"Not really." She puts her hand over mine, still clamped around the shovel, and gives it a squeeze. Her eyes meet mine and send some unwelcome butterflies swirling up inside me. *Now is not the time.* I swallow them down as best as I can and smile.

"Molly McDaniel," I say, going along with it. "I'm pleased to finally meet you, Shani. Otis speaks very highly of you."

She laughs at that, a genuine one, and it's hard not to feel like I just won a prize. This is the closest I have ever come to seeing her with her guard down, and I'm not taking it for granted, even if hot horse girls are better left on my e-reader than in real life.

She looks down for a beat, and then meets my eyes. "Look," she says, rubbing the back of her neck. "I was pretty pissed off about you getting this place. I've been being an asshole about it, but I know it's not your fault."

"Shani Thomas," I say, tilting my head at her. "Is that an apology I just heard?"

"No, ma'am," she says. "Just a statement of facts. But how about I help you finish up in this stall, and then you help me with Gideon's. You already got all the stuff out. No sense putting it away when I'll need it later anyway."

And is this . . . is she asking me to hang out with her? I mean, sure, when I envisioned us around hay it was more as in "rolling in the" and less "scooping shit out of," but still. This feels loaded. I mean, I *do* only have a few weeks to live out my rodeo fantasies before I'm back in the real world, behind the milk frother at The Grind, waiting for Ashley to find me a life-changing fairy godmother—or a potential buyer, whichever.

"Sounds like I'm getting the better part of the deal," I say, passing her a shovel. She does a cute little hop before taking it, and if I wasn't crushing on her before, I definitely am now. Especially once she takes her gear off and tosses it over the stall door. She adds her flannel to the pile—her arm and back muscles now on full display—and I have to fight the urge to stare.

Think of horseshit, Molly, I tell myself. *You're basically standing in a giant litter box right now. This isn't sexy. This can't be sexy.*

We work in silence for a few minutes, and I wonder if she's having as much trouble with behaving appropriately as I am. One glance tells me she's all business though, her face perfectly neutral as she shovels out the filthy shavings. I need to rein it in. I need to harness every single butterfly that reared up in my belly when she took my hand and send them straight to the kill pen. She's offered me a reset, a second chance, and I'm not going to blow it this time.

Given the fact that I'm getting more and more desperate to jump her bones each time she bends over and her tank hangs loose would be the *definition* of blowing it. She's not making it easy though.

As the time passes, I swear she's making excuses to lean over, to lean closer, to stay in my line of vision. If I wasn't so sure she didn't like me, I would think she was crushing on me right back.

I decide she's just oblivious at best, and deliberately fucking with me at worst.

"How did you get into horse hooves," I blurt out, desperate to focus on something, anything, besides the tornado of butterflies screaming through my body.

"I don't really know that anyone has put it like that to me before." She laughs. "Farriers are more than just hooves though. We're kinda like . . . well, people come to us like vets. Technically, that's outside of our purview but owners always end up calling us for everything, especially out here where equine vets are few and far between and the ones we have don't offer credit or payment options like I do."

"So you, what, do this to 'help the people'?" I ask, even making air quotes.

Shani laughs. "Not really. It's just kind of always been something that interested me. When I was little, my family traveled a lot with our horses, and my dad's best friend was a farrier who usually came along with us. She was always showing me how to do stuff; pick hooves, wrap them, medicate them. Then as I got older, she started showing me more about how to make a living off of it."

"Your dad traveled with his farrier? That is a devotion to horse feet I did not know existed."

She shakes her head. "No, he was on the rodeo circuit and we all followed along. He got her a job on the circuit too so they could hang out. I think they were probably more than buddies for a bit, but I don't want to know."

"That's kind of cool though."

"I guess."

"Are you and your dad close then?"

She clears her throat, clearly uncomfortable. "He, uh, he died a few years back so, I don't know. I guess? We talked regularly, he checked in, but we weren't all up in each other's business."

"Oh, sorry."

She waves me off. "You didn't know."

I want to ask what happened to him—if it was cancer like Christina too—but the hard expression on her face makes it clear that this line of conversation is over.

"Was your mom in the rodeo too?"

She sucks air through her teeth, narrowing her eyes as she looks at me. "My mom took off long before Daddy died. Me and my brother stayed here, with Christina, when we weren't on the circuit with him."

"Oh. How did I not know that? That's . . . wow. So, she raised you?"

"Basically. My father was always on tour, so he left us here more than he didn't. Lochlin joined him full-time when he turned fifteen. He had fallen in love with the circuit too and couldn't wait any longer. After that it was just me and Christina, and . . . now it's just me."

"Wait, were you here that summer I was? I don't remember you."

Shani shakes her head. "No, I always spent a few weeks in the summer with my dad. We missed each other by like a week. You left your awful drawings all over my room though," she says, with a little smile. "Why did every horse have blue eyes? It was creepy."

"I have no idea." I laugh. "You know, I did wonder why Christina had so many clothes in my size."

"You wore my clothes?" she gasps, fake scandalized.

"My mom sent me with like a dozen sundresses! What was I supposed to wear!"

"Man, you just love helping yourself to my stuff, don't you," she says, teasingly . . . but my face falls anyway.

"Shani—"

"Anyway," she says, cutting me off with a look that tells me not to press it. "Long story short, I hated school, but I loved horses, so your aunt bribed me and said as long as I graduated, she would set me up with an apprenticeship for a farrier she knew, since my dad's friend was still working the rodeos. I kept my word, she kept hers, and here we are. It's hard work, but it's honest work, and you feel like you're making a difference. Unlike jumping on the back of some poor abused bronco and getting thrown around like a rag doll."

"Is that what your dad did?"

She laughs, but it's bitter. "No, he mostly just got high and hung out by the time I was born. Occasionally, he tended to the stables and whatnot. That's why they let him stay even after he couldn't ride anymore." She sighs. "The broncos are what my ridiculous brother does. He claims it's safer than bull riding but it all looks stupidly risky to me. I don't know. These boots I'm wearing came from his sponsorship deals, so I suppose I can't complain too much. At least he keeps me looking good."

"That hat his too?" I ask, letting what she said sink in. I don't know how all this works really; I've never even been to a rodeo let alone been in one, but having multiple sponsorship deals makes me think her brother might be kind of a big deal. Add it to the list of things I need to google later.

"Nah, the hat was Christina's. She gave it to me when I finished my apprenticeship and started working on my own clients. I used to steal it all the time when I was little. It meant a lot when she hung it on my head and said I'd earned it."

"I'm sorry I never knew how close you and she were . . ." I trail off, not sure what else to say.

"Closest thing I had to family besides my dumbass brother," she snorts. "Or at least that's how it felt on my end. With her leaving you this place though, I guess I don't really know what to think anymore."

"I'm sorry," I say again because what else can I? I didn't realize this was her home, her surrogate mom, her whole life before I crowded in it.

"For what? Existing?" she asks, and I try not to fixate on the way her biceps flex as she throws another shovelful into the wheelbarrow.

"For intruding."

She pauses then, like I caught her off guard, and studies my face. Whatever she's looking for, she seems to find, because the smallest smile appears on her lips, along with a little crinkle in her eyes. "I really might have been wrong about you," she says.

Before I can respond though, Ashley bursts into the barn apparently finished with her assessment. "There you are! I've been looking for you," she says, the heels of her shoes clicking on the hard barn floor. "I should have everything I need for now, and the sooner we can get into that other house—and maybe even get rid of the renter depending on what their contract says—the better. I may have someone in mind already." She beams. "He reached out to an associate of mine recently and I know he's been looking for land that would work for duplexes and condos. This could fit the bill if we can raze the structures on it and the town agrees to subdivide. While I make some calls to that end, I'll email you a list of repairs to look over and see what you can reasonably get done before you head back down to the city."

My face flushes hot as Shani's gentle smile fades into first confusion, and then realization.

"I . . . thank you," I say but Ashley's already heading out to her car. She gives me a quick wave, writing in her notebook as she walks.

I turn back to Shani with a guilty expression. This isn't how I wanted her to find out about this and I can tell by her face whatever warmth was blooming between us is ice-cold now.

"You're selling it," she says, and I can see the hurt and anger flare up in her eyes.

"I don't know the first thing about horses," I say, realizing how bad this makes me sound. Shani just confided in me about how much this place means to her, and now not only did I take it from her, but I'm most likely going to sell it to somebody who will probably turn it into condos.

"You could learn," she says. "You *are* learning."

"I need the money. I'm trying to start a—"

"Forget it. I don't care about your excuses." She snorts. "This is just never gonna make sense to me. I was the one here by her side the entire time. Right in the room next door from beginning to end with this cancer thing. You didn't even call. You didn't even come!"

"I didn't know," I say, like that even matters.

Wait, the room next door? The locked room? It was Shani's? I don't get to ask before she continues.

"Of course you didn't, probably because of your goddamn mother, right?"

"Hey! Leave my mom out of this!"

"You know, Christina actually convinced herself that the only reason you didn't respond to all the cards and checks she sent you over the years was because you were *so loyal*. She was *proud* of you for standing by your mother, can you believe that?"

"What are you talking about?" I snap, my mind spinning at the fact that Shani seems to know a hell of a lot more than I do about what happened between them.

"You're not loyal though, Molly, are you? Just greedy. Just selfish. You showed up to the will reading like a vulture picking at the scraps of your aunt's life and I had you pegged right there. But then I saw you trying. Even Otis and Edward warmed up to you and they basically hate everybody but me. I thought, maybe I misjudged you, and you weren't just looking to fatten your bank account off a tragedy. Maybe there was some reason I just didn't see yet that made Christina give you the place." She shakes her head. "I guess that just makes me as stupid as her, now doesn't it."

"That's not fair! You don't even know me!"

"You want to talk to *me* about fairness, Molly? How fair is it that Christina got sick? How fair is it that she went and died on me? *How fair is* it that some stranger gets to decide if I lose everything else now too?" She huffs out a harsh breath, like the reality of her situation just punched her right in the stomach. I take a step toward her, but she holds up her hand. "Go on, Molly, I'll finish these stalls up on my own."

"Shani—"

"Go on, Molly," she says again, this time more firmly.

So I do.

Chapter Seven

I'm baking cookies for Shani.

I don't know what else to do. I've been alternating these last few days between being mad at her for blaming me for something I have no control over and breaking my own heart imagining how she must be feeling. The way Shani talked about how much Christina meant to her . . . Not to mention her finding out like that that I'm selling right out from under her. I feel like a monster.

An intensely curious monster though. She seems to know a lot about what went down between my mom and Christina. Way more than I do. My mom was over the moon when I called her that night after my fight with Shani . . . until she realized I wanted to talk about her and Christina's falling-out. She said it was none of my business, to leave it buried, and then changed the subject to ask me if I really wanted to toss out all those NFL jerseys I acquired dating Blake. She thought she might be able to sell them on consignment for a little bit of extra cash instead.

I told her to go wild, I didn't care about them anymore, and after two more failed attempts to get her to talk about Christina, made an excuse to get off the phone. When Mom doesn't want to talk about something, you can't change her mind. I must get my stubbornness from her.

It's been a few days since the real estate agent came and blew everything up—yes, Ashley did send me the list of tasks, but no, I haven't looked through them yet. I tried, I swear, but when I saw how long the list was, I immediately panicked and noped out.

Nat and KiKi are coming out in a couple days, and we'll look through them together and come up with a plan. At least I think it's tomorrow, time gets a little blurry here, especially now that I'm not even working the call center job. Every day, I just wake up, throw on some jeans and a ponytail and fuss around with a grumpy horse and his little donkey in between barn chores.

I tried to explain to Nat on the phone how awful I felt about everything with Shani, but she didn't really get it. She accused me of falling into my old patterns again, as if feeling really guilty about selling someone's home they expected to inherit was just me being extra about things. I think her exact words to me were "by all means have fantastic fucking sex with the cowgirl, but don't start thinking you're going to go all desperado and live your life out there mending fences. Get over the guilt, it's a wasted emotion."

She's right, on like a really superficial level, I guess. None of this was my choice, and I'm doing the best I can, but I can't shake the growing pit in my stomach about it all. The feeling that I've taken something from Shani, stolen it, even if that isn't true.

The guilt is overwhelming.

Thus, the cookie baking. Guilt cookies. Guilt-kies, if you will. I know she loved them last time—even if she pretended that she didn't. Maybe if I give her some, just for her, I'll be able to sleep again at night. *Sorry I took your inheritance, how about a little treat instead?*

I groan and slide the cookies onto the cooling rack. It's been almost three whole days and Shani is still truly avoiding me. I need her to stop—for reasons both emotional and practical— like that I really do need to get inside her house and report back to Ashley what we're working with over there.

So, I pack up the cookies, and I make my way over, and I try not to think too much about what I'm feeling and whether I should or shouldn't be feeling it.

Shani's house is small, maybe not even a thousand square feet if I had to guess (and I've gotten pretty good at guessing since Ashley keeps texting me asking to measure the bathroom, the kitchen, and various things while she puts together her ideas for "staging" purposes). It's not the fanciest house I've seen, sure, but it's much better kept up than the main house, with its missing shingles and siding. This one even looks like it's been recently painted, and the steps don't squeak or bend when I walk up onto the little front porch. Even most of the falling leaves are raked up, stashed in little bags in neat rows beside her pickup truck.

While Shani and I appear to be roughly the same age, give or take, it's clear when I see those yard bags that she is significantly more of an adult than I am. Than I probably ever will be. She uses lawn bags. She's held someone's hand through cancer. Through hospice. I couldn't even go in the backyard when my parents buried my hamster after he died of old age.

"Did you need something?" Shani asks, pulling her door open before I can even knock.

I stand there awkwardly shifting from foot to foot—my words failing me as I realize she must have just gotten out of the shower. Her hair is wet and a few stray strings trail in front of her eyes, which she brushes back impatiently, still blocking the door and definitely not making any move to let me in.

She's wearing the coziest-looking pair of burnt-orange sweatpants I've ever seen, along with her signature white tank top—but the sports bra is missing, and I can see the outline of her nipples in the cold night air. I look away, blushing furiously.

This time instead of leaning into the flirting, she crosses her arms, her eyebrows raising as she fixes a frown on her face. "Molly," she says and now her voice is somehow even harder. Less welcoming. "Why are you here?"

"I made these," I say, thrusting the plastic container full of cookies in her direction. "The chocolate chip cookies you liked along with some biscotti. It's . . . I only really know how to bake stuff I learned at the café, but I think you'll like it. I hope you . . ." I trail off.

She takes them from my hand but scrunches up her face as she inspects them, as if they might be poisoned or something. "What's this for? Are you trying to butter me up before you evict me? Do you need to measure the square footage of my bedroom? Count the bathrooms or something?"

"No! Well, technically, yes, I do need to do that," I say, deciding at the last second to be honest, "but that's not why I'm here. Can I come in?"

Shani hesitates for a moment, looking between me and the cookies.

"Please?" I add. She shrugs and pulls the door wider, stepping back to let me in.

I'm not sure what to expect when I walk into her house, but it isn't this. There's a new-looking woodstove in the corner, letting off a warm, dry heat that I didn't even know was possible to accomplish—especially after staying in my aunt's old drafty farmhouse. The décor is basic, but nice. The walls are a clean white, the floors hardwood, and a modern gray couch sits facing a large television, which is paused on what looks like a rodeo competition. Beside it is a large industrial-looking black lamp with an Edison bulb, casting light over a stack of books I definitely want to investigate more.

"Is that your brother?" I gesture toward the screen.

"Yeah," she says, still standing rigidly by the door. "I record them and watch them after I'm sure he didn't die. I like to have them, just in case."

Just in case of what, I wonder, but I don't ask.

"Can I sit?" I ask, even though the annoyance radiates off Shani in waves.

"What do you want, Molly?" she asks, her voice more resigned now. I'll take that as a no.

I sigh. "What am I supposed to do in this situation? I know you're pissed I'm selling, and I fully get that," I say, the words falling out before I can swallow them. "I don't know why she left this place to me and not you! I haven't ridden a horse in sixteen years, and even then, it was just for the summer . . . but my back is against the wall, okay?! I don't have a choice here. I have sixty-five thousand dollars in student loans and a job pouring coffee. Before this happened, I was living in my childhood bedroom because I can't afford rent *and* the minimum payments, with a mom who alternates between treating me like her stand-in husband or a little kid—who won't even tell me what went down between her and Christina, even though maybe that would give me some semblance of a clue about why I'm here. Not that you'll talk to me about it either, because of course you hate me again! Why wouldn't you? You see me as a *vulture*," I say, desperately trying to hold it together.

Shani seems confused by my outburst and leans back against the door. Always leaning. Always watching. It drives me crazy in the best and worst ways.

"Everything I need to start my life is on the other side of this sale. I can pay off my loans, get an apartment, and hopefully even have enough left over to start my business, if things really go my way."

"Your business?"

"Event planning, like weddings and milestone birthdays and anniversaries, things like that. Immaculate Events," I say, because if I say it enough maybe it's real. "I want to make people happy, and make their special days awesome, basically. I'm sure you think that's silly but that's like my whole thing. I might not ever get my happily ever after, my relationships tend to explode, but I can help other people have them! I can make anyone's dream wedding a reality. I'm good at it! No, I'm great at it!" I say. "But instead of doing that, I'm stuck. I'm double stuck, because for me to have the life I've been working for and dreaming about, I have to basically kick you out of your home. Not to mention kicking out all of the boarders, and who knows what's going to happen to Otis and Eddie—"

"I wouldn't let anything happen to them."

"Well, good," I say, not realizing how on the verge of tears I am until I wipe at my eyes. "Sorry." I sniffle. "I just came here to give you guilt-kies and now I'm dumping all my problems all over your nice living room and I—"

"Guilt-kies?"

"Shit, I didn't mean to call them that." I rub my temples, a headache coming on fast and strong.

"I thought you said it was chocolate chip?"

"Yeah, I just . . . I made them for you because I feel so freaking guilty, and I started calling them guilt cookies in my head and then—"

"You shortened it to guilt-kies?"

Her eyebrows scrunch together as she looks back down at the container in her hand. And god, I'm making a mess of this. I always make a mess of things. I just try so damn hard, with everyone, to be everything, and I screw it all up. Jesus, I can't even hand over cookies properly.

Shani sighs, finally stepping away from the door.

"If these were apology cookies, I might eat them," she snaps, handing them back to me. "But guilt cookies, no thanks. That's to make you feel better, not me."

And that does it. The straw that broke the camel's back or whatever. Before I know it, or have any prayer of making a graceful exit, I'm bursting into tears in the middle of my very hot, very angry, farrier's living room. Screw this.

Too late, I try to bolt to the door, but she blocks me. "Hey, hey, hey, hang on," she says, holding up her hands in surrender. "What's with the tears? Just . . . hang on a second."

And god, I wish she'd make up her mind. First, she wouldn't let me in, and now she won't let me leave.

"It's fine," I say, trying to step around her, but she shifts to stay in my way.

"It's not fine. You're crying."

I shake my head, clutching the cookies even tighter. "Just ignore me, okay? I was trying to make things right, but I made them worse. Again. I'm sorry, I shouldn't have come over here."

"Well, you did, and I'm not about to let you run out into the night, crying your eyes out across a pasture." I think she's being nice until she adds, "All I need right now is you breaking your leg on some hole you can't see and making things even harder on all of us. Lita just got back on her morning rotation at the hospital since you're here to turn the horses out. I'm not making her give that up again."

And okay, fuck you very much.

"I won't break my leg, don't worry." I push past her and storm out, slamming her door behind me. I march down her steps and practically catapult myself into the pasture that serves as the quickest cut through between my house and hers.

Break my leg. Break my leg. How stupid does she think I am that I'll—

My foot slides on a particularly muddy patch and I fall on my ass spectacularly, cookie tin flying in the air, because of course. Of course! Before I can stand up on my own, a hand grabs my arm, and helps me to stand. It's Shani, because the universe hates me. And also, because I barely made it ten feet into the pasture before falling, so I'm sure she witnessed it all going down.

"Are you just here to gloat?" I grumble, scooping up the cookies and wiping the mud off my jeans.

"No," she says and clicks on a huge flashlight. "I just want you to get home safe."

"Do you seriously not even have enough faith in me to walk across a field by myself?"

"That's not why. Can I please just walk you home?"

"Then why?" I practically shout, anger replacing my mortification.

"You brought me guilt cookies, right?" Shani says, waving her arms around in exasperation. "Consider this my guilt flashlight, okay? And it's here to get you home safely."

I roll my eyes, but there's really no heat behind the action. I can get behind a guilt flashlight, I guess. If I have to. I *did* bring guilt cookies first. I take a deep breath, rubbing the mud off my hands a little harder. "Whatever, let's just go."

I think I see a hint of a smile, but I can't be sure in the dark.

We walk silently through the field together then—Shani carefully lighting the way and occasionally tugging me to the side to avoid every mud patch or dip in the earth. She seems to have every blade of grass memorized and I wonder how many times she's walked this path in her life. How many times it took before she decided to just move back into the room beside Aunt Christina's.

Which, speaking of.

"Hey, you used to stay in the one room upstairs, right? The locked one?"

"Yeah," she answers, and I can tell she's uncomfortable talking about it.

"Do you happen to have the key for that?"

"Lost it," she says, and picks up the pace.

I think she's lying but decide not to push it tonight. It's not an emergency anyway. The list Ashley sent me was long enough to keep me busy for a bit.

"Oh," I say.

"Yeah." Even though Shani is clearly uncomfortable now, her hand stays steady against my arm—warm and heavy, and peeking out from an oversized flannel she threw over her tank at some point before rushing after me. And damn, it looks soft.

No, it looks cozy; everything she wears is so fucking cozy. Which is so damn opposite of her personality that it's short-circuiting my brain. It's not a crush, I decide. It's just . . . attractive confusion.

Right. That.

When we finally make it to the other side, Shani pulls the gate open at the edge of my yard. I think this is where she'll stop, but she doesn't. She sees me all the way to the door, her hand still guiding my elbow gently and her light shining the way.

She's being pretty nice for an asshole. I huff out a tiny laugh at this newest contradiction, and she scrunches up her face.

"What?" she asks, apprehensive but clearly curious.

"I was just wondering to myself how someone as prickly as you could be so polite and freaking cozy all the time. It's not fair."

And there she goes, trying to hold in her smirk again. She looks down, hiding any proof of humor from me. "You think I'm cozy?"

"I think you're an asshole."

"But I'm a cozy asshole?" she asks.

I shake my head, fighting a smile of my own. "Irrelevant," I say, pushing open my door. I try to shut it, but she blocks it with her boot, and it bounces back open.

"It might be a little relevant," she says, and my jaw hits the floor.

"Are you . . . flirting with me right now?"

"Would you like it if I was?" she asks, like that's any sort of answer.

"You're giving me whiplash."

"That's funny, considering you're the one flipping my life upside down," she says, all hint of teasing gone.

"I didn't do this to you," I say, gently.

"But you're the one who's here, Molly," she says, suddenly studying the scuff marks on her boots. "I can't yell at her. I can't ask her why."

"I'm sorry," I say, because what else is there.

She crosses her arms and leans against the doorframe. "You're for sure gonna sell, then?"

"I don't have a choice," I say, and then it hits me. "Wait, what if *you* bought this place from me? That would solve everything."

She blows out a long breath. "There's no way I could. Believe me, I looked into it immediately when I found out you were getting it, no offense."

"None taken."

"Unfortunately, I'm out of the running. I do okay as a farrier, but I lost a lot of my business helping Christina this last year. I let some things slip with my credit, and I lived off a lot of my savings. I gotta build my clients back up first and get everything sorted with my bills. Lenders look at last year's taxes and my credit score and they'll run screaming."

Great. Not only can she not buy it, but the reason she can't buy it is because she was taking care of my aunt. What the hell, universe?

"What am I supposed to do?" I whisper, more to myself than her, but she answers me anyway.

"Otis already likes you and you know how to sling shit, that's half the battle," she teases. "Plus, it's kinda funny watching you flail around in the barn with that chart Lita made you."

"If I didn't know better, I'd almost think you liked having me around." I laugh.

Shani doesn't respond right away, just chews the inside of her lip, before finally saying, "Christina made a nice living off this place. I could help you build it back up if you wanted. I won't bullshit you about bills, I know what it's like to hit tough times, but you could at least run the numbers to see if they worked," she says. When I don't answer right away, she looks embarrassed. "I wouldn't have to be involved, if that's the problem."

"It's not," I say, too quickly. "That's really unexpectedly sweet—"

"Coming from someone as big of an asshole as I am?" she asks, her eyes glinting in the porch light as she pushes off the doorframe and steps closer.

"Coming from anyone," I say, my heart thrumming from her nearness as I look up at her.

"Then I better quit while I'm ahead." Her gaze dips down to my lips and then back to my eyes, and I almost incinerate when she gives me a crooked smile. "Don't decide anything yet, Molly, either way. At least run the numbers first."

"Shani—" I say, but she holds up her hand to cut me off.

"I like not being mad at you for once," she says, shifting the tiniest bit closer, all clean laundry and cologne and that smile. That smile. It takes all my willpower not to close the distance between us with a soft mouth and a curious tongue. "Let's just leave it, and take that win for the night."

She runs her hand down the side of my arm as she dips her head toward me. My eyes close, hoping for a kiss that doesn't come. She steps back instead, clearing her throat and putting a safe distance between us.

I huff out an embarrassed laugh, doing my part to break the tension. "Yes, yeah," I say, not even sure what I just agreed to, but knowing that if I stare at Shani's mouth for one more second, I'm going to do something I might regret. No scratch that. I won't regret it, but maybe *she* will, and I can't risk that.

"Okay," she says, taking the cookies from my hand and definitively ending whatever moment we just had. "On that note, me and my guilt flashlight are gonna head home to finish watching my brother ride on the back of an angry animal while I eat your stale, dry, guilt-kies in peace. You—" She waves her hand around me. "You have a good night over here too. Neither one of us needs to talk about anything else or go running out into the dark again. Deal?"

"Deal," I say, quietly, my whole body humming at the sight of her pulling her flannel tighter against the wind as she turns to leave.

"Wait, Shani?" I call out, just as she reaches the gate at the edge of my property.

She looks at me but doesn't say anything.

"Just . . . thanks for walking me home tonight," I say, a million other thoughts crowding my head, like *stay* and *kiss me*—all things that should be swallowed instead of spoken.

Shani nods and turns home. Pretty soon, she's just a slash of light cutting through the enveloping darkness as she makes her way through the field. But I saw it, even if she didn't mean for me to. I saw her smile, and she smiled like she meant it. And I felt it, even if she didn't want me to, that almost kiss. That ghost of what could have been.

And maybe, I think, as I watch her all the way until she's safely inside, maybe I could stay . . . just a little bit longer. Turn the renovations down from a rush job to a nice steady pace. Just for a second.

Chapter Eight

I could help you build it back up if you wanted.

Shani's words are still echoing in my head the next morning, even as I look over the email with the list of repairs and staging recommendations from Ashley, and the fifty-seven TikToks and memes my mother has sent me this morning with the heading "Can't wait till you're back home." Most of them won't even load since my cell service is so weak, so I can only imagine what they are.

I can't believe I'm actually considering staying, even if it is the teeniest tiniest bit of my brain. I can't believe I'd even *want* to consider it. It's true that feeding and loving on Otis is turning into the highlight of my day—shit, even the donkey is getting pretty obsessed with me, although that probably has something to do with how often I sneak into the paddock to feed him and Otis apples and peppermints when nobody is there to stop me. And it's true that getting to spend more time with Shani is definitely a draw. But is that *enough*? I don't know.

It's thoughts like this that've had me pinned to this chair on my porch, watching this little mini universe Christina created at the barn come and go without me. Most of the boarders are here today, enjoying early Saturday morning trail rides or utilizing the pens for lessons or training. JJ is filming a TikTok over in pasture two, and Lita and Aiyana are brushing out their horses together in the main barn.

Shani was here for a minute—just long enough to check Otis's foot, surprise JJ and Aiyana with coffees, and then leave without saying goodbye, so I guess Otis must be healing fine. Maybe she's feeling a little awkward after last night, but I know her professionalism would have had her on my porch if there was really a problem, and it's not like I expected a coffee anyway. Just because she said she "likes not being mad at me" doesn't mean we're *friends* or anything. Besides, she had her truck loaded up with all her farrier stuff, so I'm sure she's got a long day of work ahead of her.

I've got a long day of thinking.

The two biggest things holding me back from just jumping right in: my mother and Immaculate Events. First, I don't know what my mother would do if I ended up moving out here. An hour plus away might as well be the moon. She can barely drive, doesn't even have a car, and relies on public transportation to get everywhere she needs. I would be depriving her of companionship (which I've done before, when I moved in with Blake, but I was only a couple blocks away), half of my rent money (she can technically afford it, but still), and leaving our student loans up in the air once the forbearance ends in another month (not cool). As my cosigner, she would be on the hook if I missed a payment, so I absolutely *cannot* do that.

Even if I figured out the financial side of all of this, it still leaves the fact that my mother hated it when I lived blocks away, let alone fifty miles. She's being semi-cool right now because there's an expiration date on our distance. She knows I'm going to be back as soon as this is wrapped up. I don't know how she would react if the circumstances were different.

It's been just us for *so* long, ever since Dad left. I'd be lying if I said I didn't feel guilty about the idea of moving forward with my own life, whether that means staying here or getting my own place in the city again—for real this time though. Not like with Blake, where I still swung by almost every day to do laundry or watch a show with her or eat dinner.

I don't know.

And then there's Immaculate Events, my dream. My *lifelong* dream, that I incurred tens of thousands of dollars in debt to pursue. Walking away from it now feels a little like leaving my American Girl doll stranded at the altar . . . or myself. Am I really ready to set that aside to shovel horseshit all day? To live in this reality of crumbling fences, and vet bills, and mud, and hay instead of helping people create fantasies of beautiful cakes, and flowers, and gowns so beautiful it takes your breath away?

But then there's Shani and our almost kiss, and the horses, and all the new friends I'm making, and the fact that for once in my life I feel a little bit useful instead of totally stuck. It's an intoxicating combination.

Almost too intoxicating.

I need advice, and I need it stat. I'm pretty sure Nat's at the coffee shop right now for the weekend morning rush, so I text instead of call. Just a simple:

Hey what if I kept the place though?

My phone starts ringing before I even have a chance to set it back down.

"Have you lost your ever-loving mind?" Nat asks, without so much as a greeting.

"Hello to you too." I laugh.

"You can't keep the place, Molly. You have no money, you have no experience, you weren't even a horse girl in elementary school! You can't just become one now!"

"Oh, is that the rule? I didn't realize I was closing a door when I doodled kittens instead of ponies in my third-grade composition notebook," I scoff.

"Is this about the hot horseshoe woman?"

"No." *Yes.*

"Don't lie to me, Molly! You suck at it. Please, you cannot keep an entire freaking stable as a grand gesture to win over some girl you're into."

"That's not what I'm doing!"

"Of course it is, that's what you always do! You become them and then you break up and you cry and then you're on to the next one."

"That's kind of fucking hurtful, Nat," I say.

"Well, sorry, but I'm currently hiding in a bathroom stall, while Randy handles the rush, because I had to pretend to have a stomach issue to call you back! It's not easy without you here, you know. I couldn't even go to an open audition yesterday because we were so short-staffed."

"Shit, really?" I hadn't considered how my absence might be affecting Nat *and* the coffee shop, not just my mom and me.

"And what about your mom? You're just going to leave her? Molly, you could barely move a mile down the road from her last time!"

"I know, I know," I say, just as another text from my mom comes in. This one is a picture of two Redbox movies, followed by missing our movie nights! Love, mom ☺

Impeccable timing.

"This is like when you pretended to love football, because Blake did. You blew all that money you had set aside for Immaculate Inc. or whatever to freeze your ass off at stadiums and cosplay being a fanatic. Now everything's packed up in a box labeled toss and you're throwing yourself into a new daydream."

"Nat, it's not like that. I know it *sounds* like before, but I'm actually thinking this through. I promise. I'm just looking at all my options."

"Weddings, Molly. Think weddings, please. Not manure and country queers who probably voted for Trump."

"There's no way she voted for Trump."

"I'm just saying, while you're caught up in your cowgirl fantasy make sure you know where she was on January 6th."

"Jesus, Nat," I say, heading inside for a little bit more privacy.

"It's true!" she says. "I don't want you to blow a real opportunity because you have heart eyes yet again for someone you barely know."

"I just think I should consider every angle before I decide to sell," I say, trying hard not to think of Shani's face because this isn't just about her. *It isn't. Is it?*

"Look, me and KiKi will be there in a couple days, right? Like we planned? Did you get the list from the real estate agent yet?"

"Yeah," I say, resigned that I'm somehow even more confused about things than I was before.

"Cool. Forward it to me, please? I'll get some things together that we might need for repairs, and I'll make sure KiKi brings all the right tools. I promise, the second you see me you'll snap out of this. You're just trapped right now in this bargain basement cowboy movie, and maybe it feels like you're the main character of a rom-com but you're not. You're not! Do not be the sophisticated city girl who moves to a small town to bake cookies all day or something. Keep your 401k and your future and your bennies!"

I don't bother mentioning that Randy doesn't offer a 401k, or any other benefits for that matter, and that working in a coffee shop full of asshole crypto bro customers and harried stay-at-home moms with their financial sector spouses isn't exactly the height of city sophistication . . . in fact, I do more cookie baking *there* than I've done here.

"That's not . . ." I trail off when I notice JJ running up the path to my house with a giant coffee and a paper. "Hang on a second, Nat," I say, stepping back out onto my porch. "JJ?"

"Morning, Moll," he says cheerfully. "Shani asked me to run this over to you. She had to jet. Some emergency at the Smith farm and all that."

"Nat, I have to go," I say. "Call me back after work?"

"Whatever, I have to get back out there anyway," she says, clearly still annoyed when she hangs up.

I push open the screen door and JJ holds out a large, iced coffee with a smile. "She didn't know what to put in it, so she gave me this." He holds up a paper bag bursting with straws, sugar, and creamers. "We have oat milk in the office too, if you'd prefer that."

I take it from him, confused. "This is from Shani?"

"Right? I'm just as weirded out as you are. Maybe test it for poison first? She shoved it in my hands, told me to run it up here and then took off like something was chasing her. I had to finish my TikToks for the week first, so, sorry. But it's cold anyway and you were on the phone, so I didn't think you'd really care that it was a little late."

"That's so nice. Tell her thank you."

"Or you could tell her." He laughs. "I know you have her number. You found enough reasons to talk to her last week."

"Well, I'm *also* sure she could've taken two seconds to walk the coffee up here herself, but here we are. Thank you for being our middleman."

JJ shakes his head as he walks away. I swear I hear him mutter "hopeless." And yeah. Maybe. But it looks like I'm not the only one.

* * *

A KNOCK ON my door pulls me out of my cleaning trance. It's evening already, well past dinner. I must have lost track of time. Today, I tackled the kitchen, scrubbing every bit of it to within an inch of its life. If I do decide to sell, there are things on the list like "repaint cabinets" and "remove torn wallpaper," that have to be done regardless, and if I don't . . . well, I need the space clean anyway. It felt like a logical place to start.

I pull the side door open, expecting to see Lita or maybe JJ again, but instead it's Shani standing there, all hot and sheepish, doing her signature half lean against the doorframe.

"Hey," she says quietly.

"Hey yourself," I say, stepping back to let her in.

I wish I wasn't in a ratty Nirvana shirt that I got from the clearance section of Target. I wish I wasn't covered in dust and grime and smelling like oven cleaner right now. Because she smells like crisp autumn air and leather, and something else I can't quite place that makes me want to bury my face against her neck and breathe in forever.

"I saw the light was on, so I thought I'd swing by. Sorry I had to rush out this morning. JJ bring you the coffee?" she asks, like it's the most normal thing. Like she didn't still hate me thirty-one hours ago. She pulls her hat off her head and sets it on the table, and I pretend it doesn't thrill me to see it sitting there like she plans to stay awhile.

"Yeah, he brought it," I say, "and about half the creamer in the whole county."

She laughs. "I was trying to be diligent."

"You were," I say, setting my rag down. "Two creams, one sugar, by the way."

"Hmm?"

"For next time," I say, hoping to god there is a next time.

"Looks good in here," she says, looking around and not acknowledging what I just said. "I don't think it's been this clean since before Christina was sick. You could eat off the floors when she was in her prime."

"Really?" I ask, because while the house wasn't, like, disgusting, it was nowhere near eat-off-the-floors clean when I moved in.

Shani sighs. "Yeah, we let things slip a little. Everyone was chipping in at the end, coming or going when they had a second. We kinda just wanted to be by her bed, you know, not scrubbing toilets or stocking cabinets." She has the good sense to look guiltily down at her own boots—still on her feet, on my clean floor.

"I get that," I say, and then we stand there in silence for a minute. "So," I say when I can't take it anymore. "Did you want something to eat?" I want her to say yes so bad, but she shakes her head.

"Nah, I'm good. I just wanted to see if you thought about last night anymore."

I resist the urge to say, *You mean when you almost kissed me?* and instead opt for a shrug. I know she means the property, I know it, but a part of me wishes she was talking about us.

Shit, maybe this *is* me falling back into old habits. Old habits I promised Nat I was breaking after what happened with Blake.

"About keeping this place, I mean," she adds, like she knows what I'm thinking.

Or maybe she doesn't and last night was all in my head. If Nat's right, I can't trust what I'm feeling right now.

"I don't know. I'm considering things."

"Considering things?" she asks, a hint of a smile in her eyes. "Well, don't consider things too long, you're making me antsy."

"Yeah, well, I guess antsy is better than pissed," I tease.

She ducks her head before looking back up to meet my eyes. "You tryna make me apologize again?"

"If I remember right, you said you were stating facts last night, *not* apologizing."

She purses her lips and huffs out a breath that sounds suspiciously like a laugh. "Fine. I'm willing to admit that there is a small chance that I may have misjudged you, and that, plus my feelings about Christina leaving you this place, led to us getting off on the wrong foot. I apologize, Molly," she says, with an exaggerated bow.

"Thank you," I say. "But a small chance? That's not exactly a glowing review."

She crosses her arms with a good-natured sigh, like I'm pushing it, but she doesn't quite mind. "I don't let my guard down easy," she finally says. "Me saying it's a small chance *is* a glowing review."

"Okay." I laugh. "So yesterday you were *sure* I was a money-hungry parasite that you hated, but now you're confirming there's at least one percent of you that might feel differently?"

She huffs out another laugh as she grabs her hat off the table and walks to the door.

"Something like that."

And wait, that, that's it?

"Shani," I say, when her hand hits the door.

She turns to look at me, adding in an eyebrow raise when I hesitate.

"Is that really the only reason you came tonight?" I ask finally. "To ask about my plans?"

"Is there something else you want me to be asking you about?" A grin splashes across her face. She knows. She knows what she's doing to me. I squirm a little under her gaze.

"I—no—well?"

"Well?"

"No," I say, losing my nerve.

"All right then," she says, giving me a little wink as she drops the hat back on her head and disappears out the door. "Later, Molly."

Damn.

Chapter Nine

The horses are screaming.

That's the first thought that crosses my mind as my eyes shoot open. The second is that it is fuck-off early o'clock and I should not be awake. Especially since I was out in the barn last night having a heart-to-heart with Otis about my history of losing myself in romantic relationships until well after midnight.

But then I hear them again. A chorus of whinnies and shrieks and stomps.

The sound continues, growing louder and I'm suddenly aware of just how alone I am out here, at the end of a long dark driveway, in the middle of nowhere. I should hide. No, I should check that the doors are locked and then hide—but the distress in the horses' voices compels me out of bed and to get dressed. I grab the baseball bat that I found while cleaning out the hall closet yesterday and make my way to the window. The barn is dark. The yard is dark. In fact, everything is dark here, dark and claustrophobic.

Without sparing too much thought, I grab my phone, shove my feet into my boots, and go running out—charging, really—with my bat held high and ready to swing. I'm sure my neighbors would be laughing at me, back in the city. I bet I'm quite the sight in my old, worn Home Alone pajama pants and Hello Kitty T-shirt, buried under my aunt's two-sizes-too-big Carhartt jacket and old boots, swinging a bat around like I'm looking to score a home run or take someone's head off.

But there's no time to worry about that now as I rush into the barn, ready to attack whatever's hurting my horses. *My* horses, I realize as I rush in and flick on the barn light. For the first time ever they feel like mine, and I've got a duty to protect them.

The bright overhead lamps flood brightness into every corner, blinding me for a second and making me swing out in fear, but as my eyes adjust, I see that I'm alone. Definitely alone. The horses all chuff or whinny, heavy hooves scraping against the floors and stall doors as they shift restlessly. I swear they're urging me on, somehow, even though that sounds absurd. I do as they ask, checking in each stall as I go.

Otis is missing, I think, taking a head count as I walk, but then realize he's not. He's there, on the ground, trying to . . . I don't know? Is he playing? Did he wake me up in the middle of the night because he was bored and wanted some more attention? Anger rushes through me white-hot as I watch him roll on the ground like a baby, his feet clanking against everything, but then he cries, actually cries and it's not happy, it's not a sound of mischief, it's the unmistakable whine of pain.

I pull up Shani's number as fast as I can. "It's Otis," I shout, the second she answers, her voice sleep worn and worried. "Something's really wrong with him. You have to come. Now!"

I don't even bother to hang up, throwing the phone down as I rip open his stall door and try to get close. He's twisting and thrashing on the ground, and I dodge hooves as I try to get to his head. If I can just hold him, if I can comfort him, if he knows I'm there . . . A rumble of a truck barely registers, followed by footsteps, running, but I'm too busy trying to get closer to Otis to care.

"Christ, Molly, you're going to get killed," Shani says, pulling me up and tossing me out of the stall. "Easy, Otis, easy."

"What's wrong with him?"

"Come on, boy," she says, ignoring me. "Come on, now."

"Is he going to be okay? What do I . . . What do I do?"

"Call the vet. Now! The number's in the office. His cell, it's in pen, not his main line. They aren't open this late. Go!"

I run to the office and search the desk, tears blurring everything, until I finally realize she means the numbers bulletin board. I scan the list of numbers written in fading pencil, until I come to one that says "Chet the vet," which might have made me laugh under different circumstances. I skip the first number and go straight to the one labeled "cell" written in scratchy red pen.

"Hello?" a man's voice answers. "Who is this?"

"It's Molly. You don't know me but, I'm at Christina's farm, shit, I don't know the address. Shani! Shani what is the—"

"I know who you are," he says, in a calm, sleep-scratched voice. "Everyone knows what happened with Christina's place. I'm very sorry about your aunt. But do you mind telling me why this call couldn't wait till morning?"

"It's Otis. He's an old horse we have here, like real old—"

"I know Otis," he says, sighing now like he's annoyed. "What do you need?"

"He's rolling around. I thought he was playing, but he's screaming almost. And Shani's here but she said to call and . . . so . . . I did. I don't know . . ."

"Has Shani given him any Banamine yet? I think I left some last time I was there. Did she get him up and walking?"

"I don't know!" I cry, panicking. "I don't know what she's doing. Will you just come? Please!"

"All right, okay," he says, his voice switching back to soothing. "Take a deep breath. Where are you? You in the office?"

"Yeah," I say, trying to catch my breath from crying.

"I need you to go walk out to Shani and see what she's doing. If you can, give her the phone. If not, you're gonna relay some messages for me. Can you do that, Molly?"

"Y . . . yeah," I say, wiping at my eyes as I walk out into the barn. "She's got him up," I say, relief flooding me at the sight of Shani standing beside an unsteady Otis. "He's standing."

"Good, that's good, see if you can put her on the phone."

"He wants to talk to you," I say, holding it out to her.

She takes it, and hands me his lead. "Keep him walking, slow and gentle. He's gonna wanna drop and roll some more but you don't let him, okay? I'll be right here, getting some meds together, okay? Just walk him up and down the aisle." I nod and she turns her attention to the man on the phone. "Yeah, I'm getting it now," I hear her say, but I don't turn to look at what she's doing. "I didn't think I was gonna be able to get him up without you . . . yeah, it's a bad one this time."

I keep my eye on Otis, nice and steady, as we take one step after the next. It takes forever to reach the end of the aisle, and he pulls on his lead a couple times, standing still and going rigid, but I don't let him down. I beg, plead, and cry, offering him a lifetime of peppermint candy and apples if he stays standing. "Don't you sink on me, Otis," I say when he goes particularly still. "You cannot die, I refuse! You can't do this to me. I love you, okay? You cannot leave me here alone, you overgrown fuzzball! Please, don't do this to me," I say, full-on snotting at this point. "Walk, dammit!"

He huffs like he understands and maybe thinks I'm ridiculous for it, but then starts walking again. "Thank you," I say, tears falling uncontrollably until Shani comes and stops us.

She's got something in her hand, and I turn and bury my face in Otis's neck. I can't bear to watch whatever she is going to do to him next. "It's okay," Shani says, and then adds, "Molly." I thought she was comforting Otis, but no. I turn my head and watch her giving him some kind of paste to eat.

"Banamine," she says, like I know what that means. She must see the confusion in my face because she adds, "for pain. Why don't you go on up to the house and get some sleep."

"No, I want to . . ."

"You crying on him and stressing him out isn't gonna help. If you want to do something, go take all the food, water, and hay out of his stall. I'm gonna walk him for a while, keep him moving. We don't want him eating anything when this kicks in and he starts to feel better."

"What's wrong with him?"

"Colic, as far as we can tell. I'm gonna monitor him tonight. If nothing changes, Chet's gonna swing by around seven A.M. to check on him."

"What if it does change?"

"Then I'll trailer him up and take him to the hospital. If you consent, that is. I guess he's technically yours. Could get pricey if he needs surgery."

"Christina only left a few thousand but . . . I have a credit card, I guess. I don't know. He's an old horse, should we really—"

"He's Christina's horse, Molly," she says, her voice almost pleading. "You can't just kill him because he's inconvenient."

"I didn't say he was inconvenient."

"Then finish your sentence."

"What?"

"You said, 'he's an old horse, should we really . . .' and then I interrupted. What were you going to say then?" Her eyes flare in anger, but I can hear hurt beneath it all.

"Nothing," I say, ashamed.

"Two minutes ago, you were hugging him and crying that you loved him but now that money's involved it's 'oh, he's old anyway.' Some things are bigger than money, Molly." Her voice cracks. "Don't you fucking get that yet?"

"Don't do that to me," I say, because I'm not sure if we're still talking about Otis, or about me selling the place, or about how the reason she can't buy it is because she put Christina ahead of her farrier business, but it doesn't feel fair regardless. "You're the one who just said it would get pricey! I'm broke! And Christina barely had anything and I—"

"Forget it, Molly, let's just hope this works. It's fine."

"No, it's not fine. You act like I'm being selfish when I'm just being realistic!"

"Realistic?" She nearly sneers, all the hurt in her eyes turning to icy rage. "Is that what we're calling this?"

"One of us has to be," I say, sounding more like Nat than I mean to, and as soon as the words are out of my mouth, I regret it.

Shani scowls, leading Otis on before I even get to say goodbye. I watch them for a moment, before going to empty his stall of everything that could hurt him, or that he could eat, or that he could bang into. And once I'm sure there's nothing left to be done, I head up to the house. Alone.

* * *

CHET ARRIVES AT seven on the dot, but I stay in the house like a coward, afraid he'll only have bad news and feeling like a jerk from what I said last night . . . even though I was technically right. You can't pull money out of thin air and Shani herself said the vets don't work on credit.

Aiyana comes right after, turning out her horse into one of the smaller paddocks for a minute and backing up her trailer. She's got a show today, I forgot.

I figure Shani will come up and tell me what's going on when there's something to know, so I set to work baking some muffins for us to eat after he leaves. Guilt muffins . . . but also an excuse to keep hiding away, trying not to cry. "Crying on him doesn't help any," mixes with "You can't kill him because it's inconvenient" in my head and there's not enough flour and sugar in the world to make me feel better today.

The vet doesn't stay long, but Shani never comes with an update either. I wait as long as I can, another hour, practically burning the last batch of muffins, before I head out to the barn with a plate of them.

Aiyana is giving Otis all of the pets when I walk up, but Shani's nowhere in sight. Her truck's still here, but I suppose she could have walked home. I just didn't think she would have left without checking in.

"Muffin," I say, offering Aiyana the plate. Otis tries to take one too, and I'm half-tempted to give in, but Aiyana pushes the plate away and rubs his nose.

"None for you, eating too much is probably what got you into this mess in the first place, sir."

"Eating?"

"Yeah, he probably got into something weird in the field or broke into some grain when no one was looking. Somehow, he got—"

I nearly drop my plate. "I fed him extra last night before bed. We were hanging out and . . ."

Aiyana tilts her head. "What do you mean?"

"I like to come out here and talk to him at night, you know? Last night, I was venting about my problems and he was nosing around, acting hungry. So I just . . . gave him another big pile of grain to be nice." *Guilt grain.*

Aiyana's eyebrows hit the ceiling. "He's not like a dog you can just give a little extra to and deal with some puke or something. They have no way to get it back up. If you overfeed them—"

"Is this my fault?" I ask, my blood running cold.

"He's really prone to this kind of thing anyway," she says, not meeting my eyes. "Just promise me you'll keep to the schedule Lita gave you. And don't do that with the other horses here either. I . . . someone should have told you how important that was. This is on us. We forget that you don't know this stuff."

"I hurt him?" I say quietly. "This was all because of me?"

And then I balked over the cost of a hospital. Great. Perfect. Love this for me.

"You didn't know," Aiyana says, and I feel like I'm going to be sick.

"I . . . shit. Where's Shani?" I ask, feeling like I need to confess or be punished or at least hand over these guilt muffins extra now. *What kind of monster am I?*

"She went in the office after Chet left. She asked me to keep an eye on Otis. Molly, seriously, it's not your—"

"Thanks," I say, rushing down the aisle and waving her off.

I step inside the office, ignoring the closed door. I expect to see Shani digging through some papers or waiting to yell at me, but instead find her curled up on the couch, her hat resting over her face. I can tell by the slow, steady rise and fall of her chest that she's asleep.

I think about waking her up, telling her what I did, letting her scream at me or something until we both feel better. But I don't. I spy an old, heavy blanket shoved in the corner and shake off the dust and the hay before covering her up with it as gently as I can.

She stirs when I tuck it around her but doesn't wake.

I leave the muffins on the desk where she'll find them, and then head back to Otis to relieve Aiyana, hugging him and apologizing until my voice gives out.

Chapter Ten

I scurry out of the barn the second I hear Shani moving around the office, dipping out the side door before she has a chance to see me. While I don't *think* Aiyana is going to rat me out for overfeeding Otis off schedule, I'm sure Shani is probably putting it together by now anyway. I decide to drown my sorrow in bad coffee and work, setting about going through Aunt Christina's things to stay busy. I'm still hoping that I find a random key to that locked room, but there's definitely enough to do in the meantime.

Aunt Christina wasn't so much a hoarder as she was sentimental, and there's a lot here. In the kitchen closet—which I think is *supposed* to be a pantry—I find everything from boxes of photo albums to old, dented trophies, to what I can only imagine are halters and leads with some kind of emotional significance.

I even find the aforementioned stack of blue-eyed horse pictures that I drew during my one fateful summer here. I'm tempted to text pictures of them all to Nat. They may not have been in my composition notebook, but regardless I feel like I deserve at least a smidge of credit. I wasn't a horse girl . . . but this is proof I was at least horse girl *adjacent*. I send them to my mom instead, who extols my potential as the next Picasso. We text back and forth for a while—her dipping and dodging my questions about Christina, me trying to think up new ways to get her to talk—but when she starts grilling me about the exact day I'm coming back home, I make an excuse to get back to work.

The kitchen pantry is fully gleaming by the time I'm done, and thanks to another trip to the store, fairly well stocked, so I decide to tackle the downstairs bathroom next, aka my makeshift closet.

As unglamorous as it sounds, I was sure that it hadn't been taken care of in months and there's a catharsis to all this cleaning. I can't control what's going on with Otis, or how Shani feels, and I have no idea what the future holds for me and this place, but I *can* control the lime stains in the bathroom sink and the ring around the tub.

"I don't want these." Shani's voice makes me jump. I'm elbow deep in the toilet, trying to work out the hard water stains before my cheap yellow gloves disintegrate when she walks in. I jerk away, pelting both of us with drops of toilet water. Wonderful.

"What the hell?" I say, jumping up. "You scared the crap out of me. You can't just walk in here without even knocking." When she doesn't reply, I sigh. "Is Otis still okay?"

"I said I don't want these." She's holding the plate of guilt muffins, the ones I left for her when she was sleeping.

I pull my gloves off and stand up. If she's going to be obnoxious, I'm not going to keep scrubbing the toilet while she does it. I wash my hands off with the extra foamy soap Nat sent me, my favorite from Bath & Body Works. Then, with as much dignity as I can muster, I take the plate and push past her into the kitchen.

She follows after me, clearly itching for a fight. "Aren't you going to say anything?" Shani asks, her voice rough and angry.

"Thank you for taking care of Otis."

"I didn't do it for you," she says, and oh, that shouldn't hurt me as much as it does, but it does.

I take a deep breath. "Well, thanks all the same."

"You don't belong here," she says, watching me.

"Right," I say. "I got that." I drop into one of the kitchen chairs and bury my head in my hands, exhaustion and emotion combining overwhelmingly inside my skull. I'm not going to cry in front of this woman again, I'm not. But her words echo in my head anyway, each one burrowing beneath my skin like a tiny, vicious sliver.

I try to rub the hot sting out of my eyes, taking a shaky breath before I look up at her. "I'm sorry," I say. "I get why you can't stand me, after what I did. I didn't know though, you have to believe that. I didn't hurt him on purpose. I just thought I was giving him an extra treat."

"What?" she asks, looking genuinely confused, and oh, maybe she hadn't figured it out at all.

"You didn't know?" I ask quietly. "Then why are you so mad?"

"Didn't know what?"

I'm tempted to say nothing. To just pretend I don't know anything, but my honesty gets the better of me. "Aiyana says I caused the colic. I overfed Otis last night and—"

"Yeah, obviously. I figured that out pretty quick when I saw how low his oats were in the feed room last night. Why would I be mad about that? You made a mistake that we didn't warn you about. I'm not a total fucking asshole, you know."

"You could have fooled me!" I snap.

"You would have let him die if he needed surgery. I'm allowed to be pissed about that."

"I didn't say that."

"You said 'he's an old horse,' like that matters! People like you are how Christina ended up with so many rescue horses in the first place. You don't see them as living things, or this as their home. It's just dollar signs to you. Oh, what's Otis going to cost you? Oh, what's the barn worth? How much can I get for the land it sits on?" she snaps. "How many pairs of fancy shoes can I buy with other people's lives?"

I huff out an angry laugh and shake my head at her. "You don't know *anything* about me!"

"I know you're a spoiled brat, just like your mother."

I sigh, resigned. "If you have something to say about my mother, just say it, because I'm getting nowhere with her, and all this hinting you're doing is getting ridiculous."

She looks at me in disbelief. "Okay, let's be real. How can you seriously not know about the money thing?"

"What money thing?" I snap, rubbing my temples, because none of this makes any sense and I'm so, so tired of getting blindsided.

"How she showed up here after your dad left with her hand out! Christina didn't have any money to spare, because she had just started up her rescue program and it was eating up every dime she had. Your mom was furious!"

"No, that's not how it went," I say, meeting her eyes. "Christina came to our house! My mom never came here. I might not have heard their whole fight, but I *clearly* remember that part."

"Well, I was here when she showed up, whether you want to believe me or not. Your 'wonderful' mother looked right at me when she said that maybe Christina should 'worry a little more about her own family and a little less about rescues.'" Shani swallows, clenching her jaw hard as she looks away.

I'm up, moving toward her before I can stop myself. "Shani, I—"

"Don't," she says, jerking back before I can even reach out.

"I don't get it." I step back, giving her the space she so clearly wants, confusion clouding my thoughts. "I remember them fighting, but it *wasn't* here . . ."

"Christina *did* go there too; that's probably what you remember. She was being eaten alive by guilt and tried to convince your mother to have you two move here with us. That wasn't good enough for your mom either. Too many *rescues* around here." Shani flashes a bitter smile. "I guess the apple doesn't fall far from the tree."

"This doesn't make any sense."

"It's what happened," she says, her voice hard. "Just like this is happening now."

I pull back my hair, frustrated. "Whatever did or didn't happen back then isn't my fault though. Like *this* isn't my fault," I say, gesturing to the house around us. "You can't expect me to throw my life away out of guilt. I won't do it. I can't."

"Great. Fine." She shoves the plate roughly across the table. "Then stop doing shit like this!"

"Like what?"

She's practically vibrating with anger as she glares at me. "Don't you dare come into my barn again and—"

"It's not your barn, Shani, no matter how much you pretend it is. Christina left it to me. To get *my* life on track, and that's what I'm going to do," I say, and the way her face crumples tells me my arrows hit their mark.

Neither of us say anything then, the sound of our angry breaths echoing in the stillness of the room. I look away, unable to meet her eyes.

"Do what you have to do, Molly," she says, hurt and anger washing over her voice. "But don't tuck me in and leave me muffins, and act like you want to kiss me, when you don't mean any of it. Got it? You want to sell this place, fine, but quit messing with my head in the meantime."

"Shani, I'm not—" I say, but she's gone, the door slamming behind her so loud I jump.

And what just happened. What. Just. Happened?

Chapter Eleven

Nat and KiKi show up bright and early the next morning, ready to get to work. I'm still thrown from my conversation with Shani last night—and a shitty call with my mom this morning—but I'm trying to rally.

I don't know what I expected when I called Mom to confront her about what Shani told me, but all I got was: "It was a long time ago, there were hurts on both sides. You need to quit harping on it. Focus on getting the place listed," and then she begged off the call saying she was going to be late for work.

I didn't even have time to process that before Nat and KiKi were pulling in.

"What's wrong with you?" KiKi asks, carrying in an armful of painting supplies.

"Obviously, she just missed us," Nat teases, pulling some papers out of one of the bags. Apparently, Nat used Randy's office to helpfully print and laminate three copies of the repair list from Ashley—and even brought a fresh pack of dry-erase markers for us—so that we can all coordinate together with ease. I'm grateful when she sets to work dividing the tasks, circling what each of us will be responsible for, organized and strategic as usual. She is the big sister who saves the day, always.

KiKi watches Nat with a smile as she sets up her stuff—a tool kit, a small step stool, some paint rollers and the fuzzy things you stuff on them. KiKi is quiet, always has been, but the love she feels for Nat just radiates off her in waves. It used to make me jealous—Blake and I (hell, anyone and I) were never like that. I don't know what it makes me feel now. Hopeful, maybe, that something like that could exist.

I try to soak it up, to push out all thoughts of my mom and of Shani's accusation that I'm messing with her head. *Me? Messing with her?* It's clearly the other way around. I think I'm doing a semi-decent job of pulling it off too, until KiKi heads outside to investigate if there's anything useful in the old tool shed out back and Nat turns back to me with a frown.

"Okay, enough of this, why are you moping?" she asks, grabbing one of the apology muffins that Shani returned last night. At least someone will enjoy them.

"We should get started," I say, not wanting to talk about it, not wanting to *think* about it anymore this morning.

"We're taking a fifteen," she replies. "Why. Are. You. Moping?"

"Can we take a fifteen when we haven't even started?" I pour myself some coffee, deliberately going out of my way to not meet her eyes. "I'm not moping, I'm just tired." *And confused. And concerned. And, okay, more than a little mad.*

The more I think about our conversation yesterday, the more I wonder where Shani gets off acting like I'm the problem here, or the one leading someone on, when clearly, it's her. I'm sorry that I have to worry about money, but I do. I'm also sorry that I act like

I want to kiss her, *but I do*. She's the one leading *me* on, if anything, with her stupid charming face and her ridiculous chivalry and her lips that pout in an entirely delectable way whenever she gives me that grumpy puppy look.

"I've known you since your freshman year, Molly. I think I know the difference between tired and moping," Nat says. "What's up? Is this because I said you shouldn't keep this place?"

"Nothing is up," I insist a little too hard. "I just want to get this stuff done and get out of here."

"Good."

"Yeah, good," I say, trying to walk past her to where we were working in the living room.

"Wait," Nat says, holding out her arm to stop me before narrowing her eyes. "A few days ago, I was worried we'd have to host an intervention to get you to still sell. Now suddenly you can't wait to leave? What happened? Did you and the cowgirl get in a fight or something?"

"There is no 'me and the cowgirl,'" I huff.

"Hmmm," Nat says, narrowing her eyes.

A truck rumbles up the driveway—Shani, because of course. Almost as if on cue, really. I know she's shoeing Aiyana's and JJ's horses today. (Not that I asked, I swear; they both "helpfully" mentioned it all on their own.)

I hold my breath as she gets out of the truck, hoping she'll— I don't know, come up to say hi? Ask me to talk more? Anything? Nothing? I don't even know what I'm wishing for. She notices me standing on the porch with Nat. I raise my hand in a hesitant half wave, and she shoots me a glare that makes me want to melt into the floor before disappearing into the barn.

"Ouch," Nat says, as I grab a scraper out of the toolbox and rush inside to the first wall I see to start ripping into ragged wallpaper.

I hear Nat come up behind me, but I just keep scraping, needing to do something, anything, right now.

"The sex was that bad?" she laughs and I know she's just trying to lighten the mood, but I hate it.

"Let's just work," I say, pulling down another strip of torn wallpaper with a satisfying rip.

Nat sighs, and leans against the wall, giving me her best "concerned mother" face. "No. Spill. What's going on?"

"Nothing," I say, and it shouldn't bother me that it's technically the truth, but it does anyway.

"Okay, then I guess it won't matter if I walk down to the barn and see if she wants to join us for some shitty frozen pizza later."

I grab her arm as she walks away. "That's not funny."

"Then *spill*," she says again, a satisfied look on her face. "Obviously there's something going on."

I weigh my options: I could keep this to myself and make the whole day awkward for both of us—she's not going to stop asking—or I can just tell her everything and get it over with. I mean, she's my best friend. I should *want* her to know this stuff. Right?

I sigh and pass her the scraper. "I'll tell you everything while we work. You scrape, I pull. Deal?"

"Deal." She smiles, turning toward the wall to start.

Over the next couple hours, I tell her everything. I tell her about Otis getting sick, about Shani—how she walked me home, and about our almost kiss, and about how mad she got at me, the stuff she said about my mother, and how confused I am about all of the above—but mostly about how none of it even matters because I have to clean this place up and sell it. I know I do.

Halfway through the story, KiKi comes back through and announces she's heading off to Home Depot with a hastily scratched out list of everything that she *didn't* find in the shed or the basement. I notice a look pass between Nat and her, and I feel like it was about me, but I don't ask. I feel bad enough already.

"You like this woman," Nat says sadly, when I finish my story.

"I don't know her enough to like her."

"Since when have you ever had to know someone to be into them? You've fallen in love on first dates since I've known you."

"So did you and KiKi though."

"Yeah, but I was still being logical. I was into her, but I didn't *turn* into her. I didn't magically become obsessed with all of her favorite things the way you do. I didn't even let her move in until I was convinced that we'd get married eventually, maybe have her pop out a few kids."

"Ew, don't say pop out."

"I'm just saying! She's happy to play stay-at-home mom while I'm walking the red carpets." Nat fans herself comically. "And I love that for us."

"Speaking of, did you get a callback for the Pepto commercial yet?"

She frowns. "Not yet. But we're not talking about me; we're talking about you and your obsessive need to pin your future on other people."

"Yeah, well, lucky for my future apparently, Shani hates me again."

"I'm not sure that that's true, but let's just go with it, so you can hurry up and list this place and get back to the city with me, where you belong," Nat says, flashing me a goofy grin.

I sigh, wishing I could just give in to her good mood.

Nat pretends to bang her head against the wall. "Fine, what do we have to do?"

"What?"

"What do we have to do to get you over this? Can we skip past all the drama this time, and just get to the part where you re-member that you are a strong, independent woman, who should be focusing on launching that damn event business?" She shakes my shoulders gently, her eyebrows practically to her hairline as if they are punctuating the point. "You are too awesome to spend this much of your life pining!"

I start to tell her that I'm not pining. I'm not. This is different . . . but is it?

"Molly," she says seriously. "Staying would be a mistake."

"I'm not staying," I say, glancing out the window to the barn. I can see Aiyana's horse in the crossties, Shani hunched over, filing its hoof. My chest tightens at the sight of her, but maybe it shouldn't. Maybe it's better for both of us—easier even—if she can't stand me.

Nat watches me as I take out my phone and pull up Shani's number to fire off a text. No, not a text, an arrow, an arrow meant to ruin it all. To burn whatever this was all down between us before it goes any further:

I need to get into your house so the real estate agent can measure.

Nat reads over my shoulder, but I don't take my eyes off Shani. She straightens, checks her phone, and then looks up at the house. I know she can't see me in here, but somehow it still feels like she's looking right at me.

"What'd I miss," KiKi asks, walking in with two paper bags.

"Shh!" Nat says. "Molly's growing a spine!"

"It's about time," she mumbles, setting the bags down and looking out the window to see what we're staring at.

Outside, Shani looks up at the sky for a beat, and then shoves her phone back in her pocket, getting back to work. Like it didn't even matter. Like she didn't even care.

Chapter Twelve

The next few days pass in a blur of painting and scraping. KiKi finishes most of the exterior windowsills, so all that's left now is to caulk around them and scrub the glass. Nat and I have managed to paint the bathroom and kitchen a pristine white, fix up the kitchen cabinets, and even get most of the wallpaper down in the living room. Not too bad for a couple days work, and over far too soon.

The house falls eerily quiet once they leave late Tuesday night. I wish they would have stayed but KiKi has another job lined up for the rest of the week, and Nat has two different auditions—another commercial, and a student film—and a shift at the coffee shop, so I don't even bother trying to guilt them into it.

Instead, I bake myself muffins and watch them go stale as I spend the rest of the week scraping and cleaning by myself. Every day, I hear Shani's truck go up the shared driveway on her way out to work or to my barn to check on the horses and, every time, I peek out through the cheap Walmart curtains Nat brought me and feel more and more alone.

I spend my nights pacing the house, having long rambling conversations with my mom on Christina's old cordless phone.

I try to get her to talk to me about her fight with Christina—as if proving Shani was lying will somehow make me feel better about how things all went down—but Mom is adept at redirection. Instead, she rambles on about the new neighbors and the movies she's watching, and how she's practically counting down the minutes until I get home.

If nothing else, hearing her sound just as desperately lonely as I am confirms I'm doing the right thing by not staying here. Maybe it doesn't matter what happened with her and Aunt Christina anyway. The past is in the past, there's no changing it now.

When my hands refuse to touch another cleaner or any more wallpaper dissolver, and I've thrown out whatever there is to throw out downstairs into the little dumpster bag KiKi grabbed for me at the hardware store, I know it's time to handle what's upstairs, and maybe, finally sort through Christina's stuff.

After all, the only other option is to go down to the barn and risk running into everybody. I've been avoiding the whole crew the last few days, not just Shani. I've made it quick work every morning to turn out the horses, and feed who needs feeding and clean what needs cleaning, and then I rush back up to the farmhouse and lock myself in. I'm sure Shani has told everyone by now my plans to sell. I can't help but feel like I've let them all down.

I need a cup of coffee.

A noise pulls my gaze from the coffee grinder that KiKi helpfully left behind, and I snap my head up just in time to see Shani's truck backing up toward the barn. Weird for two reasons: one, she's normally at work this time of day, and two, there's a trailer attached.

I'd be lying if I said I wasn't instantly glued to the window. And I'd be double lying if I said I wasn't dying the second I saw her load up Gideon with the lure of some alfalfa. Shani shuts the door of the trailer and then glances right up at my window, catching my eyes.

I jump back, bumping the edge of the table, and letting the curtains fall into place. I stop rubbing my hip long enough to peek through the curtain again, only to see her walking toward the house with an exasperated look on her face.

Shit. We haven't so much as acknowledged each other's existence since I sent that text. Naturally, I do what any dignified woman would do—fall to the ground and army crawl my way over to the living room, where I deftly hide behind some furniture. My kitchen is easy to see into, the gauzy curtains not providing too much cover, and while I'm sure she's seen me spying, if I don't answer the door, maybe we can both pretend none of this ever happened.

Her boots clomp up the steps, and I hold my breath, waiting. Only, instead of the knock I'm expecting—or hell, just the sound of the door opening since she seems fond of walking right in— I hear the rusty clang of the mailbox by the door snapping open and shut. There's a single knock on the door, and I fight the urge to get up and open it, because I know what this is now—I've been through it a thousand times before, starting with my dad and ending, most recently, with Blake. She's leaving and I don't want to look at her while she does.

I crouch lower behind the couch and try to negotiate with my brain, which is currently screaming at me to get up and talk to her. To stop her. *This is a good thing*, I tell myself. *It's what I* *wanted, right? It will be a lot easier around here without her stupid hot face and her stupid little freckles and her stupid . . . but before I can even finish that sentence, she's gone. Like well and truly gone, as in boots down my steps and across my lawn and then back in her truck, coasting down and out of my driveway.

And ugh, if this is supposed to be for the best, then why does it feel so awful? *Pull it together, Molly. Come on. You don't need her or her condescending attitude.*

I'll show her.

I hop up and take a quick peek out of the curtain to be sure she's gone, and, seeing the driveway empty for once, I storm out of the house and to the barn, ignoring whatever she left in the mailbox. I don't need it. I don't want it.

She wants to leave without saying goodbye? Then good riddance.

I head straight into the stall where her horse used to be and start tearing down the rickety old makeshift hay feeder in there. It wasn't on the list of things that had to be fixed before listing—it's still functional and safe, just a total eyesore.

It's not going to matter if whoever buys it just razes the barn anyway, but I tell myself I want it gone for staging purposes. Out with the old, in with the new. Well, sort of—there's no point in replacing it; it's not like I'm going to take on any more boarders or anything.

But still. Some people cut their hair after a breakup—not that this is a breakup, god—but I apparently remove hay feeders. *Be the change* and all that.

Okay, fine, maybe I just feel like breaking something.

"Oh cool, you're fixing up Gideon's stall?"

I turn, covered in sweat and bits of hay to find JJ standing there with Lita. Her eyes are narrowed, like she knows exactly why I'm tearing apart the stall, and JJ is no better, with his raised eyebrows and knowing smirk.

"The real estate agent wanted it down before she comes and takes the listing pictures," I lie.

"Sure, yeah," JJ says. "I know Shani will appreciate you replacing that anyway. Are you going to do all of them or . . ." And it barely registers that he's fishing to see if I'm getting a new one for Marlowe because I'm too confused by the first thing he said.

"Why would Shani care what I do to this stall?"

"Because it's where Gideon lives and she . . . loves him?" he says slowly, like I'm ridiculous.

I scrunch up my forehead in confusion. He said *lives*, not *lived*. He was down here already when Shani was loading Gideon up, and he notices *everything*. Does that mean she's coming back? Shit, maybe I *should* have looked at whatever Shani left in my mailbox before I went in here ripping things off barn walls.

"Right yeah," I say, trying to play it off. "Of course, this is where Gideon lives." Lita and JJ exchange looks.

"I'm sure she'll be surprised when she's back from the rodeo circuit in a few days," Lita says, meeting me dead in the eye for that last part.

JJ, seemingly bored of this, nods in agreement and then heads down to Marlowe's stall to get on with his day.

Lita, however, steps into the stall with me. "You need a hand with that?" she asks, gesturing to the fractured pieces of feeder that I've managed to rip down off the wall with my bare hands— which are now full of little cuts. "Maybe you should go grab us some gloves first."

I nod and head into the office to grab a couple pairs, passing the extra to her as we lift the old hay feeder up and carry it out into the aisle. It's a two-person job, I'm suddenly realizing—and I follow Lita's lead out behind the donkey pen, where she shoves it in yet another overfilled shed that I didn't know existed.

"Will you two ever just talk like adults?" Lita asks, startling me. I pretend I don't know what she means, but she just rolls her eyes and shuts the shed door. "You're as stubborn as Ed."

"She's stubborn," I grumble under my breath, but apparently not quietly enough.

"No, she's grieving," Lita says, which makes me feel worse than I already did. "And you've turned her whole life upside down. You've turned all our lives upside down, actually. When were you going to tell us you were selling?"

Edward Cullen brays at us, annoyed that we're standing so close and not even giving him treats. "You're mad," I say, resigned. Edward hangs his head over the gate, demanding ear scritches and I quickly oblige, just happy *one* thing doesn't hate me here.

"I'm not mad. I understand. I just wish you were up-front about it. Finding a new barn, moving horses, it takes a lot of work, especially when you're not a cute, rich white girl."

I glance up at her. "I'm not rich."

She laughs. "I wasn't talking about you. I was talking about the general population of the horse industry, but I'm glad to know you think you're cute."

My cheeks flame with embarrassment as she leans against the gate beside me.

"Christina worked hard to make this barn a safe place for everyone; you don't always see that around here. It's not a secret this industry isn't exactly welcoming to Black riders . . . and forget about Aiyana. It can take us a little longer to find the right place."

"Aiyana?"

"She's Seneca Nation. She never told you? Sure, I get hit with the standard racist fare—you know people assuming I'm just a groom or having to straighten my hair to fit show standards—but she gets that, plus people assuming she's gonna have some extra 'tribal' element to her exhibitions," Lita says, making air quotes. "Don't get me started on all the garbage 'cowboys and Indians' shit she has to hear too. It's disgusting."

"Oh my god," I say, quietly.

"That's actually how we met Christina. A couple girls were harassing Aiyana at one of the shows and your aunt came flying out of the barn with her iPhone up telling them, and I quote, 'I can't wait to show your racist asses to your bosses, the competition judges, and my entire Facebook group.' The way those girls started crying and carrying on. I bought her a beer after that. The video's still up too, all these years later."

"I wish I had the chance to get to know her," I say, trying to picture her as Lita sees her, and not the way my mom does.

Lita pushes off the fence and looks at me. "Yeah, she was one of the few good ones around here. We kept crossing paths at shows and stuff and pretty soon, I decided that hers was a barn I wanted to support. As soon as Aiyana graduated college, she moved her horse down here too. Your aunt had a knack for finding people who could use a friend and turning them into family. So yes, even though I get why you're planning on selling, it doesn't mean it's not breaking my heart."

I drop my head back with a heavy sigh. "I didn't ask for any of this."

"No, but you have it just the same, and I think you could do a better job being kind to the people who think of it as home."

"Like Shani," I sigh.

"Not just Shani, but yeah."

"Where is she, anyway? I thought she hated that rodeo stuff."

"Her brother called her."

"And?"

"And Shani might have her shortcomings, but loyalty isn't one of them." Lita smiles. "That boy says he needs her, and she goes running every time."

"Is he . . . hurt?" I ask, thinking back to when I saw him getting violently tossed around on a bronco.

"Not yet." Lita sighs, seemingly taking pity on me. "They had a farrier issue. Lochlin might be reckless, but he takes his animals' safety very seriously. Their next tour stop was supposed to have someone on standby to touch up the horses' hooves and check one that went lame. The guy no-showed, and the horse is doing poorly now. Shani's heading out to join him for a bit and take care of things with the animals. She'll check on what needs checking on and head back. She probably won't even be gone a week."

"Why'd she take Gideon then?"

"She never told you about that horse?"

"I mean, not beyond telling me not to feed him or turn him out, or touch him, or look at him or . . ."

Lita laughs. "That horse is her baby; I'll give you that. But if that's all he was, then Shani would have still left him here—just in my care, not yours."

"Okay, what then? Is Gideon, like, her assistant farrier or her emotional support animal or what?"

"That horse whose shit we're about to shovel," Lita says, ending our walk right where it started, "is a championship barrel racer. Broke some records even."

"What? Seriously?" I ask, grabbing a shovel. "And Shani's just lending him to her brother?" I snort. "I'm not allowed to give Gideon a treat, but she'll let some random people race him all around an arena? See? I told you she hated me."

Lita full-on belly laughs. "No, Molly, Shani will ride him herself."

My mouth falls open. "Wait, *Shani* is also a champion barrel racer? Shani who hates the rodeo?"

"When she chooses to be," Lita says. "I don't think she'll ever completely quit it, just like I can't ever turn away from Happy and our hunter/jumper shows, even though it's getting harder to find ones at the level I ride at."

"Why is it harder?"

"A lot of barns and promoters went belly-up a few years back. When everybody went into lockdown at the start of the pandemic, a lot of horses got surrendered or sent to auction. People couldn't afford them. Some barns really made out adjusting to promote outdoor activities and stuff, but a lot didn't. There are fewer people to put on shows and fewer people who want to spend money on the low-level ones, where Happy and I compete. Higher levels bounced back pretty quick, but those are serious horse people who aren't going to let anything stop them. It's mainly the hobbyists like me taking the hit. Two of the barns that used to host semi-local events closed up shop. The closest competition site now is hours away."

"It got that bad?"

"Molly, a lot of those horses you saw running around the first time you came here were boarders that Christina couldn't bear to send to auction. She kept them herself, hoping the owners would reclaim them once they got back on their feet. Some of the people occasionally visit, but most of them didn't look back, especially knowing they were safe here with her. A horse isn't exactly a cheap pet. Shani and I have been splitting the cost of their feed while we try to find them new homes as fast as we can. I'm just glad you haven't seemed to notice the space the last few take up yet or that you could be charging for it."

I huff out a small laugh. "Well, at least I'm not the only one who's been keeping a secret. What's going to happen to the ones that are left when I sell this place?"

"That's up to you, I guess."

"Shani said she'd take Otis," I offer. "Maybe I could hide Edward in my mom's apartment."

"Shani can't afford Otis. Not with Gideon too, and having to find a whole new barn to board them at. I don't see how. Farrier jobs are picking up again, sure, but she's got a lot of digging out to do after taking so much time off."

"But she said—"

"If you sell this place to someone that doesn't want to keep it as it is, I'd imagine you'd have a tough time unloading Otis anywhere but the slaughterhouse. The rescues are all overrun around here."

"No, she'd figure something out." Otis peeks his head out from the stall beside us, probably hearing his name, and I rub his velvety muzzle and pick some stay bits of hay out of his forelock. I smile as he nudges me, hoping to find some contraband treats.

Nice try, buddy.

"Look, Molly, I get that you were thrown into this, but trying to sugarcoat things isn't doing you any favors. If you want to treat this place as an asset to sell off, then you need to realize that that's all any of Christina's animals are. Shani can spare your feelings by selling you a fairy tale where she runs off into the sunset with all the orphans, but she already told me she can't keep that horse."

I stare at her, my mouth gaping. *Why would Shani lie to me?*

Lita looks at me, clearly feeling a little guilty.

"I . . . I have to get back to work on the house," I lie, needing to be away from this nice woman who's going to have to find a new barn, and this sweet old horse that might end up in a kill pen because of me. I turn and race back up to the house before Lita can stop me—hesitating only when I see the mailbox and remember Shani left something in it.

There's a key—which is confusing since everyone says she's coming back—but there's also a note. I unfold it, smiling at her handwriting, which is far loopier and fancier than her exterior would suggest. It reminds me of Christina's, when she used to send me Christmas cards. I imagine them both sitting at that table in the kitchen, little Shani practicing her writing over and over until it was just as pretty.

I smooth out the note, pushing all other thoughts out of my head as I do.

Molly,

Heading out to visit Lochlin for a few days. I know you
wanted to get the real estate agent into my place to
take a few measurements or whatever. I'm leaving you
my key so you can get it over with while I'm gone.
Stay the fuck out of my stuff though. Don't know when
I'll be back, but I left Otis's med schedule and revised
feeding schedule tacked up in the office. Don't kill him
while I'm gone.

—S

I stare down at the note for another second, it seems almost . . .
nice? Somehow? Reluctantly?

And then I take the key, and head inside.

Chapter Thirteen

Ashley meets me early the next morning on Shani's porch, clutching the same leather-bound notebook stamped with the real estate office's logo and passing me a to-go cup of coffee. It feels weird to be here without Shani, intrusive, but she left me her key, and we do need to get measurements and pics.

"Oh, this is in much better condition than I expected after seeing the main house," Ashley says. For the first time, I wonder how much work Shani has put into this place—and how much of making it nice was with her own money, for her *own* life. Great, like I needed another reminder of how much I'm taking away from her for my own chance at a happily ever after.

It's for the best, I remind myself. It *has* to be.

"This place gets beautiful light," Ashley continues, walking through Shani's home. Her shoes click on the gleaming hardwood floors, and it bothers me that she didn't take them off. I fixate on the tiny bit of mud Ashley trails through the otherwise pristine area as I pull off my own shoes and set them nicely on the mat beside the door—equal parts politeness and apology—my discomfort growing every minute.

"Maybe we should do this another day," I say, but Ashley just ignores me and continues snapping pictures. Maybe she didn't hear me, but I doubt it.

I think about saying it again, but don't. There's really no point. We need the pictures; it's not going to make any difference whether Shani is here or not. Besides, Shani would probably prefer it this way. Not having to watch it all go down and all.

My eyes catch on a massive, framed picture mounted over the mantel. It's a giant black-and-white side shot of a horse galloping around a cloud of dust, one denim-clad leg the only visible part of the rider. All of the focus is on the rippling muscles of the animal and the pounding sand around it. It's Gideon, I can tell, and I wonder if it's a shot from them barrel racing. If the hint of denim is Shani.

It has to be.

I spent all last night googling stuff on my phone, pacing around until I found a spot in the front yard with good enough connection to let the videos of random women barrel racing finally load. The sport didn't make sense to me before, and it still doesn't even after watching. All that dirt, all the running and training, for what? A fifteen-second ride where you try not to knock over a barrel or run too wide?

I wanted to fall in love with it, but instead I was left even more confused. If anything, it just further highlighted how different Shani and I are, how badly we don't belong in the same worlds. How much she's right about me not belonging here.

I even almost googled Shani's name in a moment of weakness—as if watching her ride would somehow fix everything. I had it all typed in, just waiting to hit enter—if her record was as good as Lita implied, I'm sure there would be a million hits—but instead

I closed the browser, and even went inside for good measure so I couldn't be tempted.

It wasn't because I didn't want to see her. It was because I was scared that once I did, it would all make sense to me. Like seeing Shani racing through the arena in front of all those cheering people would make something click, and suddenly riding a horse around a giant barrel would seem like the best idea anyone ever had. Would make me care all over again.

I don't want to care. I can't afford that—as in literally cannot afford it. No matter how sentimental or sad I was when Shani left, I have to stay focused. My mom is sounding more and more desperate every time we talk, Nat is working doubles because Randy's still holding my job, and Immaculate Events isn't going to jump-start itself. I have a life to get back to, with friends, and dreams, and obligations. I'd do well to remember it.

"Should we take this to the bedroom?" Ashley asks with a laugh.

And oh. *Oh.* I hadn't thought about the fact that we might actually have to go into her bedroom. Where she sleeps. And maybe does other stuff. Stuff that I should definitely not be envisioning right now. "Can we skip that part?"

Ashley's face pinches up. "If we're going to show the layout of the place, we have to include the bedrooms, otherwise people will think we're hiding something. Which brings up another thing I need to talk to you about . . ."

"Oh yeah?" I ask, desperate to avoid the bedroom for as long as I can. "What's that?"

"I heard back from that developer friend, and he's very interested if the price is right. I think we could get there with him; I really do. It would save you from having to do the rest of the repairs, since it would be a teardown anyway."

"You really think that's the best option?" I ask, glancing out the window to where Otis is grazing in the field between our houses.

"The main house is in really bad shape," Ashley says. "This guest home has potential, but that doesn't mean much. I've given you mostly cosmetic things, lipstick on a pig, but let's face it. There's going to be a lot of things that pop up on a home inspection from a private buyer. Working with a developer is going to be the easiest option—especially this one. It's a local couple, they're very nice and pay cash, my favorite. They just want the land—we'd get to skip all the home inspections and allowances and things like that. They don't even write contingencies into their contracts."

She smiles like she just gave me the best news of my life. I should be happy. Having a buyer already interested, getting out of home repairs, being able to start my new life now instead of months from now—but I can't shake the sick feeling in the pit of my stomach.

And I can't tear my eyes away from Otis. Sweet, old Otis, who wouldn't just be losing his home, but also maybe his life. Or of Lita and all the other boarders. This is so much bigger than just me and Shani.

"I don't know," I say, sounding more unsure than I'd like to. "I think we should try to find a private buyer still, someone who will keep this a barn."

"Okayyyy," Ashley says, dragging out the word. "Not the answer I was expecting, but we can work with it. I do think you should at least hear out their offer before deciding. In the meantime, you're going to have to let me take pictures of the bedroom and prepare yourself for the reality that the property will probably sit for a while, then. You'll need to keep chipping away on that repair list I sent you while it does."

"Right, of course." I nod, following her down the short hallway, which feels even shorter as it propels me into Shani's room.

I don't know what I was expecting her bedroom to be like, or if I was even expecting anything, but I'm taken aback once I step inside. It smells like Shani, like leather and petrichor and a hint of woodsy bodywash. It's stronger here than in the rest of the house, as if it's imbued in the thick navy-blue comforter neatly made over her farmhouse bed, turning this room into my very own hot-girl potpourri. *I should absolutely not be in here.*

Next to the bed, there is a single bedside table, a lamp with another Edison bulb—that must be her thing—that looks antique but probably isn't, and a stack of books piled up haphazardly. I sneak a closer look, surprised to find that they're mostly romances. I spy the latest Ashley Herring Blake, a couple of Alexandria Bellefleurs, and a stray Emily Henry and smile. At least our taste in books is the same.

Ashley opens the closet to take some pictures, and I look away, my quick glimpse of flannels and neatly stacked denim inside the small walk-in closet feeling wrong. Overwhelming. Secret, somehow. Like Shani should be the one to show me, to let me borrow things from it when I'm cold.

Jesus, what am I doing?

That is not our situation. We don't have a situation. She is my tenant. I am her landlord and anything beyond that is—who am I kidding?

"I'll be on the porch," I say, wanting to be anywhere but here. Shani hates me. She *hates* me, and I need to respect that. No matter what the butterflies in my belly are whispering to me right now.

Snooping around her house won't do either of us any good.

* * *

JJ AND AIYANA are trailering their horses together by the time I make the trek back across the pasture. I was slowed by a pit stop to visit Otis for a little bit, scratching behind his ears and reassuring him that Gideon would be back soon. He looks as mopey as I feel, so I snuck him a vet-approved cookie that I stashed in my pocket and hoped that cheered him up some.

"Where are you two off to?" I ask, clicking the pasture gate shut behind me and stepping onto the front lawn.

"Horse show day," JJ laughs, throwing up jazz hands. At least I think it's jazz hands . . . but then it turns into elaborate moves that look like a cross between the macarena and competitive cheer. Aiyana elbows him as she walks up, and he goes back to fastening the trailer gate.

"You want to come watch us kick everybody's ass?" Aiyana asks, with a big grin.

And yeah, I realize. I think I do.

Chapter Fourteen

It's going to be an overnight trip, so I convince Lita to take over the rest of the turnouts and feeds for tonight and tomorrow in exchange for a discount off stall rent, and then rush to pack a bag, grateful that Lita has this weekend off and doesn't mind spending it with the horses.

Soon, Aiyana, JJ, and I cram into Aiyana's truck for the drive to the show. It's an old Dodge Ram with only one bench seat, leaving me to take the middle. In most other circumstances, this would probably be a little annoying or humiliating, but in this one? It feels kind of cozy and fun, like we're off on a little adventure and nothing else matters.

Especially not the real estate agent that I left poking around in Shani's house.

JJ is more anxious than I've ever seen him and won't stop chewing on his lip—not in a "trying to look hot for TikTok" way, but in a "compulsion I can't stop till I bleed" way. I resist the urge to tell him to relax, even though he's setting off my own anxiety.

To be fair, I don't even know what a "hunter/jumper" competition even is, so I'm not about to tell someone to chill. For all I know he could have to spend the entire afternoon defusing nuclear bombs on horseback. Probably not, right, but if you asked me a few days ago, I *also* wouldn't have believed that people can become champions of running tight circles around glorified kegs, but here we are. Or, well, there Shani is, I guess.

Aiyana flips on what she calls her and JJ's "pump up playlist" which is mostly depressing Taylor Swift and Billie Eilish songs, with the occasional Selena Gomez song mixed in, but again, who am I to judge?

The drive passes faster than expected, and before I know it, I'm wandering around the event area while they go off to check in and get the horses settled. They have to do something called "schooling" this morning, which apparently means practice riding the horses around, getting them used to the place, and getting their nervous energy out. Aiyana said to consider horses "big dumb guinea pigs who are terrified of anything new" but JJ elbowed her and said to speak for herself because "Marlowe is brave and smart, thank you very much."

I noticed he still took her out to ride, though, as soon as we got settled.

I don't know what I expected as I wander around the facility, but it wasn't *this*. I understood JJ and his endless TikToks weren't exactly *traditional western things* per se—like he doesn't even have the hat like Shani does—but I didn't realize their stuff was this far removed from it. Nary a bucking bronco or cowboy hat in sight.

In fact, everyone's horse is gleaming and athletic and the people . . . the people! They're all dressed in minisuits, rich black riding jackets atop tan pants, their boots gleaming as brightly as their horses' shiny coats in the sun. And sure, almost every horse is brown—sorry, *bay*, Aiyana lost it on me for calling her horse brown once—but they're still gorgeous. JJ's white horse is definitely going to stand out here.

I can't help but compare the two facilities as I walk. The event's host arena isn't that much bigger than Christina's place—or I guess my place, for now—although it's much, *much* better maintained.

The central barn looks new, with heavy doors and labeled stalls that haven't been chewed to bits. There are several arenas, a few about the same size as the larger paddocks back home, and I head toward the biggest one, only to find it strewn with random fences and walls and so many flowers.

Even the sand is perfectly curated (minus the hoofprints of course), everything combed and groomed within an inch of its life. There is a sheet by the main gate with an event listing and times, but since none of the competitors are actually listed, I'm not sure when Aiyana and JJ will ride. All signs point to this being a well-orchestrated event designed to go off without a hitch, and I'm a little jealous.

It reminds me of when I was interning with a wedding planner right after I graduated college. All these different vendors and clients had to work together, deliveries and events happening in tandem, to pull off one incredible experience for people to share.

It turned into a job offer, but one so low that I couldn't make it work. It was a nearly sixty-hour-a-week commitment (unofficially; officially it was "forty with long, restorative lunches," ha) and thus didn't leave much time in the evenings to make up the income with coffee shop and call center work. Factor in the student loans and massive health insurance premiums, and I had to step away.

It was the hardest thing I've had to do, and the memory only serves to remind me what I'd be giving up if I stayed in this world. Why I *can't* stay, even if this updated and renovated horse space does give me inspiration for what Christina's place could become.

Maybe it can still become this, just not with me involved.

If I can find just the right buyer, one who will fix it up and make it shine like this place, it will be the best of both worlds. Shani could stay, the boarders could stay, and I would still get seed money—the perfect solution. I fire off a quick text to Ashley before I lose my nerve, letting her know that I don't need to hear the offer from the developers; we're going private sale for sure. I smile, running my hands along the fence and finally feeling good about a decision.

When Aiyana reappears a couple hours later, she's alone and dressed just as gloriously as everyone else.

"There you are," I say, still studying the ornate silk flowers that adorn the posts and jumps. I've used this same exact brand at weddings before, and never thought I'd see them at a farm, even one as nice as this. They are pricy with a capital *P*.

"Here I am," she says. "I thought you might want to watch JJ. He's riding soon in the main arena—let's go grab seats before we miss him."

"Obviously." I smile, following her and feeling some of that same nervous energy JJ clearly was feeling in the car. I want him to do well, whatever that means in this context.

She weaves me through the crowd of spectators, trainers, entrants—pushes through a herd of nervous moms watching their children in the novice competition—and then leads me up to a spectator area set up behind the arena. A bunch of collapsible bleachers are lined up on one side, right behind the judge's table.

We climb up to empty seats in the middle of the stand. Rows of other people look excitedly into the ring, which is set up like the other one was, with various jumps in the center painted a brilliant white. Little makeshift hedges and silk floral arrangements pull it all together into something that looks almost magical.

"Now this is a little bit different from my event," she says, pointing out how the rider in the ring is doing a canter around the edge of the area. "Hunters have to look *pretty* while they compete."

"And jumpers don't?" I ask.

"We just have to be fast. We're much cooler that way," she laughs, fanning her face.

I'm about to reply that JJ might have a different opinion on that, when I hear his name announced over the speakers. He trots his horse into the ring, and gone is the goofy guy, determined to film as many flamboyant TikToks as he can possibly fit in a day. Instead, I see a side I've never seen before. He looks serious, somehow regal even, atop Marlowe who herself looks perfectly calm—her perked ears and flaring nostrils are the only hints that she's feeling the same degree of emotion that her rider was on the whole drive up.

Suddenly JJ is off, his trot turning into a canter around the ring. In a heartbeat, he's switched gears, weaving between the obstacles: jumping, running, and looking fabulous. Marlowe's tail is in what Aiyana calls the "perfect" position, although it doesn't really look all that different to me, but even I can tell his seat makes him look like he's floating. The whole thing just looks . . . effortless.

I stand up and whoop after a particularly high jump, but Aiyana shushes me and drags me back down into my seat, embarrassed. But still, worth it. JJ is incredible, and every second of his run left me breathless and thrilled. The sound of Marlowe's hooves thunders around the area, muffled only slightly by the sand, matching the rhythm of my heartbeat.

It's perfect. It's brilliant. And it's over far, far too soon.

I eagerly watch as the judges tally up their scores, utterly disappointed when Aiyana tells me they won't announce them till the end of the show.

"Come on," she says, pulling me up behind her. "I'm up soon. I'll show you where to sit."

"You don't ride here too?"

"No," she laughs. "There's about a billion more hunters to go. Come on, I'll take you over to where the cool kids are."

* * *

AIYANA IS RIGHT, her event is completely different. It's like the hunter competition, but a little rougher around the edges. It reminds me more of those barrel racing videos I was watching last night.

The horses aren't prancing in, they're galloping; muscles bunching, drool flying—something Aiyana says is a good thing actually—the timer counting as they zip around impossibly fast. The riders are wearing a haphazard mix of whatever they want, some like Aiyana are similar to JJ's uniform, others clearly mixing and matching. It's fun, it's fast, and it's occasionally terrifying. It's magic. I don't know how else to explain it, and I can't tear my eyes away.

Even after JJ comes over and Aiyana's done eventing, they sit and let me watch, utterly mesmerized. They fill me in on all the little details of the sport, relaxing now that their show nerves have calmed. I think I'm most shocked to hear that at the more prestigious shows, you don't ride your own horse at all, but rather are randomly assigned one. They laugh at my surprise—I don't know that I would trust a random animal to do what I saw them do today—but they explain it's to keep everything fair. Still though, wouldn't be me!

Later, when their horses are settled in their borrowed stalls for the night—all cooled down and locked up tight with the other temporary boarders who decided not to drive out till tomorrow morning—Aiyana can't stop teasing me for not knowing there was more to horsemanship than trail rides and, as of last night, barrel racing.

"Wait," she says in between laughs. "You really thought western was the only way to ride?"

"I don't know! My mind was blown from barrel racing! I didn't know they could leap small buildings in a single bound and look good doing it," I say, gesturing back toward the now empty arenas as we walk to the truck.

Aiyana has long since unhooked the trailer, saying there's no use wasting the extra gas on the weight when they don't need it until tomorrow. The barn owner, a good friend of hers, was all too happy to let her leave it overnight while we hole up at a cheap motel the next town over.

JJ is laughing so hard he's wheezing, and I'm half-scared he's going to die. "You're hopeless, Molly, but we love you," he says, between gasping laughs. "Oh my god. Oh my god, Aiyana! Imagine me in a cowboy hat?" He imitates putting one on and pulling it down low. "Howdy, pardner."

I shake my head in a pout, but he just adds "Giddy-up!" in a deep and terrible Southern accent, and then erupts into a fresh round of giggles.

"Ha. Ha. You two," I say, crossing my arms, though I'm not really annoyed. It's nice to see them all relaxed and happy again, even if it is coming at my expense. "To be fair though," I add, intent on keeping the good mood going. "I don't really know what a western rider does either."

This sets JJ off all over again, but instead of joining in, Aiyana crinkles her forehead. "Hey, what time is it again?"

I check my phone. "About five. Why?"

"Hmm." She grabs her own phone out of her pocket and types something in, eventually holding up a map to show a route leading about an hour's drive from here. "What do you think, JJ?" she asks, completely ignoring me.

JJ's eyes go wide. "Oh my god, we have to!"

"Have to what?" I ask, looking back and forth between them.

Aiyana grins and hits a button to make her phone spew directions to the mystery place.

"You ever been to a rodeo, Molly?" JJ asks, putting his arm around me.

"No," I say, looking between them suspiciously. "Why?"

"Because you're about to!" He laughs, squeezing me even tighter, and oh. Oh no.

Chapter Fifteen

Rodeos smell. Like a lot.

While Aiyana and JJ's horse show smelled like sand, gardenias, and sure, the occasional whiff of horse, this one smells like cows and hay and shit. Old shit, specifically. That's been sitting in the sun for a while.

A lot of people are walking around in chaps and cowboy hats, and there's just a lot of . . . leather. A lot of leather . . . and flannel . . . and beer . . . and shit.

I look at Aiyana in despair and she crinkles her nose. "Okay, so maybe this isn't a great one to start with. Most of them are *much* nicer."

"There are nice rodeos?" I ask as I step over a suspicious-looking puddle of what seems to be the remnants of someone's corn dog that didn't stay down.

"Oh yeah, for sure," JJ says, backing her up. "I mean they aren't really my vibe, but a lot of the title rounds take place in actual arenas instead of creepy barns best known for their haunted hayrides. This is *not* representative, trust me."

"Then why are we here?" *And why is Shani? If her brother is so big-time, it doesn't make sense.*

JJ shrugs. "Lochlin's buddy bought this place a few years back, so he makes sure to draw an audience here whenever they're passing through on the circuit."

"Hooking up your friends seems to be a reoccurring theme in this industry," I say, thinking about how Aiyana was also friends with the owner of the barn where she just competed.

"Kind of! The horse community is massive, sure," Aiyana says. "But regionally you get to know all the players. When you see the same people time after time, it starts to feel smaller and homier. You'll see." She catches herself and holds up a hand like she didn't mean what she just said. "Or you won't. Whatever. This is me, fully accepting that Christina's barn is a stepping stone for you. Just a slip of the tongue, I swear," she says, rambling. "But if you do sell on us, you're going to have to promise to give me a discount on your wedding planning if I ever get married."

"Same," JJ says, nudging me.

"Naturally," I laugh, even though it makes me feel a little sad. "I think it's cool though, the community you've all built. I never really experienced anything like that. I didn't do any sports growing up, and trying to get a job in the event space is pretty cutthroat. I interned for this one wedding planner, and her main competitor called and had the flowers canceled like a week before our wedding event just to fuck with her because she thought she stole the client."

"Oh my god."

"Yeah, so . . . event planning is kind of drama."

"I'm not saying the horse world is drama free. We have more than our fair share, for sure," Aiyana says. "But why would you want to go into a career knowing it's going to be cutthroat drama from the jump?" she asks.

"I just . . . I love it." I shrug. "Life is so unpredictable; people get divorced, die, stop talking to each other," I say, thinking about my mom and Christina. "But for that one day, I can give people the fantasy of happily ever after in a real, tangible way. I can create a perfect event for them, and it feels really special to be a part of that."

"Wait, what happened with the flowers though?" JJ asks, sparing me from having to explain myself any further, because I know what Aiyana is really asking, and it's more along the lines of "Why would you ever choose that over this?" A question I'm already tired of feeling like I have to answer.

"Oh, I spent every day that week sourcing new stems and driving all over the state to get them. We pulled it off, and the bride had no idea," I say, a little pride flushing my chest. "I know I should be pissed that the other planner did that, but I like doing stuff like that. Like finding all those flowers, making sure the bride stayed calm, and everything went off without a hitch? I was really proud of myself for pulling that off."

JJ looks at me with a smile. "Yeah, I kinda get that with Marlowe, but instead of an angry bride I'm dealing with a thousand-pound animal that could trample me whenever she wants. Much worse."

"Spoken like someone who's never met a bridezilla before."

"True," he laughs, and I'm relieved when even Aiyana joins in.

"Hey, come on over here," she says, gesturing to a small open arena flanked by rickety bleachers. It's packed with even more people in cowboy hats and flannel, most of them cheering. Popcorn and beer both flow in abundance and everybody looks like they're having a blast and aren't afraid to show it. It's a very different crowd than the last horseshow and while maybe the last one is more in tune with my aesthetic preferences, the enthusiasm here is catching.

"Wait, is that Shani?" JJ asks, gesturing into the arena where a woman is currently making a tight, tight turn around a bright orange barrel. I've never seen a horse run so fast, or a rider look so confident. If I thought she had swagger before . . . but I can barely focus on that before she's flying back out the arena door, right under the bleachers and into a holding area out of view from the public. The way Aiyana yips and cheers though, I'm guessing Shani did very well.

"Dammit," Aiyana says, turning toward us, "I was hoping we would catch her whole ride."

Me too, I think, but don't say it out loud. I don't know where I stand with Shani right now, and now here I come crashing her rodeo like a lovesick puppy. I'm sure I'm the last person she'd want to see.

"We should go find her," JJ says. Aiyana nods enthusiastically as they quickly get up and head down the steps back to the arena.

I pull away when they turn toward the holding area in the back. "Actually, I think I'm gonna go grab some dinner. Those . . . corn dogs . . . look great?"

"Molly," Aiyana says, with a little frown.

"I'm . . . I'm hungry," I say, praying she hears what I really mean, which is that I can't do this right now. Not with an audience and definitely not in public. I'm not ready to see her after the way we left things and I'm sure she doesn't want to see me either.

"Don't be a—" JJ starts.

Aiyana smacks him in the arm. "Okay, we'll catch back up with you in a little while. I'll shoot you a text when we're done."

"Awesome," I say, grateful that she's dropping it.

I watch them disappear to what is no doubt going to be a surprised and happy welcome from Shani—and do my best to ignore the way that it twists my stomach that I won't be a part of it—and that it definitely wouldn't be a warm or happy greeting if I was.

I make my way through the row of vendors in the alley between the large sandy arena, pausing to look at some leather pants that look kind of like what Shani wears to do hooves. For half a second I imagine surprising her with them, but that would just be me bringing the guilt gifts to a whole new level. Besides, a) I'm completely broke and b) she probably wouldn't even accept them, and I'm not about to ask what the return policy is on a pair of glorified leather chaps.

I walk around a little more, grabbing some fries at one of the food trucks and dodging more drunk cowboys than I can count. Somehow, I find myself standing by the rail of the massive arena in the back, surrounded by another large-ish crowd of spectators.

There're clowns in the middle of this one, and I'm confused for a second—is this the kids' show or something?—until a chute opens from the side and a massive bronco comes flying out, a rag doll of a man on it as the animal whips around and jumps trying to fling the rider off its back. It's violent and horrible, and I turn to go just as the rider falls, followed by a sickening crunch as the horse's back feet make contact with the man's torso.

Everything goes silent and still in the arena as the clowns and handlers rush the bronco back to the chute. In the dirt, the man stays very, very still and I hold my breath, waiting for him to get up. I want to run away, forget I've ever seen this, but I'm pinned against the gate by the crowd.

A gruff man starts yelling and pushing everyone backward and out of the way, pulling open the entire side of the arena which I didn't even realize was a gate. A moment later an ambulance comes slowly backing up. We all watch as the rider is carefully loaded up onto the gurney and put in the back of the ambulance. He's hurt pretty bad, if I had to guess, but I see him shift a little. Everyone cheers and claps when he gives a weak thumbs-up just before the doors shut and the ambulance carts him away.

Still, I feel like I'm going to be sick. I don't know how anyone could do this. I don't know how anyone could watch this. I don't know how anyone could think this place was fun.

I storm off in the direction of Aiyana's truck—I'll just wait for them there—but my phone buzzes in my hand before I'm even to the exit.

> Where are you???? Lochlin got really messed up by the bronco he pulled. I'm driving Shani to the hospital in her truck. JJ will wait for you by mine.

Oh my god.
That was Lochlin? As in, Shani's brother Lochlin?

I fight the urge to say I'm coming too. Even though I know Shani hates me right now, I just . . . I want to be there for her, make it better somehow. Make her *all* of the coffee, bake her *all* the muffins. Fuck. This isn't about me, and Shani doesn't need my bullshit right now. Maybe I can just wait in the lobby for them or something. Be nearby in case I'm needed, but not actively in the way?

JJ flashes the high beams when he sees me walking up the row, and gestures for me to get in the passenger side.

"I'm driving," he says, putting it in reverse when I've barely shut the door. Good, I want to get there fast . . . which is why I'm so confused when he enters the name of our motel an hour away into the GPS.

"What are you doing?"

"Going back to check on the horses and get some sleep. What else?"

"Aren't we going to the hospital?"

He looks at me like I have two heads. "You didn't even want to say hi to her and now you want to crash the waiting room? No. We're definitely *not* doing that."

I sigh. He's right. I know he's right. But I wish he wasn't.

"I have specific instructions to bring you back to the motel," he adds.

"From who?" I don't know why I need to know if it was Shani sending me away, but I do.

"Aiyana. She'll send us updates when there's anything to know. In the morning, you can help me trailer the horses. Aiyana's asking her friend if we can borrow a bigger trailer so we can come back and grab Gideon tomorrow too. It's probably going to be a very long day."

"Right, of course," I say, not sure if I feel better or worse that it's Aiyana banning me from the waiting room and not Shani herself. "What about Aiyana though? How's she going to get back to the motel tonight?"

"There's no way she's leaving Shani alone. She'll catch a ride back to town with her whenever the time comes. I told her we'd take good care of her horse until then."

"Yeah," I say, trying to get the sound of the bronco kicking Lochlin out of my head.

"Scary as hell," JJ says, more to himself than to me. "Really reminds you that we're dealing with animals here, and they don't always follow the plan."

"He gave a thumbs-up," I say after a beat of silence. JJ looks at me, probably surprised I was over at the bronco riding arena. "I was right there when it happened. It looked really bad, but he gave a thumbs-up on the stretcher. That has to count for something, right? It's a good sign?"

"Yeah, that's good," JJ says. "That's really good." But I don't miss the tightness of his jaw or the way his knuckles go white as he squeezes the steering wheel.

Chapter Sixteen

Driving home is a somber affair the next day.

Aiyana didn't text us until well after midnight to tell us that Lochlin was awake and doing well. Or at least as well as someone can when they have a shattered arm, multiple broken ribs, a punctured lung, and a pretty bad concussion. JJ says Lochlin got very, very lucky and well, if that's true, I hope I never see what unlucky looks like. I get now why Shani doesn't ever like to watch these things live. I know I never will again. I desperately hope no one recorded it this time, and that she'll never see it.

Aiyana gets us a bigger trailer to borrow and we run back up to the rodeo arena to grab Gideon, just like JJ predicted. It's an hour out of our way but neither of us mind. Bringing Shani's horse home at least makes us feel like we're doing something.

JJ and I barely talk the entire ride home—gone is the fun of the experience, even though he's got a fresh new trophy to show for it and so does Aiyana. It just doesn't seem like the right time to be celebrating.

I help him unload the horses as soon as we get home, and I'm not at all surprised that JJ promptly hops in his own little Honda Civic and takes off the second we're done. Last night was heavy, really heavy, and I would be tempted to drive off too if I could. But there're chores to be done, and fewer people to do them now, so I get to work.

I take my time giving everyone hay and grain, so relieved to see Otis that I basically collapse against him. He nuzzles me for a few minutes as if he missed me too, even letting me hug extra tight, before abandoning me for the fresh hay I just shoved in his feeder.

It's when I see his feeder that I remember. *Shit.*

I look over to Gideon, remembering now that I tore out his during my little temper tantrum the other day. *Get it together, Molly. Jesus.*

A quick text and a Venmo request for way more than I expect has Lita arriving with a brand-new slow feeder about an hour or so later. My nearly maxed credit card is going to be sad to see another high-dollar purchase, but hopefully Shani will be happy when she gets back. It feels like the least I could do.

Lita gives me an impromptu lesson when she arrives, telling me that spreading hay on the ground would have been just as effective—something about the position allowing mucus to drain or whatever—but I can't imagine anybody wanting to eat their food off of pine shavings on the floor, so I let it go. As a compromise, she says, she bought me a slow feeder that slings low into the stall. A huge improvement over what used to be there apparently. If I'm going to go new, I might as well do it right.

"Like I said though, Gideon was fine," Lita says when we get to the stall and find him foraging on the ground for any dropped grain or hay.

"I get it. And I really, really, appreciate you grabbing this for me. I guess I just . . ." I trail off, surprised that I feel like crying.

"Why do I feel like this isn't really about replacing a feeder," Lita says, giving me a gentle pat on the shoulder.

"No," I sniffle, wishing I could inhale my half-shed tears. "I saw Lochlin get hurt. I don't know if JJ told you that, but I did. It was scary before I knew who the rider was, and a thousand times worse after. I can't do anything to make it better for Shani, you know? So, I just wanted to do something to at least not make it worse. I need to feel like I'm doing something right now."

Lita studies my face, a soft smile spreading across her lips. "Let me show you how to set it up and then I'll be out of your hair."

* * *

Okay, well, Lita definitely made it look easier than it was when she explained the directions before she took off to get back home—apparently the only reason her partner wasn't mad about me interrupting their Sunday night was because Lita promised to come right back. If I'd known they had plans, I never would have asked her to come, but . . . maybe she just needed to feel like she was doing something too.

Still, it's almost impossible to get it installed right, and not just because Gideon is towering over me, extremely curious about everything I'm doing to his stall. I eventually give up and put him out in the crossties so I can have more room, except now he's just nipping at my arm every time I move past to grab another tool out of the office—as if I broke some sacred trust between us by not letting him nibble on the screws that I accidentally spilled all over the ground.

I get it, he's probably just as exhausted as I am after the drive, but I'm trying to do something nice here . . . If he would stop chomping on me, that would be great.

I grab my AirPods on my next tool-finding trip to the office, desperate to drown out the stomps and sighs of the horses as they complain about the barn light still being on. I scroll down to the *Midnights* album and push play, letting the opening notes of "Lavender Haze" settle me down. *I wish I was in a lavender haze right now*, I think, as Taylor Swift croons in my ear. Instead, I'm in a let's-take-turns-hating-each-other situationship. No, not even a situationship. This is barely more than an acquaintance-ship, a bitter acquaintanceship at best after that last text I sent her about measuring her place.

Fuck. I didn't have to be such a dick about it.

I go back to struggling with the feeder, earbuds firmly in place now, still dodging Gideon's incessant nipping, until a tap on my shoulder has me spinning around with a scream. An extremely exhausted-looking Shani catches my arm right before I hit her, instincts on overdrive.

"Oh, Jesus! Sorry, Shani! I'm gonna put a bell on you so you can't sneak up on me anymore," I yelp, pulling out my AirPods and shoving them in my pocket. "I . . . you're home! I didn't expect you so soon." I pull her into a hug, just relieved to see her again, but realize my mistake when I feel her stiffen in my grasp, her arms pinned tightly to her sides. "Sorry, sorry," I say, jumping back, embarrassed.

"It's fine, Molly," she says, sounding tired, the bone-deep kind of tired that even a hot bath and a good podcast can't fix. "I was just coming to check on Gideon, and then I got worried when I realized he was in the aisle. I thought maybe JJ left him in—"

"Oh no, JJ was great. Got him all settled in, even put down hay for him but I . . ." I trail off, gesturing hopelessly behind me to the hay feeder. "I got you this."

"That's a nice feeder," Shani says, leaning past me to peer in the stall. "The real estate agent wanted that?"

"No, when you left, I noticed his old one was kind of in shambles, so I took it down," I say, skirting the truth. "Then we brought Gideon home for you, and I realized that meant he didn't have one anymore. Lita was all, 'hay on the ground is fine, let him drain his mucus' or whatever and 'you don't really need a feeder, calm down!' But he had a feeder when you left, you know! And now he was going to not have one? I couldn't let that happen." I'm rambling and I can't make it stop.

Shani pinches the bridge of her nose, rubbing it hard. "Look, it's late and I have a killer headache. Just bill me for the feeder—"

"Yeah, of course you're exhausted, sorry. I'm not . . . I'm not charging you for this though. I just wanted you to come home to something nice."

"Why?" she asks, her tone wary and suspicious, and her face even more so.

"Because I . . ." I trail off, not sure how to finish the sentence.

"I'm too tired for this," Shani says, turning to go. "Just please, make sure he's in his stall before you leave."

"Because I was worried about your brother!" I blurt out, and she turns back to me, surprised. "And you! And I know that text I sent you was an asshole move. I'm sorry. No matter what happens with this place, you deserve way better." I look back in the stall, trying to hide the sincerity of those words. "I was trying to be nice, but this screw would *not* go in and Gideon was biting me the whole time. So now, instead of coming home to something awesome, you came home to your pissed-off horse and a broken stall and . . ." I sigh. "I just keep fucking everything up when I'm trying to— Look, I'll figure it out. You do *not* need to deal with this. I'll put him in his stall as soon as I'm done. You can trust me. Seriously."

Stunned realization crosses Shani's face and I realize far too late that I just admitted I was doing this all for her. I look down, my cheeks burning. "Where's the screw?" she asks, eventually.

I hold it up weakly and step out of her way. She studies the hay feeder for a moment and then goes out to her truck, returning a few minutes later with a drill in her hand.

In seconds, she has that screw in and has tightened all the ones that I (poorly) attempted to do by hand. Right. A drill. I'm an idiot. I think KiKi even brought one on her last visit. It's probably in my kitchen right now. Why didn't I think of that?

"I didn't mean to make more work for you, Shani. I swear I would have put him away safely," I say, as Shani leads Gideon into his stall. The horse eagerly inspects the new feeder and, seemingly satisfied, drops his head low to pull out some non–pine-shavings-covered hay. He whinnies in approval as he leans into Shani, who is now resting her forehead against him in a half hug.

I step out, giving them a moment, glad Gideon seems to be done biting people for the night.

"You didn't have to do that, but thanks," Shani says, when she finally steps out and locks the stall door behind her. "I know you would have gotten the screw eventually, but I had the drill right there and I needed a Gideon hug anyway. The hospital was . . . hard."

"How's Lochlin?" I ask, trying not to dwell too much on the way my heart picks up at the idea that she believed I could have handled it. That she could have trusted me with her horse.

"Stubborn. Frustrating. I'm gonna bring him back here to recover and rehab his arm, if it's okay with you. If I don't, he'll just get right back up on another horse before he's healed. I can go stay with him somewhere else if you don't want him to, but the man needs a babysitter."

"Yeah, yes, of course it's fine. Whatever he needs. Whatever you need."

She looks at me once more, surprised, and I've said too much again.

"Molly—"

"I told Ashley that I don't want to go with a developer," I say, before she can say anything else.

"Are you thinking of . . . ?"

"I'm still going to look for private offers. I can't keep this place, Shani, but I can make sure it stays what it is. It's the best I can do. I'm really trying here."

She hangs her head for a second, nodding for herself like she should have known, but when she looks up at me again, she doesn't look mad like I was expecting. She looks . . . touched?

"Makes sense," she says, her voice quiet. "Aiyana was telling me about your plans a little. I think she was just trying to keep my mind off things while we sat in that waiting room all night. It means a lot that you would try to find a private buyer, and I appreciate you fixing it up in the meantime," she says, gesturing toward the stall. "I mean that. Gideon's never gotten an *apology hay feeder* before."

"You're welcome," I say, utterly lost in her tired smile. And god, I know it's not the time, but when she looks at me like that? Like I made this day suck a tiny bit less? I can almost imagine what it would feel like to be the one that always gets to comfort her, hold her, kiss her . . .

"I'm gonna go get some sleep. I'll see you tomorrow, yeah?" she finally says, but I hear the real question beneath it. *Are we good now?* and maybe even a little *I'm sorry for my part in this mess too.*

"Yeah, I'll see you tomorrow," I say, and she doesn't hug me exactly, but she leans in and gives my shoulder a little squeeze as she walks by.

I float on air all the way back to my house.

Chapter Seventeen

Hey darlin," Lochlin says, walking—well, limping really—up to where Lita and I are working in the main barn on a sunny Friday afternoon. He got released from the hospital late last week, but I didn't realize he was in up-and-walking-around condition yet.

Lita is cleaning out a stall she stashed an extra horse in for a friend the other day—I didn't charge as long as she cleaned up after it—while I continue my eternal paint scraping in the little lounge across from her. It's a near constant effort to clean this place in the hopes that Ashley can take better pictures next time she's here. The listing is going live soon, showcasing only the areas we have fixed up and the information on the land and houses, but every new area I finish gives her an excuse to update it and send a new mailer out to relevant buyers.

Shani's brother being here will be a welcome distraction from all of that.

"Lochlin!" Lita says, dropping her shovel as she rushes over to give him a hug that's somehow both fierce and gentle all at once. I grin, happy to see him back on his feet, even if Shani probably wishes he wasn't. Although she *did* feel comfortable enough to head out to work today, catching up on her backlog of clients from while she's been busy tending to her brother, so that has to be a good sign.

In fact, the mood around the barn has steadily improved as Lochlin got settled in and we all realized he was out of the woods for good. Well, maybe not for good, given that he's already talking about getting back on the horse (literally), but for now, at least.

Shani left us this morning with instructions to call her if Lochlin dared leave the house, and while Lita and I both swore we would, neither of us seem inclined to at the moment.

"You should be in bed," I say, popping my head out of the office, because yeah, I might not rat him out to his sister, but I'm also not going to completely abandon my post on Lochlin watch. Shani and I have been getting along much better since she realized I wasn't going to sell to the developer, and I don't want to do anything to ruin it.

"Oh," he says, turning to me with gleaming eyes and a smile I can't help but drown in. "I knew Shani was gonna have spies. I just didn't realize they'd be so pretty."

Lita laughs and mumbles something that sounds like a drawn out "wow," before turning back to her work in the stall, leaving me to deal with him alone.

I blush, never having the full force of Lochlin's glow I've heard so much about turned on me. "I won't tell, if you get back into bed right now."

"You care to join me?" he asks, arching an eyebrow. I realize too late how it must have sounded. Rather than getting embarrassed, I turn it right back around on him.

I gently pat the cast on his arm. "You couldn't handle me on the best of days, and you're definitely not having the best of days right now," I snark, knowing he's full of shit.

"Is that so?" he asks, his eyes flashing. "I think I could surprise you."

"Bad news, I don't like surprises."

Lochlin comes a little closer, clearly enjoying our easy banter as much as I am. "Then I'd have to walk you through it, take it *real* slow, you know?" he says, as he flashes me a devilish grin. "But what kind of girl doesn't like surprises?"

"The kind with daddy issues and a lot of debt," I say, going back to scraping. "You practice that look in the mirror or was it just trial and error with your fans?"

He laughs, caught off guard, and his whole demeanor changes. His swagger seems to drop as he shifts closer to the wall, trading his cocky lean for actually resting against the wall and letting it hold him up. His smirk gives way to a warm smile, even his aggressively attractive dimples seem to shift into something gentler, lighter.

"I can relate to that," he says, watching me continue to strip the wall.

"I thought you might," I say. "Is that why you jump on the back of feral horses?"

He rubs his chin, considering. "Nah, I do that for the fun of it. Just everything else . . ."

"Oh, is that all." I smile. I like him. I didn't expect to like him, not with the way he first came in. Maybe we could even be friends someday, if he sticks around long enough.

"How much time you got?" he teases. "It's a long story."

"Not long enough," I say, trying not to think about the mile-long to-do list I have for the day.

"That's too bad," he says, and it sounds like he means it. "You're kinda fun."

"Now there's something I never get called." I laugh, pausing my work to look at him. "Not that I'm not enjoying this conversation, but I did promise your sister I would call if you escaped. You need to be resting."

He grins and shakes his head. "Despite what you may have heard from my jailor sister this morning, I have been paroled."

I narrow my eyes, not believing him.

"Not forever mind you, just a short reprieve. I'm waiting for my buddy, Tyler, to get here. It's hell trying to find the little turnoff for Shani's place, so I told him to come to the main house. God knows you can't miss the fucking ugly Christina's Corrals sign."

"Hey!" I say, even though I agree. It hits different when it's someone else saying it.

"Wait, you walked all the way over here? Shani approved that?" Lita asks, poking her head back out of Happy's stall, and I'm glad she's the one doing the grilling. "I'll just give her a quick call to—"

"No, don't!" He looks at Lita, scandalized, but before he can say anything else, an old antique pickup truck comes roaring up the drive, kicking up a cloud of dust behind it. Lochlin grins and makes his way to the front of the barn as fast as he can. He waves to his friend as he steps, or hops really, out into the sunshine.

Tyler, a slim-built, white, cowboy-looking dude in his late

twenties, complete with light brown hair and eyes so blue you could swim in them, parks his car and walks over. I have to lift my head to look up at his six-foot-plus frame, but it's endearing, the way he pulls off his hat as soon as he gets to us.

He nods at me and slaps his hat against Lochlin's unhurt arm in greeting. "Morning, ma'am. Hope this one here hasn't been too much trouble." His voice comes out in a low, Southern drawl that in another time and another place might have had me tearing off my clothes.

Lochlin shakes his head. "You know I don't actually *need* a babysitter, Ty."

Tyler raises his eyebrows. "That's not what Shani said when she told me to get my ass out here so she could go back to work." He glances at me, a new bashfulness taking over his features. "Pardon my language."

"It's fine. Call me Molly, not ma'am. Please!"

"Apologies, ma—Molly," he catches himself.

"Fuck me, did she seriously call you?" Lochlin groans. "Is that why you *suddenly* had some time off to come hang? You're such an asshole."

Tyler looks quite pleased with himself and gestures toward his car. "Maybe, but I'm the asshole that's gonna give you a ride back and get you into bed. I can see how you're sweating. You don't have to be such a stubborn fool and refuse pain meds, you know."

"Leave it, Ty." Lochlin clenches his jaw and with a curt nod in my direction, limps his way toward the truck. Tyler offers a quick apology and quickly follows after him.

"That boy . . ." Lita says, turning to get back to work once again.

I know I should follow her lead and return to both minding my business and scraping paint off the ten thousand walls I seem to be responsible for, but curiosity gnaws at me. I set my scraper down and follow her as she picks up the end of the wheelbarrow and carts it out back.

"So . . . Lochlin had a drug problem or something?" I ask. "It's like someone dumped a bucket of ice water over him as soon as Tyler—"

"Some things are sensitive," she says, clearly considering her words carefully.

"You don't have to tell me. I just didn't want to accidentally step in it with Shani when we're just starting to get along again, ya know?"

Lita sighs and dumps all the mess she cleaned out of the barn. Fitting for what I'm asking her to spill right now. "Shani didn't just choose to stay here. Her dad lost custody," Lita says, and I try not to act surprised.

"Oh. That's . . . yeah."

"Lochlin was about ten and well on his way to being a rodeo whiz when his father got himself tangled up on pain pills, and Shani was only twelve. Lochlin was able to convince another rodeo family to take him in pretty easily since he was doing well homeschooling on his own and already competing in all the junior events with their kids.

"They couldn't keep Shani too though, and thank god for that. Your aunt stepped up to take her in and became her legal guardian until she turned eighteen. It was . . . rough. Their dad went from having a big name with a family legacy and kids riding right after him, to . . . a drug addict, basically. It wasn't his fault—"

"How can you say that?" I ask, incredulous.

"Eh, bronc riders all have this stupid machismo attitude," Lita says, finishing up with the wheelbarrow. "Like take Lochlin, right? A bunch of broken ribs, broken arm, fresh from the hospital. He shouldn't be walking farther than the bathroom, yet he's marching all the way across the field to look strong for his friend."

"Ridiculous," I snort.

"Yeah, but because of his dad, Lochlin won't take anything stronger than Tylenol. That boy looked like he was about to pass out just from standing here—and he was still trying to play it off. It's not a great way to live. I don't think he was pissed Tyler brought up the meds though, but because he brought up *the pain*."

"What do you mean? Obviously he's in pain—"

"It's all part of the show."

"But why go through that?"

"They all have their reasons. You'd have to ask Lochlin for his. He's one of the luckier ones too. He does well for himself, so he can afford to miss some time, but most of them can't. They have to ride if they want to eat. Time off can screw you over in a way you can't recover from. If you don't have any education or experience besides sitting on an animal for three seconds every other night, that's a scary proposition."

"Damn." I always pictured it as more of a hobby, not a way to earn a living, even though I knew objectively that's what Lochlin had been doing. I guess I always figured Shani was subsidizing some of that for him, like the dutiful sister she seems to be. "Is barrel racing the same way?"

"What do you mean?"

"I mean, I saw the tail end of Shani and her horse. People seemed very excited she was there, but JJ said it wasn't a comeback or anything, sometimes she just goes out like that and gives herself a little taste of it."

"No." Lita considers her answer. "I see barrel races as just another aspect of horsemanship, like hunting, jumping, or equitation. It's not really the same as the bulls and broncs, although you can get sucked into the lifestyle in general just as easy with any one of them."

"Then why doesn't Shani do it anymore, if it makes her happy?"

"Why don't you just ask her," Lita says with a gentle smile. "I've told you more than I should have about her brother and their business already. You want to know more? Go to the source."

"I'm trying to stay on her good side for once," I laugh. "I doubt digging up her past is gonna keep me there."

"I don't know," Lita says, getting back to work. "She might like knowing you're interested."

Chapter Eighteen

The next week passes by in a busy blur. I keep tackling the list from Ashley and actually make a solid dent—and I start to get used to Lochlin hanging around whenever he finds a way to sneak past both Shani *and* Tyler to come hang out in the barn with me.

He's fully dropped the pretense of "flirty cowboy with swagger to spare," and now most of our conversations center around the horses and fixing up the barn, with more than a few critiques of my skills at both. If I'm being honest though, it's nice to have someone to talk to when I'm doing hours of chores and repairs, even if he does occasionally piss me off by insisting that I use sandpaper instead of a scraper on certain areas or a different size screw for something else.

Nat and KiKi pop over again as soon as they're able. KiKi's just coming for the day, but Nat is staying over for a girls' night, so they had to take two cars—something KiKi complains about loudly when she arrives, worried about gas money and putting miles on both.

It's awkward but we all try to shake it off as we get to work. They've come to help me fix up some areas of the fence I'm struggling with—but Randy has Nat working double time, and that plus auditions has her so exhausted that she pretty much just watches KiKi and me work.

It's mostly fine, even if KiKi occasionally sighs loud enough to make me feel guilty down to my toes.

"Thanks for doing this," I say to her, hours in, when Nat leaves to get us water. Maybe if we address the elephant in the room, it'll cut some of the tension. "I'm sure there are other things you'd like to be doing with your day off. I mean it, I really appreciate your help here."

KiKi shrugs. "This is what Nat wants to do so . . ." she says, which doesn't exactly make me feel any better.

"Is everything okay?" I ask, dreading the answer.

She hammers in a post a little harder than is strictly necessary. "Why wouldn't it be?"

"I don't know, you just seem . . . annoyed? Maybe?"

She pauses, meeting my eyes. "Now, how could I be annoyed when I'm lucky enough to spend all my time out here in the middle of nowhere fixing up your house for free?"

"Hey!" I say, rearing my head back. "I didn't ask you to come out here and do this. Nat offered!"

"No, you never ask, do you? You just expect us to show up. Fix your life, fix your house. What's next? You want to move in with us too?"

"I—"

"Who's thirsty?" Nat calls in a singsong voice as she walks up from the house, effectively cutting me off. She's brought my sleeping bag out too, along with a bag of chips. She makes herself at home, lying down to watch us. "What did I miss?" she asks, glancing between us.

"Nothing," KiKi says, grabbing one of the bottles of water. "Just getting tired. I have to head back soon."

I start to say something—wanting to settle this or fight it out or tell KiKi to leave if that's how she feels—but the glare she shoots me, followed by the gentle look she gives Nat, has me swallowing my words.

Nat seems content to fill up the space between us anyway, so we both just let her. She dives right into complaining about Randy, about the man who continues to not ask for creamer space and then inevitably spills, and about how the only thing she's booked this year has been a diarrhea medication commercial—things I used to care about more than anything.

Except, as we pack up and head into the house—where KiKi leaves after just a quick kiss to Nat and not even a goodbye to me—I realize that I don't miss it.

I miss Nat, sure, and my mom, of course, even if she is still dodging every question I have about her and Christina, but I don't miss the job. I don't miss that *life*. Plus, now that I've finally taken a minute to get a handle on the books for the barn, I have a much clearer picture of where things stand. While I wouldn't say the business is *firmly* profitable, it is, at least, teetering on the line between red and black. Which means that its little savings, combined with mine, have been enough to live off and fix the place up. Barely. If you squint.

Sure, my diet has been more pasta than steak lately, but it's been nice. I feel useful here, in a way I'm not sure I ever have before.

"Why do you look like a confused wombat right now?" Nat asks, tilting her head.

"A confused wombat?"

"I don't know. Have you ever seen the video before where it's like this creature that's all . . . never mind, forget it. What's going on in your head?"

"I was just listening to you talk and thinking about how much I don't miss the coffee shop or living in the city. You sound completely burnt out right now."

"Fuck you too," she laughs, pouring herself more wine.

"No, I'm being serious," I say, and her face falls. "I know we had this dream of living in the city, with these great jobs and—"

"It's not a dream, it's a *plan*," she says sharply.

I don't bother pointing out that that "plan" doesn't seem to be working out for either of us. "Yeah," I say instead, biting my lip and realizing I should have probably just kept that thought to myself. "I guess."

"What is going on with you," Nat says, taking a sip. "I feel like I'm losing you lately. It was bad enough when you were always busy with work or your mom—at least we had our shifts together at the coffee shop. Now, it's like this place is your only focus."

"You say that like it's not a huge responsibility," I laugh, pouring my own glass.

"It's not supposed to be though," she says, meeting my eyes. "Why are you wasting your time on fences and wallpaper when you could just sell to the developer and be done?"

"Trust me, this is the right thing."

Nat sighs. "Is this about that woman?"

"It's about a lot more than just that."

Nat pinches the bridge of her nose. "This isn't a Hallmark

movie, Molly. You're not rich enough to be the city girl who falls for the lumberjack with the Christmas tree farm or whatever."

"I'm not falling for anybody," I say, right as there's a knock on the edge of my screen door.

"Well, that's certainly good to know," Lochlin says through the screen, slipping back into performance mode when he spies Nat. "I'd hate to think I missed my chance. May I come in?"

"We're kind of in the middle of something," Nat snaps, not even asking to be introduced.

"Hey, Loch," I say cheerfully, trying to cover for her rudeness. "Do you have permission to be out and about?" Tyler comes up the steps behind him and flashes me a little thumbs-up that suggests this is, in fact, a sanctioned visit.

"Yes, this time." Lochlin grins. "But you didn't seem all that worried about me sneaking around when I distracted that old horse for you this morning," he teases. "Sometimes I wonder if you're just using me, Molly McDaniel."

"Charming," Nat grumbles.

"Be nice," I say quietly, and she rolls her eyes. "Hang on, guys, let me get the latch." I casually peek out on the porch as I let them in.

I like hanging out with Lochlin, don't get me wrong, but I'd be lying if I didn't say I wished his sister was also standing on my porch right now. Other than a "hi" or "bye," Shani just tends her horse or rushes off to work. I wonder if she's working double time to avoid me, or to cover hospital bills, or just to make up for the time she missed. No matter the answer, it sucks.

I make introductions all around, and notice that the cast on Lochlin's arm has changed from its original white to a bright pink. I raise my eyebrow, but he just laughs. "They cut the old one off for an X-ray today. I didn't mind. It was dirty anyway," he says with a grin.

"As if he doesn't like being dirty." Tyler nudges him and, if I'm not wrong, Lochlin's ears get a little blush from the teasing.

"So, what's up?" I ask now that we're all awkwardly standing around my kitchen.

"I can't believe how much nicer this place looks," Lochlin says, but I block him from looking in the living room—which is still sadly operating as my bedroom. While I've gotten Aunt Christina's room mostly emptied out, I still can't get the door to the other room open. I know it's ridiculous and even a little sad or rude maybe, but the idea of sleeping in the room where she died freaks me out.

"You came all this way just to say good job?" I tease.

"That's not why we really came here, Molly," Tyler says. "Although it does look good."

"Thank you," I say, looking between them, still confused as to why they are here. "Everything okay with Shani?"

"Yes. In fact, the warden has given me an evening pass," Lochlin says, standing a little bit straighter. And okay, now it's Nat's turn to look every bit the confused wombat as I do.

"Shani's letting him go out tonight," Tyler helpfully translates. "His appointment with his ortho went well enough today they're starting to talk about PT and massage therapy."

"And if I'm healthy enough to be tortured with physical therapy, then I'm healthy enough to go out to The Whiskey Boot."

"That dingy-looking bar on Main?" I ask, incredulously.

"Okay, so it's doing the best impression of a country western bar as it can in the state of New York, but it's better than nothing. They even allegedly have line dancing tonight, although I don't expect many people will participate."

"You line dance?" I shriek, barely able to control my laughter.

"You are brutal, you know that, Molly?" Lochlin laughs. "Yes, I do line dance on occasion. I won't make it on the floor long, but there's no crime against drinking and watching."

"I don't know about the line dancing, but he's definitely good at the drinking and watching part," Tyler helpfully supplies.

"Hey!" Lochlin pouts. "Just because you're actually from Tennessee, and I'm not, doesn't mean I'm not every bit as country as you."

"It literally does," I snort.

Lochlin shakes his head. "Well, either way, we're just missing one thing."

"Which is?" I ask, already dreading his answer.

"Pretty girls on our arms."

Tyler has the good sense to duck his head and look embarrassed, but Lochlin gives puppy-dog eyes to Nat like he didn't just say the most ridiculous pickup line I've ever heard.

"I see." I fake a grimace. "And what's in it for me?"

"My shining company," he says, pretending to be offended through his laughter.

I turn to Nat. "What do you think?"

"No. Way."

"Please? You want to spend more time together, right? When's the last time we were able to go out like this?" Nat crosses her arms, clearly still not happy with me, but I don't give up. "You just said you wanted to spend time together that doesn't have to do with this farm. Let's go! I happen to know you look really cute in denim too, so . . ."

"Ugh, fine," she says, downing the rest of her glass of wine. "But I meant what I said about us needing to talk more."

"Yes," I say. "Fun now, talk tomorrow, I promise."

Nat sighs. "Okay, so what do you have that I can wear?"

* * *

WE CHASE THE boys out so we can get ready, promising to meet them over at Shani's around seven P.M. so we can all take one car. Nat raids all the clothing boxes in the storage shed while I take a shower.

She appears a little while later with an assortment of "the most country looking clothes I could find," which mostly just consists of bedazzled denim—let's just say I do not share the same love of rhinestones that Christina obviously had. There is *some* stuff I like though.

I settle on a pair of jeans that look like I was poured into them, and a pair of Christina's cowboy boots that miraculously look like they've never been worn. Nat also found us both what she calls "flirty flannel shirts," which she insists we tie up around our waists over some of my old cropped tank tops.

She even helps me do my hair, and I help her do her makeup, and by six forty-five we're the country bumpkin version of dressed to kill, and all that weird tension between us is gone . . . at least for the moment. It was *fun* getting ready with her. I forgot how great that was. We're both laughing and smiling as we make our way over to Shani's—it almost feels like old times.

Tyler pulls the door open, looking spit shined and ready to go and is that a freaking bolo tie? One with a tiny ornate bull skull in the center? Dork.

An attractive dork, but still.

"Hey." Tyler smiles. "Lochlin's drowning himself in Drakkar to make up for the pink cast. Please come in."

"I haven't worn Drakkar since middle school, thank you very much," Lochlin says, coming out of the guest room. And Jesus, he cleans up nice.

"You two look beautiful," he says, looking between Nat and me.

Which is the exact moment Shani decides to come out of her bedroom. She looks a little flushed and annoyed when she sees me, and while a "Hey, how are you" or something would be nice, it doesn't happen. Instead, I get, "Why are you dressed like that, Molly?"

Her words are harsh, but it comes out in an almost whine. I fight hard to ignore the way my belly flip-flops at the idea that she might *like* me all done up like a country girl—or "buckle bunny" I think is what Aiyana called me when she saw us walking over. I'll have to ask her what that means later when she meets us at the bar after putting away her horse.

"What's wrong with how I'm dressed?" I laugh.

Shani tilts her head, like she's trying to puzzle me out. "Are you and Nat going out or something?"

"Yeah," I say. "Lochlin and Tyler invited us to join them."

She flashes an angry look at Lochlin, but he just grins and holds up his hands. "Just making nice with the new owner, Shan," he says.

She looks like she wants to say something else but instead turns back to me. "He's taking you to The Whiskey Boot?"

"Yeah. It should be pretty f—"

"Wait here," she says, and disappears down the hall into her room.

Lochlin groans. "What the hell, Shani, we're trying to leave."

"Fucking hold on," she calls from her room.

She returns a second later with a cowboy hat in her hand. *Her* cowboy hat. She drops it onto my head, and I'm instantly lost in the smell of leather and *Shani*. I swallow hard while she adjusts it, leaning so close to me that if we didn't have an audience, I might have lost my mind and tried to kiss her. Again. And again. And again.

God, she makes this impossible.

"There," she says, stepping back to admire her work. "Now your cowgirl cosplay is complete."

I touch the soft leather brim of her well-loved, broken in hat. "Are you sure you want me to wear this tonight?"

"Positive," she says, pushing me out to the front porch where everyone else is already waiting. "Have fun."

And once again, I'm left trying to quiet the stupid butterflies screaming in my head over the fact that Shani's letting me borrow her hat. I glance at Lochlin, surprised to see him shaking his head at his sister as she shuts the door behind us.

"Ready?" I ask him, and his face clears.

"You know you don't actually have to wear that, right?" he asks.

"It's cute," I say, as I follow him down the steps.

"Okay," Lochlin says, drawing out the word as Tyler tries to hold in a laugh.

I narrow my eyes, glancing between them. *What did I just miss?*

Chapter Nineteen

The mood in Tyler's truck is more subdued than it was when we got there. Nat and I are crammed into the back, trading equally confused looks, while Lochlin and Tyler sit up front, whispering and shaking their heads. I can't help but feel like the guys are sharing some joke that we're not in on, and I kind of hate it.

"*This* is where we're going?" Nat asks as we pull into the little bar on the outskirts of town. There's a giant sign out front of a neon cowboy boot kicking over an equally bright glass of what I'm guessing is supposed to be whiskey, and a few Harleys dotting the parking lot, but mostly it's just other pickups and the occasional car. The parking lot is fuller than I expected for a random weeknight.

I walk in with wide eyes, determined to take it all in with an open mind. The bar is much bigger than it looked from the outside, and what it's lacking in width it makes up for in length. A large scratched-up oak bar runs halfway down one side, crowded by people in cowboy hats and fringe, and where I felt a little silly before—what did Shani say? that I was "cosplaying cowgirl?"—I now realize that I actually fit right in.

The entire middle of the place is taken up by a large dance

floor, where a DJ is playing some old Sam Hunt song that I remember hit the Top 40 stations a few years ago. A smattering of people clutters the dance floor, but most are around the bar or at the various tables dotting the outside of the walls. In the far back, stands a crowd almost as big as the one by the bar. I go up on my tiptoes to get a better look and see a woman riding what looks to be a mechanical bull. Or at least I think that's what it's supposed to be, considering that it doesn't actually have a head or legs or anything.

"See, I told you this was a real country bar," Lochlin laughs.

"No, it's not," Tyler sighs, pinching the bridge of his nose.

I narrow my eyes at Lochlin. "Don't get any ideas, sir," I say, gently tapping the bright pink cast on his arm. "No bull riding for you."

Lochlin pouts at me, but there's no heat behind it. He flicks the brim of my hat before walking off, greeting some girl he seems to know from way back when, judging by how tightly she's hugging him. I look at Nat, but she either doesn't notice or doesn't care, because she just says "come on" and pulls me over to the bar.

Within minutes, Lochlin is swarmed by a small group of women, fawning over his cast and the fact that he's in town. I look on, amused, while I wait for the bartender to notice me. Tyler touches the edge of my elbow to catch my attention. "First round on me," he says. "What are y'all having?"

Nat asks for a White Claw, which gets a scrunched-up look from Tyler. I ask for a Michelob Light, because that's what most of the women around me seem to be drinking, even though I'd prefer a White Claw too.

Nat and I go and find an empty table and scrounge up enough chairs for all of us. "Nice place," Nat says, raising an eyebrow.

Before I can respond, Tyler comes back, blushing hard and complaining that he's never going to live down asking for a White Claw at a place like this. I don't bother pointing out that they wouldn't stock it if no one was ordering it, choosing to enjoy his bashfulness instead.

"Is it always like this with him?" I ask, tipping my beer toward Lochlin whose grin couldn't get any bigger if he tried. One of the women whispers in his ear. There's no way I can hear what she says over the music, but I can tell by the way his eyes widen and his ears pink up that it must have been something good.

"Yeah, pretty much," Tyler laughs. "He's got his share of buckle bunnies in almost every town we visit."

"Yeah, what is that?" Nat asks. "Aiyana used that phrase too."

"Sorry, *fans*. Fans who want to . . ." He huffs. "I really don't know how to explain this without sounding like a misogynistic asshole."

"Then maybe you should stop using misogynistic asshole terms," I say, figuring out exactly what he means. "Does your mother know that's how you talk about women?"

"I apologize, Molly. You are absolutely right. I shouldn't—"

"Relax," I laugh. "I just wanted to make you squirm. I mean, yes, you should quit instead, but I accept your apology in the meantime."

"You're a little bit evil," he says, tilting his beer at me. "I like it. I'm not allowed to like it, but I do."

Nat crosses her arms. "What's that supposed to mean?"

"I don't mess with taken women, ma'am, no matter how nice they are. Now if you'll excuse me, this shithole seems to have managed to play one good song."

I look at Nat, utterly baffled as Tyler heads over to Lochlin. They clank their beers together in celebration then head to the dance floor, along with several of the women that Lochlin was talking to. One of them wraps her arms around Tyler for good measure.

"What the hell was that about?" Nat asks.

"I have no idea," I say, watching them out on the dance floor.

"If he's implying that Lochlin called some kind of dibs on you or something, and that's why they invited us here," Nat says, "I'll make sure the next round is on him, and I don't mean paying. I mean wearing."

"I love you, but there's definitely no dibs involved. Lochlin and I are just friends." I laugh, but as I watch the guys out on the floor—Tyler seeming to know what he's doing, and Lochlin is just spinning some random girl around with his good arm—I can't shake my confusion. "It's weird though, right? What he said about me being 'taken'?"

"Maybe the horses knocked his brain too many times." She shrugs and takes another sip of her drink. "Which speaking of, let's go get in line for that bull."

"What?"

"Come on, when are we *ever* going to be at a place like this again? Don't tell me you're not at least a little curious," she says, gesturing toward the back where someone in a bridal veil and sash is riding the mechanical bull, surrounded by a whooping and cheering group of her friends.

Huh, maybe I should add this to my list of offered bridal planning amenities.

"Molly." Nat hops off her chair. "Please?"

"No, no way," I say. "I do not need broken bones when I'm busy trying to fix up the barn."

"Don't be a baby." She laughs. "I'm asking you to hop up on a glorified rocking horse surrounded by four feet of gym padding and have a little fun. You do remember what that is, right? Or have the paint fumes made you forget that part of your life too?"

"Nat!"

"It's this or dancing," she says, gesturing to the floor where Lochlin is laughing, limping along, with Tyler beside him. It's the absolute dorkiest thing I've ever seen in my life.

"The bull, definitely the bull."

* * *

I DON'T KNOW how I got roped in to riding it ahead of Nat, and I definitely don't know how the woman in front of me made it seem so easy, but a half second in, I know I've made a horrible mistake. The mechanical bull weaves and bobs beneath me, slow enough that I think I've got a chance, and then it jerks me so hard to the side that it hurts. My entire spine snaps forward and back, and my hat—Shani's hat—goes flying off onto one of the blue pads that make up the surrounding floor.

Nat whoops loud enough to get the attention of the boys, who immediately quit their dancing—if that's really what we want to call it—and come over to watch, making me hang on out of sheer stubbornness even though my body is screaming at me to let go.

The woman before me managed to make it look sexy somehow, gyrating her hips with every twist and turn of the bull. It was clear that this was not her first rodeo.

I, however, am positive that I must look more akin to a rag doll caught in a tornado than anything remotely in the realm of beauty or grace . . . *but* the sign did say if you make it twenty seconds you get a free beer. That was motivation enough but now, given the guys are watching too, letting go is the last thing I plan to do.

The person running the machine kicks things up a notch, so the jerking goes from uncomfortable with occasional jolts of pain to *holy shit I have whiplash please someone reserve a bed for me at urgent care*, but I grit my teeth and hold on tight, utterly determined.

A particularly nasty buck and twist combo sends me flying off despite my best efforts, and I land hard on my shoulder to a chorus of "ooooohs" and sharply inhaled breaths. And yeah, I bet it looks like it hurt, because it really, really, does.

I stand up, angry at first, and lock eyes with Lochlin, who looks like he's about to fall over and propose. What. The. Fuck. I thank the guy running the bull for ruining my life and storm out of the little padded arena, pissed I didn't get my free beer, and that Lochlin and Tyler just saw me fall on my ass.

"Hey," Aiyana says, when I push past her, desperate to get back to the table.

"Oh my god," I say, stopping to hug her with the one arm that doesn't hurt. "I didn't see you come in."

"Yeah, that's because you were kicking butt on that bull up there. You were amazing!"

"But at what cost." I rub my shoulder. "I didn't even get the free beer."

"It's a scam, no one could ever stay on for twenty seconds." Aiyana makes a show of looking around the bar at everyone. "But I'm pretty sure everyone here is in love with you after that little show, so I doubt free beers are going to be a problem for you tonight."

I laugh, just as Lochlin comes up behind me and lifts me up, broken arm and all, to pretend like he's carrying me off. "That's it. Every man has a limit and seeing you up there was mine."

"Yeah, you wish," I say, wriggling out of his hands and darting back over to where Nat is guarding our table.

Tyler comes up then, a soft friendly smile on his face and my hat in his hands. "You left this over there, Moll," he says, setting it on my head and biting back a smile when a few guys that were clearly coming my way turn tail at the last second.

Nat thankfully looks just as confused as I do, but Aiyana is sitting there with wide eyes and a hilarious expression. "Are you kidding me right now?" she shrieks through laughter.

"About what?"

She covers her mouth, shaking her head. "Where'd you get that hat?"

"Shani gave it to me. Why?" I ask, slowly and suspiciously. "She said it completed the outfit."

"Oh, I bet she did," Aiyana says. "Especially knowing the type of people that hang around this place."

I rip it off my head, expecting to see, I don't know, a *kick me* sign or something, but there's nothing. The hat's just as perfect as it is when it's on Shani's head. "Okay, what am I missing? Do I look ridiculous in it or—" And I'm seething because I don't know how or what, but I know Shani did something, pranked me in some way, made me out to be the fool in some way.

"Do you . . ." Aiyana says, choking out words in between laughing her ass off. "Do you seriously not know about the hat rule?"

I lean forward, getting annoyed. "What hat rule?"

"Oh, this is gold," Tyler says, his eyes going huge as he joins in the laughter.

Embarrassment creeps over me, making my skin feel hot and too tight. "Will someone please just tell me?" I beg, wishing the words came out sharp instead of embarrassed. "What's wrong with it?"

"There's nothing wrong with it, darlin'," Tyler says, taking pity on me while Aiyana is still dying across the table. "It's just a thing. When you wear someone's hat . . . it's . . ."

"What? Bad luck? Embarrassing? Where are we going with this?"

He lets out the longest sigh, looking back at Aiyana like he's asking for permission. "All right," he says, resigned. "You ever heard the phrase, 'wear the hat, ride the cowboy'?" he asks, struggling to keep his face neutral. "Usually when you wear the hat, it means you and the hat owner are . . . it's a—"

"Aiyana, can I borrow your car?" I ask, grabbing her keys off the table.

"You're leaving?!" Nat yelps, but I'm too furious right now to be stopped.

"You can drive everybody back to Shani's, right, Tyler?" I ask.

"Yes, ma'am—I mean, Molly," he says. "But I do want to remind you that Shani—"

"Is gonna fucking die," I say, with a smile, as I storm out the front door.

Chapter Twenty

Shani's house is dark when I pull up, but I don't let it stop me. I pound on the door anyway, louder and harder than is strictly necessary. It's late enough that she could still be inside, just asleep. I'm angry enough that I don't care if that's the case. *Wear the hat, ride the cowboy.* Screw her and her mixed signals and her cockblocking assholery all to hell.

I wait a minute, and then pound again.

It's becoming clear now that she's either not home or not coming to the door, so I storm off. I make it halfway across the field, falling on my ass twice in the dark before I remember that I could have just driven back around. Goddamn it. I brush myself off, stomping even harder across the grass.

I just about make it to the porch, still mumbling expletives, when it hits me that the lights are on in the barn. The lights should definitely *not* be on in the barn. It could be Lita, or another boarder I suppose, but I doubt it. Still, I slide inside quietly, just in case.

But it's not, of course it's not. It's Shani, looking infuriatingly hot while giving Otis his nightly medicine. I resist the urge to slam the door and start screaming at her immediately; it's not

Otis's fault he's getting help from the Wicked Witch of the . . .
I guess East. However, I'm not above *quietly* storming over to
her after *gently* shutting the barn door behind me.

"You're back early." She smirks, actually smirks, when she
sees me.

I'm going to kill her. Oh, I'm going to kill her. I throw the hat
at her. I've been gripping it in my fist since I got in Aiyana's car,
but Shani manages to smack it away before it hits her. It lands
on the floor between us with an impotent thump. Not exactly
the effect I was going for.

"*Wear the hat, ride the cowboy*, Shani? Really?"

Her smirk widens as she struggles not to laugh, and oh. Oh!
I have had my fill of being laughed at today. I am absolutely
DONE with it. Fuck her. Fuck this. Fuck everyone all to hell.

"Am I just a joke to you?" I snap. I mean to sound angry, but
it comes out sounding smaller, more plaintive and hurt than I'd
like.

Her laughter dies in her throat as she bends down to pick up
her hat. "A joke? No. An infuriating pain in the ass?" she asks,
wiping her hat off on her jeans and then placing it onto her own
head. "Yes, for sure."

"You cockblocked me tonight and didn't even have the decency
to tell me you were doing it."

"I cockblocked you?" she growls. "So you *were* planning to
hook up? With who? Tyler? Lochlin? Or were you just trying
to be another notch in some drugstore cowboy's bedpost?" She
storms past me into the feed room and I stomp after her.

"If you must know, for the record, no I wasn't looking for anything tonight. *But if I was*, it wouldn't be any of your business

anyway! Okay? Sure, it was more of a hypothetical cockblock *this time*, but you still had no right!" I shout, raising my hands in annoyance. "Why do you even care *what* I do?"

"You know why," she says, her eyes flashing as she stalks toward me. I take a step back out of her way, but she just keeps coming until I'm pressed against the wall behind me. "You know exactly why, Molly."

My mouth falls open as she dips her head, her mouth hovering just above mine. It would be so simple to lean forward and close that last inch, to taste her like I've wanted to since the first time I saw her. But no. No.

I'm not doing this again. I duck out from under her arm.

She huffs out a breath, shaking her head. "Yeah, that's what I thought," she says, quietly.

"What is the matter with you?" I groan in frustration. "Is there some game I don't know about, where you have to act like you want me one second and then blow me off the next? You've got me so spun around I don't even know if I'm coming or going." I drag my hand down my face. "And this hat, and you coming up to me like you just did . . ." My voice cracks and I swallow hard.

I am not going to break over this woman. She doesn't get to see how much she's affecting me. How much I wish what we had was true.

Shani turns to look at me, her green eyes pinched and worried when she takes in the sight of me trying not to cry. I look down, willing the tears away. Because this is how it always goes, right? I end up the joke, the asshole, the one who gets played. The one who needs Nat to rescue her and tell her it's going to all be okay.

"People were laughing at me tonight, you know," I say, biting my lip, my eyes darting back to hers. "I just wanted to go out and have a good time and not be the pathetic girl pining over someone who treats her like shit for once. I thought you were being nice," I scoff. "But everybody laughed at me. Because of you."

"What are you talking about?" she asks quietly, almost gently.

Fuck it.

"It's not like it's a secret how I feel about you! Even though I shouldn't! Even though I can't! So yeah, maybe I got a little thrill over you giving me your hat, and maybe I did kind of wish you were there tonight, but I didn't know you were making fun of me. I didn't know I was still a joke to you!"

"Molly, what the hell are you on about?" she asks, louder now.

"Forget it." I turn back, ready to go bury myself under my blankets on the couch and never come out. Ready to go back to avoiding Shani the way we mostly have been. Ready to peel the paint, and freshen things up, and then get out of town because if there's anything I learned tonight, it's that there is *nothing* for me here. Just more bad habits and bad luck and wishful thinking.

I hear her boots clomping after me before I feel her hands, pulling me back to face her. "What do you mean how you feel about me? How exactly do you feel about me, Molly?" she asks, even more urgently. I look away, but she tips my face back to hers, her hand firm, yet gentle along my jaw. "Don't do that. Look at me. Tell me. Please. What feelings, Molly?"

Shani's eyes are wild, desperate in a way I've never seen before. Even when everything was a mess with Otis, or when Lochlin first came, she was always so calm. So measured. This tenuous friendship was the closest I ever got to feeling like she even really cared. But now she looks lost, confused, almost feral, as she demands that I answer her. My thighs clamp together, chasing friction as I let out a shaky breath. She's coming undone right in front of me and it's turning me on.

It should not be turning me on.

"You're killing me right now. What. Feelings," she growls, her eyes burning into mine. "I didn't know there were feelings, Molly," she says, and this time her voice is softer, gentler, as her thumb moves to ghost over my lips. "You're not a joke. You're not."

"Shani," I say, a question, a plea, as she pulls me closer. I let out a shaky breath as I slide my hand lower over hers with a smile. "What are we doing?"

"What I've wanted to do for so long." Her voice is barely above a whisper, as her mouth finds the spot on my neck that makes me shiver. She softly, slowly trails her lips back up to meet mine. She kisses me, fierce at first, like she's drowning in it, and then slower, gentler. My lips part on their own accord and her tongue slips softly inside.

"Oh," I say, when we finally break apart. Her shirt is untucked, and my hair is messed up, and it feels like fireworks are dancing beneath my skin. *I want more.*

"Yeah, oh," she says, slipping some of my hair back behind my ear.

"So the hat . . ."

"Was me being a possessive prick because I'm jealous."

"*You're* jealous?" I snort, but she looks serious.

"Yes, Molly, I am!" she says, her voice desperate. "I'm jealous of how easy and relaxed you are around everyone, even my brother, in a way you never are around me. I'm jealous that other people got to go out with you tonight, and I had to sit home knowing it. And yes, maybe I lost my mind a little bit seeing you in these fucking jeans." She trails her hand up my thigh as if to prove her point. "But can you blame me?"

"So, really not a joke then," I say, mesmerized by the look on her face.

"Not polite exactly, but no, not a joke."

"I don't . . . Shani, I can't keep up with you."

"I've been trying to be good, Molly. I've been trying to stay away and do the right thing."

"Me too, but I didn't think you—"

"It didn't matter if I did or didn't. You want to sell this place, you want to go, and that makes me a complication. I'm not the woman you take to fancy planning parties or would ever be happy hanging out in the city with you. I'm the woman who shoes your horses and smells like fly spray and shit more often than I'd like to admit. I have tried my hardest not to kiss you every time you walk by me pouting or teasing. And yeah, I almost wavered a few times. But I told myself, you didn't come here for me, you're not staying here for me. You. Are. Not. For. Me."

"Shani . . ." I say, my heart melting and breaking simultaneously at this conundrum of a person standing in front of me.

"But then you came over tonight, looking beautiful and . . ." She looks away.

"You like me," I tease, gently poking her chest with my finger.

"Shut up, Molly."

"You *like*-like me," I say, grabbing the front of her shirt and pulling her back against me. I know the other stuff she said is true, the stuff about me leaving, the stuff about how different our lives are . . . but right now it's hard to feel like any of that matters.

"Yeah, well I didn't know the feeling was all the way mutual."

"This is hilarious. I practically threw myself at you this whole time!"

"When? When you were screaming at me or when you were trying to sell my home to a developer because you couldn't get out of here fast enough?"

"When I wanted to kiss you on my porch. When I came to your rodeo. When I baked for you and hung Gideon's feeder. When I turned down the developer. When I *did* kiss you a minute ago!"

"You were at my show? Aiyana said it was her and JJ."

"I was there. I even got to see most of your ride."

A corner of her mouth quirks up. "But you didn't come in the back."

"I didn't think you'd want me there." I sigh. "We're so ridiculous."

"Yes," she agrees, kissing me again. "We are."

I grab my hat off her head and settle it back on mine where it belongs. She lets out a nervous breath, smiling as she slides her hand up higher between my legs. I squirm, still searching for the friction that's just out of reach.

"You're wearing my hat, Molly."

"It's a great hat," I say, pulling her closer. I trail one of my hands lower, my fingers trembling against the button on her jeans, trying and failing to get it unhooked. But then her hand is there, on my wrist, firm, stopping me.

My eyes shoot up to hers, scared I'll find rejection in them, but I only see heat. Wanting.

"Not here," she says and then kisses me again, more careful this time. She laces our fingers together and heads toward my thankfully empty house.

Shani walks fast, but I walk faster.

Chapter Twenty-One

It's hard to think clearly with her mouth on my neck and her hands snaking beneath my shirt, but I somehow manage to get the front door unlocked and get us inside—where she promptly pushes me back against a wall. I'm starting to think this is a thing for Shani, this dominating, overpowering, manhandling vibe, and I have to say, I like it. I like it a lot.

She buries herself against me, slotting her leg between mine until there *finally* is the friction I've been desperate for. My startled gasp seems to make her more frantic, but when she pulls back to look at me, to make sure I'm as into this as she is, it's me that's wrecked. Now that we're here, finally, doing this, I don't want it to end.

And I don't want her to hold back.

"I need you," I say, the truth of those words surprising even me.

She grins as she pushes my jeans down halfway, her fingers tracing delicate lines over my panties that leave me squirming. I'm not even mad when she finally wraps her hands around the thin slip of fabric keeping us apart and tears. I arch my hips toward her, already wet, and grateful to be bare. I'm practically begging her to—

"Hold up," she says, her breath coming in heavy pants. "I'm about to say the most unromantic thing right now, and I need you to promise it won't ruin the mood."

"Oh Jesus," I groan, feeling my impending orgasm fade back to nothingness. "What could possibly be important enough to interrupt this?"

She blushes hard and looks away. "I need to wash my hands," she mumbles, and I laugh nervously, confused and maybe a little offended.

"What, do I have cooties?" I ask.

She pulls me back against her, kissing my neck. "No, but I'm covered in horsehair and just had my hands all over Otis. So . . ."

I drop back against the wall because yes, yes, that is a mood killer. Technically, I never promised it wouldn't be, but I guess she took my silence as tacit agreement. She might as well have just poured a bucket of ice water over my head. Dirty, hay-filled ice water full of Otis drool.

Dammit.

"Yeah, exactly." She sighs, leaving me standing there as she heads into my kitchen to wash up. I pull my pants back up and slide over so I can watch her, nervous—no, *excited* energy radiating off me as she somehow makes even handwashing look hot.

Shit, seeing her in my kitchen, it's like she belongs there. I can already imagine waking up like this, having coffee with her at this little table, doing dishes together. She'd flick bubbles at my face, and I would slap her with my towel. She would laugh and I . . . need to stop. Seriously.

Shani looks up at me, noticing me watching. Her eyes go soft at first, but then take on a mischievous glint when a smirk slides across her face. "Go up and wait for me on the bed. But don't take your clothes off. That's my job."

"You don't have to tell me twice," I laugh, ready to run up the stairs at a second's notice . . . but there's just one problem. There is no bedroom. Just a couch in the living room and a sleeping bag. Which I *don't* want her to see.

"What's wrong?" she asks, her smirk falling away as she dries her hands on the little cartoon rooster tea towel I picked up at a farmer's market. "If you don't want to—"

"I don't have a bed," I whine, helplessly, and she looks equal parts relieved and confused. "I just use that." I gesture toward the couch, where my pillow sits waiting, stacked neatly atop my folded-up sleeping bag.

"Please tell me you haven't been sleeping on this couch the whole time you've been here?!"

"I didn't want to sleep in the room where, you know, and then there's the room we lost the key for—KiKi's gonna take it off the hinges for me but she hasn't yet—and the other one is still full of boxes. I've been going through it, but the couch is comfortable, we can—"

She cuts me off with a kiss. "If I was going to fuck you on a couch, we wouldn't have left the barn."

"But—"

"Come on," she says, running up the stairs two at a time, like she can make a bed somehow materialize out of thin air.

She can't exactly. But also, she does.

She stands in front of the locked door looking rightfully

bashful as she fishes around on her key ring. It takes her a second to find it with all the keys that she has, but she finally settles on one. A click of a lock and the door is pushed open revealing a completely outfitted bedroom.

I bite the inside of my cheek, torn between being pissed and impressed. "You said the key was lost."

"What do you know, I just found it."

"On your key ring?"

She turns back to me, her smirk firmly back in place. "Do you want to fight, or do you want me to take you apart—taste you, lick you, touch you—until you've come too many times to count?"

She's impossibly close now, my throat gone dry at the word *taste* being used in the context of *us*. "The second thing. Definitely, the second thing."

"Then get on my fucking bed, Molly."

I don't move, mesmerized as I am by her.

"Don't make me beg," she whispers, going from overbearing and bossy to now, suddenly, sounding vulnerable.

She stands like she's bracing for something. Like I might change my mind anyway, like she might have gone too far by keeping me locked out or talking to me like that, like I might reject her now that we've both admitted there are feelings on both sides.

I meet her eyes, seeing the nervousness there, the apprehension, and I want to kiss that fear out of her. There is nothing past tense about us. Not any part of it. I lean forward to do just that . . . but at the last second, I decide to do something better instead.

I walk right past her to the bed, just like she asked.

It takes all my willpower not to look around, not to try and decipher all the stuff around me, to soak in what it meant for Shani to be here, every night, sharing a wall with . . . helping Christina to . . . No. Now isn't the time to think about that. There will be time for that later, maybe, but right now Shani's trusting me, she's letting me in, and I want to return the favor.

The wrought iron frame creaks as I climb up into the center of her queen-size bed and turn to face her. She's still standing in the doorway, watching me with so much heat that I can't take it anymore. If she's not touching me in the next second, I might die. "Please, Shani. I need you."

She huffs out a heavy breath and crosses the room, pushing my body down against the bed. Shani licks her lips and then slides down my jeans in one torturously slow fluid motion.

"Shani," I whisper, as she crawls between my legs, spreading me wide. She uses one hand to run along my center and her other to hook my knees up over her shoulders.

I take her in—her impossibly strong hands, impossibly strong shoulders, no doubt from years of working on tough horses, from years of having a tough life, everything about her tough, but as her fingers slip inside me, joined not long after by her tongue, she's gentle, gentle, gentle.

And then she's not, hitting all the right spaces, as she licks, sucks, nips, devours me until I'm coming apart on her tongue faster than I ever have with anyone else. She pulls back, a satisfied smile on her face as she drags her fingers across her wet lips, and then sucks them clean. It's incredibly filthy and incredibly perfect, and if she thinks she's going to get away with that—

But before I can speak, she's back rucking up my shirt and

yanking down my bra, her hot mouth on my breast, her fingers drifting back inside of me. My neck strains back in pleasure, my entire body a taut string about to snap. "Right there, right there," I beg, and just when I'm about to come again . . . she pulls back, her hand going still, her lips peppering chaste kisses over my breast.

"Not yet." She smiles, and my hands fist her sheets.

"Please," I beg.

She moves over and pulls my neglected breast into her mouth, her tongue swirling as she looks back up to me. I nudge against her hand between my legs, willing it to move again and she laughs.

"Please, what, Molly?"

"You know what," I say, throwing my arm over my head, embarrassed that she's turned me into a wet, writhing mess of woman so easily.

She slides up so we're face-to-face, caging me between her arms, and I whimper at the loss of contact between my legs. "Don't hide from me," she says, and I drop my arm away, feeling every bit as debauched as I probably look. "Tell me what you want, Molly," she murmurs, sliding her hands up to pin my wrists. "And you can have it."

"I want you," I say, and she smiles so big. I try to kiss her, but she leans back, keeping me carefully pinned.

"How do you want me?"

"I want your hands, your mouth. I want all of you."

"All of me?" She grins, shifting her weight to one arm so she can let the other ghost over my skin, featherlight touches that make my nipples stand at attention and my thighs press together. "You sure?"

I'm trembling again, while she traces slow circles with her fingers lower and lower until they're almost where I want them. "Yes, dammit. Please," I beg. "Please, I need to come."

This time her smile looks devious as she slides back down my body. She buries her face between my legs, sucking on my clit. She presses my hips down as I arch up against her, keeping me right where she wants me. I swear her right hand is made of stardust and magic as she curls her fingers inside of me until I'm mumbling something like "fuck," and "I can't, I can't" but she stops again just before I get my release. And then she's back on top of me, kissing me, soothing me, telling me that I can, that I'm okay, that she's going to make this so good for me.

"Easy, baby, I've got you," she says, when I whimper, so sensitive. Too sensitive, as she keeps bringing me to the edge and then pulling back. I'm lost in a haze of sparks and electricity, my entire body going boneless until her fingers are back in the softest parts of me, her hand and lips turning my world upside down when I finally, finally, get to come.

"You look so beautiful," she says, crawling back up the bed.

There're tears in my eyes—the happy, well fucked kind that I've only read about in romance books.

"I didn't know it could be like this," I say, sleepily as I nuzzle in closer.

She kisses my eyelids and my nose and then shifts to my side, pulling us together. Her heartbeat thunders against me and I turn my head and kiss her again, a soft, sloppy thing that shows just what she's done to me. I can taste myself on her lips, and my tongue searches until I find a spot that's just Shani. That's just for me.

We lay there for a while, kissing and tracing lines against our skin, until I can form a semi-coherent thought. And when I do, it's *we're still not done.*

"Jeans off. Now," I say, because it's quite possible she has reduced me to a monosyllabic buckle bunny after that last orgasm, and I don't even care about the implication. Shani hesitates but then obliges. She starts to shimmy them down slowly, sitting on the edge of the bed, but I'm impatient and move to tug them the rest of the way off myself. "What the hell," I laugh, when I realize she's somehow still got her boots on. I wonder if that's a fantasy of hers, banging in her boots, or merely a sign of just how hurried we were to get to each other.

I slip down to the floor, looking up at her as I slide her boots off and then her jeans along with them. She groans and leans back on her elbows, which is when I realize that this bed is the perfect height.

I grab one of the pillows that fell off the bed during our last show and shove it under my knees. *There, much better.*

I glance up at her quick, her pupils blown, waiting for that enthusiastic nod and grinning when it comes. I slide her cotton Jockeys off, giggling to myself at how fitting that particular brand of underwear is for her. Then I run my fingers slowly up her leg and let my hand slide home. She's soft and so wet around my fingers. Her heat, the fact that I get to touch her like this, overwhelms me. I kiss the inside of her thigh, my thumb finding the little bundle of nerves that makes her jump and then sigh. I look up to find her blushing and looking away.

"I want to make you feel good," I huff against her skin.

"Yes," she whispers, as my thumb and fingers find just the

right spot. She falls back to the bed, her hair spread out around her, and it's so fucking sexy, I can't handle it.

I lean forward and lick her center, tasting her, finally. Her legs clamp around the sides of my head, and I let out a startled laugh as I gently push them back, settling between them . . . until I realize that all of her has gone strangely tense, and not in the "I'm about to come" way. In the "I'm uncomfortable" way.

I look up to see her hand over her eyes, rubbing them the way she does whenever she's stressed. I wipe my mouth with my hand, trying to make myself presentable. "Hey," I say, tapping her thigh gently to get her to look at me.

She meets my eyes and then looks away fast—but not so fast that I can't see the nerves in them . . . the hurt? . . . and no. This isn't okay. I climb up on the bed, wrapping her in my arms, even though she keeps looking away. I tip her chin toward me and stroke the side of her face, desperate to make her feel as safe and cared for as she's made me. "You don't like that? I don't have to use my—"

"No, I do."

"Did I go too fast? Or slow? Or . . ." I ask, studying her face. "If there's something you don't like or that you *do* like that I'm not doing, you can tell me. I'm a quick study, I promise." I give her a reassuring smile, trying to lighten the mood. "You made me feel so good, Shani. I want to do that for you too."

"Yeah, it's fine. You can." She kisses me as if she's bracing for war and it breaks my heart a little.

"Shani."

She goes back to staring at the wall. "Forget I said anything, just, can we just . . . get back to it."

"Shani!" I say again, and this time she meets my eyes, trailing her hand up and down my naked back.

"I'm fine," she says, her eyes hard.

"You're not fine. And a sad 'it's fine, you can' is not the level of 'consent is sexy' I'm going for here."

"Sorry," she says, climbing off the bed and reaching past me for her jeans. I stand up, looking away while she gets dressed, feeling like I'm intruding—even though I'm the one standing here naked while she shoves her feet into her boots like she's going to leave. And holy shit, what just happened?

I pull the blanket off her bed and wrap it around myself, self-conscious. "Are you leaving?"

"I really should, Molly."

And now the tears are back, but not the fucked-out kind. The *what the fuck* kind. I raise my eyebrows, feeling stupid. "It was one thing to send mixed signals before, but this is next level, don't you think?"

"Leave it alone, please," she says, a hint of anger in her voice as she heads for the door.

"You were so worried about someone at the bar being my one-night stand, that now you're just doing it yourself?" I grab the blanket tighter. "Did you just pretend to have feelings to get me into bed? Talk to me!"

She runs her hands through her hair and turns back. I'm shocked to find her eyes just as watery as mine.

"Shani?"

She shakes her head and looks away but the hurt, the sadness radiates off her. I walk over and wrap my arms around her. She stands still at first, but then melts against me, burying her head in my neck and then finally, squeezing me back.

"What's going on?" I ask, the hardness of my voice giving way to real concern.

"It's really difficult being back in this room."

"Oh," I say. I should have thought of that.

"No, it was great with you, but then, when I was lying there, I started thinking like—god, this is gonna make me sound so pathetic." She leans back and wipes at her eyes.

"Judgment free zone," I say, explaining when she gives me a confused look. "You can say whatever you need to, and the other person just has to be there for you. No opinions or judging or anything, unless you ask for them. I'm officially invoking it right now."

She pouts her lips, turning her head to give me the side-eye, but then takes a shaky breath. "Judgment free zone," she says and scratches the back of her neck. "This is still gonna sound so ridiculous."

"Not in the judgment free zone, it won't. Get on with it."

She sucks in her lips, studying my eyes as if looking for any signs I'm lying, before she finally says, "I got overwhelmed—being here, being with you." Her voice is so quiet I can barely hear, embarrassment coating her cheeks crimson. "Finding out that not only do you not hate me, but you'd even let me have you. I got so lost in my head about it that I froze up, then I was mortified, and then I got mad about it and acted like a jerk. Now I just feel like shit for ruining everything."

"The embarrassed-to-asshole pipeline does often seem like

an exceptionally short journey for you," I tease. "But can I ask about the overwhelmed part?"

She huffs out a tiny groan and drops her head back. "I like you, okay?"

"I would hope so because you just ate me out like I was your new best friend."

She laughs at that, and it feels like hitting the lottery. I want to keep her laughing. I don't want her to feel upset or like she ruined anything. It's been barely an hour and I already love being the thing that makes her happy, that can make her feel better. And shit, *shit*, this was not what I signed up for, but it doesn't even matter right now. It can't.

"I really like you, and I loved being with you. You're so responsive and—"

"You were very mean," I point out. "I don't think I've ever been edged for that long."

"You liked it though, right?" she asks, suddenly looking nervous about a whole new thing.

"I fucking loved it, Shani. Please, let's do that again. Often."

She laughs and looks away, blush flooding her cheeks and chest. "I'd like that, but . . ."

"But?"

"But when you went down on me, I started thinking how you were leaving, and that was gonna suck, because I've had this little taste of you now, so I'll know what I'm missing when you go.

"It doesn't feel fair . . . and then I started thinking about losing the barn, and losing Christina, and I tried to fight through it because it felt incredible—you don't need any pointers from me,

Molly, seriously." She gives me a sad smile. "I just couldn't stop thinking about how I lose every good thing, and I was gonna lose you too."

"I . . ." I don't know where to start with that. I almost make a joke that clearly I do need pointers if she could think about *anything* while I was going down on her; god knows I couldn't when the roles were reversed. But the timing isn't right. She's being vulnerable, open, and this is the judgment free zone, which means I can't self-deprecate my way out of it.

"Yeah, it's a lot," she says, hanging her head. "Being back in this room is a lot. Maybe *I'm* a lot. Too much for someone who's got one foot out the door already."

"No," I say, but she steps back.

"Thank you for an unexpectedly great night, but I really do think I should head home."

"Shani—"

"What, Molly?" she asks, her eyes blazing into mine.

I want to promise her I'll stay, but more than that I want to mean it. I want it to be true. Can it be true? Is there a world where we work out?

"I could join you," I say, before I stop myself. *What am I doing?*

"Why?"

"Because I want to. Just, ya know, give me a chance to put some sweats on because it's a little cold out and I am very, very, naked under this blanket."

Shani huffs out a laugh and shakes her head. "That's extremely tempting but—"

"I don't expect us to do anything else tonight. I hear you.

I would never push you past where you want to be or rush you. I just want to spend more time with you. We could go watch a movie or something at your place. If you're open to that?"

She looks torn. "I don't do casual, and I won't be friends with benefits. I can't."

"It's just a movie."

"It's not just a movie to me, Molly," she says, rubbing her eyes again.

"Maybe it's not to me either," I say, softly. "Look, I can't promise you forever right now, but . . . do you wanna watch a movie, together? It doesn't have to be a casual one," I say, stretching the metaphor further than it really goes and hoping she gets my meaning.

She narrows her eyes, and I hop up on my tiptoes to kiss her nose, trying to be as careful with her as she was with me earlier.

"You're killing me," she says, pulling me against her and squeezing me tight. "Go get your sweats."

Chapter Twenty-Two

I'm expecting it to be awkward, and maybe it is, a little, but mostly it's just nice. I pull on some sweats and put my bra back on before I throw on a hoodie, which is kind of ridiculous because Shani definitely just had her mouth all over me so she's well aware of any jiggles or lack of perkiness I may have, but . . . I don't know, even in cozy, ratty sweats, I want to look cute for her.

I pull my hair up into a ponytail, touch up what little makeup I still have on, and find her waiting for me in the kitchen. Shani's sitting at the table just like I imagined; all that's missing is a cup of coffee. She stands up quickly, without a word, and guides me carefully across the pasture like I hadn't made the trek myself a little while ago.

"Wait, is Aiyana here?" she asks, once we reach the front of her house, and I have to explain that no, I borrowed her car, but then left her house in such a huff that I didn't realize I could have driven home until I was halfway across the field.

Shani seems to love that, shaking loose a little of her nerves and having a genuine laugh. Still, even with her warm arm around my waist, I'm shivering by the time we get back to her house. She lets me in and sets her hat on the counter, and I think about how this whole night started. I'm tempted to put it on my head again, just to let her know I still feel that way, but I can tell she's stressed . . . and I made a promise.

A movie that's not just a movie. Nothing more.

"You can, uh, sit on the couch if you want," she says, sounding uncharacteristically shy.

I do as I'm told, becoming a little bit enamored with her nervous, shy, maybe a little wounded side—and god, what does that say about me? What does it mean that I'm somehow twice as into her now that she's acting all shy and vulnerable—twice as attracted to her. Maybe I *am* a menace.

I saw a tweet once that said "women are not rehabilitation centers for men." I can't help but notice that it didn't say anything about whether it's cool if we're rehabilitation centers for hot queer farriers who can make you come multiple times in less than an hour.

"What are you thinking about?" she asks, placing a bowl of popcorn in my hands and sitting down beside me.

"Not much," I say, because I can't exactly explain that I'm apparently so messed up I think her emotional damage is sexy.

"That seems like a lie," she teases. "What goes on in that head of yours, Molly McDaniel?"

"Currently? That I've just had the best sex of my life with a woman I really care about. You?"

She sighs. "Mostly worrying that I screwed this up already."

"You didn't," I say, shifting to face her. "I'm glad that you let me know how you were feeling. It was brave."

She shakes her head. "It didn't feel brave, it felt disappointing."

I pull her face to mine and place a gentle kiss at the very edge of her lips until I feel them curve up into a smile. "There, that's better."

"Who *are* you?" she asks quietly, pulling back to look at me.

"Sometimes I don't even think I know the answer to that."

She brushes a few stray hairs that have escaped my ponytail behind my ear with a gentle sigh. "Hmm," she says quietly. "It seems like you've been doing a pretty good job of figuring it out lately."

"What does that mean?" I half laugh, studying her face. "I don't have anything figured out."

She shrugs. "You're a lot more comfortable than you used to be. A lot more confident too. That's all I meant."

"How do you even figure?" I snort.

"Are we really going to pretend that you weren't an absolute disaster every time you stepped foot in that barn when you first got here? Now, you're practically one of us."

I roll my eyes.

"Fine," she laughs. "Not exactly to our level, but you're *passable*. Otis and Eddie are obsessed with you, you're great with the boarding horses, all the people at the barn love you—"

"All the people?" I tease, and she looks away, biting her lip and going all shy again like she said too much. I lean into her line of vision with my softest smile. "I think *everyone* here is pretty great too, for the record."

She gives me a small smile, but it doesn't meet her eyes. I can see the war in them, the words she's struggling not to say.

"What?" I ask quietly, my thumb running down her jawline like I could rub out all the tension with a single, gentle touch.

She shakes her head a little, looking away from me again. "Nothing."

"No, whatever you're thinking, say; it's okay."

"It's not okay, Molly," she says, her blazing eyes meeting mine again. "It wouldn't be fair. I can't ask you to . . ." She trails off, and oh. *Oh.* "Yeah," she says, when it's clear I understand. She wants to ask me to stay again. To be the one good thing she doesn't have to lose.

"Shani—"

"If you can't tell me who you are, tell me who you've been, so I understand."

"Understand what?" I ask softly.

"Understand why you want to leave so bad."

"It's complicated."

"Life is complicated, Molly. Try me."

I sigh, and shift closer, letting her tuck me in against her chest. I don't know where to start, so I start at the beginning. I tell her about my childhood, about my father leaving us with nothing. I tell her all about Immaculate Events, and my dreams, and my student loans, and how my mother still refuses to tell me what happened between her and Christina even though there's clearly a lot more to it than she's ever let on.

I tell her about Nat, and how she's probably going to kill me for leaving her at the bar—and I definitely deserve it—but also about how Nat's always been there for me. I tell her about my tendency to get lost in things, particularly relationships. I tell her about the push and pull I feel about this place, from her, and about how attracted I was to her from the jump.

Shani repays me in kind, telling me stories of growing up and how lucky she was to have Christina. That maybe she shouldn't have said that stuff about my mother—even though it is the truth as she remembers it—but that sharing private things just to be hurtful doesn't help anything.

She holds me close, taking my hand and telling me that she still doesn't understand why Christina left me this place, but she's trying to make peace with the not knowing. No matter what happens or doesn't happen between us, she says she's glad that I came into her life. She apologizes again for ruining the night, and I swear to her she's done anything but, and that lying here with her is perfect, the happiest I've been in a long, long time.

The words just pour out of us. Sometimes it's hard and it's raw, and other times we're laughing like when she tells me stories from the rodeo circuit, and I tell her about the man who never leaves space for his creamer.

Her fingers never let go of mine and my thumb never stops tracing circles on her hand, except for once—when her breath catches as she tells me about the last few weeks with Christina, and how desperately alone she felt, even with everyone else around. I twist to hug her then, placing a soft kiss on her cheek to let her know that she's not alone, not now.

She whispers the words that she was trying so hard not to say, and I was trying so hard not to hear: "Do you really want to leave?"

God, I don't know, do I? Shouldn't I?

It scares me, how intense I feel about Shani right now, listening to her talk. How bad I want to take away all of her pain. How much I want to hold her, kiss her, reassure her, and the most terrifying part of all, is that when look in her eyes, I see the exact same thing on her face.

And it's different. *It's different.* No matter what Nat thinks, or how I've been in the past, this. Is. Different. I've never felt a pull like this toward anything or anyone, but *everything* I've been dreaming of since I was a little girl is just barely on the other side of our goodbye. Don't I owe it to myself to make a go of it?

"I don't want to leave *you*," I whisper into her neck, because it's the closest thing I can give to an answer. "I wish things weren't so complicated."

"Do you regret coming back here with me tonight? It's one hell of a complication," she says, which, wow.

Brave. Again.

I open my mouth to say no and mean it too . . . but that's exactly when Lochlin swings the door open, Tyler and Aiyana coming in right behind him.

"You guys hooked up, didn't you?" Lochlin slurs, clearly more than a little drunk as he points at us.

And okay, maybe I do regret coming over. Just a smidge, and only because of that comment.

"Fuck off, Loch," Shani says, giving him the middle finger and grabbing a remote off the coffee table. "We're just watching a movie."

"I see you got your hat back," Aiyana teases and I shoot her a glare.

"Where's Nat?" I ask, realizing she's not with them.

Tyler winces. "I dropped her at your house first," he says. "She's pretty riled about being left at the bar and she did not hold back on shots after you left. You might want to lay low for a minute."

"Oof," I say, rubbing the bridge of my nose.

"I told her that the whole 'bros before hoes' thing is negated by the hat rule but . . ." Aiyana trails off, clearly amused by the fact that something obviously happened between me and Shani.

"I'm sure that went over well. By the way, the keys are in your car," I say, and she gets the message, holding her hands up as she backs out the door.

Lochlin has limped over to us now, and I'm surprised to see that he looks downright delighted. He puts one boot up on Shani's coffee table, resting his broken arm on his knee. Tyler sheepishly locks the door once Aiyana's car starts.

"I knew you liked her," Lochlin says, looking between us. At first, I'm not sure which one of us he's talking to, until he adds, "But you're a stubborn one, just like me and Dad."

"Get your dirty boots off of my table," Shani says, shoving his foot down.

He chuckles as Tyler comes up behind him. "Admit it, me taking her to a meat market got a rise out of you," Lochlin says. "You never would have made your move if I didn't. You should both be thanking me."

"You should be going to bed," Tyler says, lacing his fingers in Lochlin's.

"Aww, come on," Lochlin whines, "five more minutes. I'm not done making fun of my sister." He slurs his words a little bit, then sways on his feet, and Tyler slips his hand free to wrap it around his friend's waist instead.

"Yes, you are," Tyler says. "Come on, it's late."

I watch in surprise, as Lochlin turns his head to snuggle in tighter to Tyler's embrace. "Fine, but you owe me a back rub . . . and a blow job."

Tyler blushes, glancing at me. "Shut up, Loch," he says through gritted teeth, before giving us a nod. "Good night, ladies. I'm gonna go put this one to bed."

And it occurs to me suddenly that Shani's house is a two-bedroom. I mean, I *knew* that—I was here for the photos, after all—but I never really gave any thought to it *only* being a two-bedroom when Tyler showed up. I guess I assumed one of them would sleep on the couch, although it's clearly not made up like that.

"Are Tyler and your brother—"

"Who knows?" Shani shrugs. "There's definitely something between them. I wouldn't be surprised if Tyler was endgame for Lochlin—he's the only one who seems to be able to handle him. It's just a matter of if he can ride it out long enough, and if my brother stops screwing it all up by trying to bang anything that moves."

"Really?"

"No matter how far Lochlin runs, or how many notches he puts on his bedpost, he seems to always go back to Ty." She runs her fingers up my leg, teasing me. "Why? You disappointed? Did you have a secret thing for my brother?"

"God no," I laugh, leaning forward to kiss her. "Just surprised."

"Yeah, well, the rodeo circuit isn't exactly known for its liberal beliefs and tolerance. If they tried to date now, their careers would be dead. Maybe when they both retire . . ." She trails off.

"Is that why you retired?" I ask, studying her face.

"No." She smiles and clicks the TV on. "I just wanted to have a home. A *real* home."

I snuggle in against her, content to feel her warm body behind me, the steady up and down breathing of her chest, but I can't shake the nagging thoughts that come once we're quiet.

Shani found a home here, made one really, and now I'm the one that might take it all away.

Chapter Twenty-Three

We spend the night on the couch watching cheesy movies. I think we both were feeling a little raw about the things we shared with each other, so it was nice to just snuggle in—to not think about what comes next or what to do or what we've been through, but to just *be*. I don't know when I fall asleep, or why I drool on her chest when I'm not normally a pillow drooler, but she takes it in good stride, even making awkward coffee and pancakes in the morning before shuffling me out.

It's not until after I'm putting on my shoes and heading to the door that I realize that there was no reason for her to sleep on the couch with me. She had a whole bed right down the hall waiting for her. I can't stop grinning over the thought that she *chose* to hold me all night. Shani looks at me, eyes narrowed like she's trying to figure out what I'm thinking, but she doesn't ask.

It's sweet and weird, walking across the pasture right as the sun comes up. It makes me feel a little bit like Mr. Darcy walking across the field to Elizabeth in the 2005 version of *Pride and Prejudice*.

Except I'm walking away.

And also, this is a walk of shame instead of a declaration of love.

Okay, fine, I'm just walking across a field at sunrise, cold enough that I can see my breath but whatever. I meant the vibes. The vibes work.

Nat's still asleep on the air mattress in the dining room when I come in, so I'm extra quiet as I grab my barn boots and warmer jacket. She's still snoring softly, no doubt aided by the bourbon she drank last night, even as I tiptoe out the door and head down to the barn. I know I'll have to face her wrath as soon as she wakes up, and I'd like to stay in my little bubble of bliss a little longer.

I'm surprised to see Lita is already there, turning out the horses and getting ready for the day. She mentioned she was taking a few days off from work this week, but I guess I didn't expect her to be spending them all at the barn. I wonder if things are going okay at home. For the first time, it hits me I don't know that much about her, even though I feel like she's become one of my closest friends.

"Rough night?" she asks, once she's back inside, and yikes, maybe I should have brushed my hair before heading out here.

"A fun night," I say, watching Happy nibble at the crossties, while Lita grabs her bridle and reins.

"Oh yeah?" she asks, carrying her saddle over.

"Nat and I went out last night with Tyler, Lochlin, and Aiyana," I say, running my hand along Happy's withers. Her back twitches as she impatiently shifts her weight from hoof to hoof. I scratch behind her ears, just like Lita showed me, and am rewarded with a little snort.

"She's such a ham." Lita laughs, throwing her saddle up on top of Happy and cinching the girth. "Did you all have fun?"

"I had a *great* time," I say, blushing when my mind conjures up a flash of Shani between my legs.

Lita stands up, looking horrified. "Oh no, tell me you didn't hook up with one of those wannabe cowboys from town just because they can ride on that fake bull long enough to get free beer."

"No," I snort. "In fact, I'm the one who rode the bull—which by the way, ouch."

"Nice," she laughs. "I'm sure that made you quite the hit at The Whiskey Boot."

"Yeah, but I didn't stay long after that. I kind of came home and hung out with Shani all night," I blurt out, my ears going hot.

"Hung out like . . ." She trails off and I bite my lip. "Molly," Lita says but it comes out more like a sigh. "What are you doing?"

"Nothing," I say, a little faster and sharper than I mean to.

"That girl's been through a lot," she says, and that makes my hackles raise.

"So have I," I say. "So what?"

"I really hope you two know what you're doing." She bites the edge of her nail like she's deciding how much more to say or if she wants to say anything at all. Finally, Lita says, "You're leaving soon."

"I'm not leaving today," I snap, because I have no idea how to respond to her, and maybe also because I know she's right.

Lita blows out a breath, shaking her head like she's done with the conversation. "You want to go grab a saddle for Otis, the light one with the thick fluffy blanket?" she asks.

"Sure," I say, grateful for an excuse to get out of the room, if even for a minute. I dart to the tack room and then drag the "light" saddle back over. She's finished tacking up Happy and is waiting for me beside Otis's stall by the time I get back. "I didn't know we could ride him. Is he cleared?"

"Yep, Shani says he's all set."

"Who's going out with you?" I ask.

"My niece, she's only eight. Otis is really good with her. I promised her a ride if she aced her science test and surprise, she knows how to study after all."

"Cute!"

"Yeah, I wanted to take her to a horse show, but I couldn't find any local ones, as usual. People either don't want to open up their barns to crowds in this post-pandemic world or they went out of business."

"I hate that," I say, thinking about how we had to drive hours to go to the last show. I couldn't imagine doing that with a kid.

"Thank god she considers a trail ride through your woods almost as cool," Lita says. "Anyway, what's on your agenda for today? Since you'll have all that 'pining for Shani' time back, maybe you could take a look at those fences on the back acre and—"

"Pining for what now?" a voice behind me says, and of course it's Shani, looking utterly fuckable with her soft hoodie and her sleepy face.

"Nothing." I groan and storm off into the office to the sound of their laughter, even though I'm not really mad. Good. Let Lita and Shani catch up. I have work to do. It was the whole reason I left Shani's so early in the first place.

I pull out Aunt Christina's old ledger again and start opening up the mail. I need to check what bills are due, and to verify account balances. I haven't yet figured out what's on autopay and what's not.

The few boarders that are left have been paying me in cash, leaving fat envelopes on the desk, or Venmo-ing me. I've been appreciative of it—it's the only way I could keep buying stuff for repairs. Unfortunately, it's also given me the illusion of money, even when there isn't any, and when the bank account *finally* loads on my phone, I see that not only is the bank account low, but it's already overdrawn.

Shit.

I quickly transfer a little bit of money I have in my own account into the business one. It eats up more of my savings than I'd like to admit, and I'm stressing about not having *any* of my own money coming in, not gonna lie, but still, I breathe a little easier when the total listed under the business account, while still very small, is at least not flashing red anymore.

All that wondering and daydreaming fades a little in the face of an overdue electric bill and dwindling funds. It's overwhelming, but I'm determined to handle it. Baby steps, one at a time. I pay the electric bill and lean back into the chair, trying to think about how to make this place profitable. Shoveling horseshit for a living is a far cry from planning weddings.

"Hey," Shani says, knocking on the doorframe and leaning inside.

"Hey yourself." I close the ledger and take my feet off the desk.

She notices the travel coffee mug she gave me this morning, half-empty now, on the desk beside me. I catch a quick smile, before she looks away, rubbing the back of her neck. "Whatcha doing in here?"

"Trying to keep the lights on."

"Good, good," she says, in a distracted way that makes me think she didn't really even hear what I said.

"Molly . . ." she starts at the same time I say, "Shani . . ."

"You go first," she laughs.

"I was just going to ask if everything was okay out there?"

"Uh, yeah, it's great," she says, shifting her weight. "I, uh, was just wondering, you know, since you have so much free time in your pining schedule now—"

I groan. "I'm going to kill Lita. You know that, right?"

Shani laughs, breaking some of the tension, but she doesn't come any farther through the door. I wasn't exactly expecting to be greeted with a kiss or anything, but she looks ready to bolt.

"Come to dinner with me," she blurts, glancing at me, and then her boots, and then back at me, her neck and ears going pink. I wonder what else is going pink.

"Shani Thomas, are you asking me on a date?"

"It depends on if you're saying yes." Okay, there it is, that little bit of swagger I'm used to, even if it is all an act.

I grin. "Then I guess you just asked me on a date."

She comes in the door then, right up to where I'm sitting in my chair, and spins me around, stepping between my legs with a lightness I've never seen before. She takes my chin and tips my face up so she can give me a quick kiss. "Great, I'll pick you up at seven. Dress nice."

I politely pretend not to notice her giving Lita a high five before she bolts out the door.

Chapter Twenty-Four

*N*at barely says a word to me when I get back to the house, and it makes me feel worse than I already do about leaving her last night. I try to apologize, to explain, to do anything to make this right, but she doesn't care. I get it—I would be pissed too if the tables were turned. Leaving her with people she only just met was definitely not cool. Even if I knew she was in good, safe hands, she didn't. It was the exact opposite of a bonding experience, and I feel like exactly as big of an asshole as I should.

"Nat, I'm really sorry," I try again, when she's finished angrily packing up her things and is shoving her feet in her shoes.

"Don't 'Nat, I'm really sorry' me! You left me at a bar! In the middle of nowhere! To go get laid!! I have *nothing* to say to you right now."

"Come on, I'm sorry," I say. "Really, truly, I am so sorry, Nat. I wasn't thinking when I left, but that's no excuse. What can I do to fix this?"

Nat scoffs. "Nothing, Molly, I just have to get over it, as usual. Just like I do every time you blow me off for your latest crush."

"It's not like that."

"It's exactly like that. It's *always* exactly like that."

"Nat, please," I say, taking the bag out of her hand as I follow her out to the car. "Just hear me out, for a second."

She hesitates, leaning against the now open car door, which is more of a chance than I thought she'd give me.

"Leaving you there was extremely messed up, and I am extremely sorry," I say, not above groveling. "You're right to be pissed about that, and I'm not excusing myself or minimizing anything. It was wrong. But I need you to know that how I feel about Shani? It's not wrong, and it's not the same. I'm not trying to lose myself in her like I always do. I feel like I'm *finding* myself when I'm with her and—"

"Molly," she interrupts, grabbing her bag from me and throwing it into her passenger seat. "I have dried your tears a dozen times after you thought you 'found yourself' in someone."

"Not *in*, Nat! With. *With.* That's what I'm trying to tell you: that's what's different. Last night, I told her things that I never thought I would. She told me stuff too and it was . . . Nat, it was so good. She wants to take me out tonight on a *real date*! When is the last time someone wanted to do that for me? Even Blake just took me out with his friends!"

"I hope you know what you're doing, Molly," she says before sliding into her seat and shutting the door.

I'm still standing there a few minutes later when I see Shani pulling out in her work truck. She gives me a little wave as she goes and I smile. I can't help it. I've got a date. *A date!* I can feel guilty about Nat later.

* * *

I'm beyond giddy as I get ready. Shani said to dress nice, and I don't want to disappoint. Unfortunately, most of my best clothes are still in the city, packed up in my mom's storage rental, but I do have a few decent things here.

I pull on a nearly sheer maroon blouse that looks appropriately classy, and pair it with thick black leggings. My shoe options are similarly limited, but I do have my black Louboutins which give me an almost four-inch lift and make my legs look amazing.

I hope she likes it. Will she like it? Will she still like me?

I know, I know, usually these kinds of nerves are reserved for *before* you've slept with someone, but I can't help it.

And while she's had sex with me . . . I guess I sort of feel like I haven't had sex with her. I know that's not *really* how it works—we were there, together, the whole time—but I can't help but feel like we're still in this weird gray zone. The next time we have sex, I'd like it to be reciprocal and with like 100 percent fewer panic attacks.

She finally knocks on my door—endearing since she usually just walks right in—and I pull it open to see—

Wow.

Shani stands in front of me in a black suit. Her shirt is low-cut silk, and her neck is adorned with a variety of gold necklaces and chains. She's got her hair styled in dark, messy, short waves that expose her undercut. She's even got on a little gloss. I pull her in enthusiastically and kiss her hard, feeling her smile spread wide as she tries to kiss me back. Damn, she looks fucking good. Emphasis on *fucking*.

"You like?" she asks, holding out her jacket and doing a little twirl. She's not wearing a bra.

"Do that again and we won't make it to dinner," I huff out.

She laughs at that and twirls her car keys in her hand. "Better go while we still can, then."

* * *

WE'RE AT THIS cute Italian bistro that I've never noticed before, tucked way back in the far corner of town. One wall is a giant mural of all the Italian greats dining here and the rest of them are textured to look like old marble or something. It's dimly lit, with occasional red glass Tiffany-style lamps and candles on every table. It's louder than I expected, band music blaring through unseen speakers, so we lean close to talk . . . which I don't mind one bit. When we aren't leaning in, I can't stop staring at her.

"What?" She smirks, tearing her roll in half as I pass her the butter.

"Nothing." I blush.

She runs her tongue across her mouth. "Do I have something in my teeth?"

"No," I laugh.

"You're making me self-conscious," she says, tossing a bread crumb toward me.

"Sorry, but I'm one hundred percent obsessed with how you look right now."

She runs her hands through her hair, shoving back some of the shaggy strands on top in a way that manages to look even more ridiculously fucking hot. "I believe it, you're practically drooling."

I kick her under the table, and she laughs. "I'm not used to seeing you like this."

"Do you like it better?"

I can tell she's doing her best to look relaxed about the question, but I can also tell that she wants an answer. I put my hand on her knee, which has suddenly started bouncing.

"No, not better," I say. Her eyes snap to mine, her bouncing leg slowing and then coming to a stop entirely.

"Is there a 'but' coming?"

"There's not. I'm just wondering something now."

"Yeah?"

"Do *you* like this better?"

"God no," she says, running her hands through her hair again. "But I wanted tonight to be . . ."

I raise my eyebrows, waiting for her to finish her thought, but she doesn't. She shoves her tongue against her cheek, looking away like she's trying and failing to find the right word. I give her knee a squeeze, letting her know I'm still here. I'm still with her.

"You're gonna think I'm so cheesy," she says.

"I already *know* you're cheesy, so no worries there." She snorts. I can tell I've caught her off guard and that she likes it. "First of all, you do horses' nails for a living. You're an equine manicurist. If that wasn't cute and cheesy enough, you made me watch the literal worst rom-com in the world last night. You could have at least put on *10 Things I Hate About You* or something."

"Excuse me! We watched an Adam Sandler movie, not a rom-com," she deadpans. "An old comedy great!"

"I don't know, it felt like a rom-com to me—a very cheesy, goofy one, but—"

"You got a problem with rom-coms?"

"No, but I've got a problem with you pretending to be a hard-ass when you're clearly a bigger mush than I am." I trail my finger up her thigh, just until she sucks in a breath, and then pull my hand back and grab a dinner roll. "And I have a problem with you dressing this hot, if it makes you uncomfortable. Because here's the thing: you always look that way to me."

She scoffs. "You don't look at me the way you're looking at me now when I'm covered in mud, trimming hooves."

"Ummmm, I definitely do." I snort. "Your back is usually to me though. Have you seen your muscles in that tank top? Plus, leather chaps? Hello! Not to mention the way you calm down these massive animals when they're scared, taking control of everything. Dreamy, all of it. The way you're dressed tonight is just a sweet little cherry on top of a big, *delicious* sundae." My voice drops when I say *delicious*, and Shani shifts in her seat, letting me know it landed right where I wanted it to.

She gives her head a little shake and smiles down at the table-cloth. "Here I thought you hated me the whole time."

"Well, we're even, because I was pretty sure you hated *me* the whole time too."

She winces. "I might have, just a little bit, in the beginning," she says, as the waitress sets down our meal—spaghetti family style, with a side of chicken parm for me and eggplant parm for her. "I seem to just keep being wrong about you."

"What does that mean?"

She waves her hand around the restaurant and then at herself. "I thought you needed something like this. I thought you might *want* all this. I was trying to impress you tonight, to show you that we do fit and that I *can* clean up nice."

"Shani, I *am* impressed, and I *do* like this, and appreciate the effort. But this isn't just my date, it's our date. I'd rather us both be having fun in sweats eating takeout than sitting at the fanciest restaurant in the city with you feeling uncomfortable."

A guilty smile crosses her face. "Do you mean that?"

"Yeah, I do. In fact, if you'd rather leave right now—" I say and then take a bite of my dinner. "Wait, no, holy shit, this food is amazing. I take it back. We can't leave yet."

"No, eat up." Shani laughs and digs into her own. "I do their horses," she says. "They give me takeout and leftovers all the time, so I'm a little bit spoiled and used to it, but I'm glad to see it meets your city-girl expectations."

And now it's my turn to laugh. "All right, so skipping out on this amazing meal is a definite no—I'm savoring every second of it. Is this homemade pasta? My god—*but* if you had something else stuffy planned for the rest of the night, we can skip. Go home and hang out or go to that bull riding bar and I can wow you with my skills. Whatever you want."

"I hate that bar, and I can think of something much better for you to ride tonight."

"Don't tease me," I whine, and she winks.

* * *

"Now PULL THAT strap through the buckle and wait for him to breathe out."

And okay, when she said she had something better for me to ride, I was totally, definitely thinking like, I don't know, her face. But no, apparently, she was being literal—as in, I'm being forced to ride old Otis like I'm Lita's elementary school niece. At least Shani's still in her suit, and I can stare straight down her shirt every time she bends over to help me with something. Which she's definitely caught on to and is, without a doubt, playing up. It's the only consolation, to be honest.

She let me change out of my heels when I realized what was happening, but other than that she just said, "Be glad you have leggings on."

When Otis is finally tacked up, Shani leads him off into the smallest paddock, with me walking beside her. She pulls a little step stool thing out of nowhere, and has him stand beside it, gesturing for me to climb up. I lose my nerve right as my foot hits the stirrup, but Shani is helping to lift me into place before I can escape. Once I'm settled in the saddle, she gets to work adjusting the reins and stirrups until they're "just right," whatever that means. Otis stands there patiently, like he's done this his whole life and it's nothing weird to have a whole entire human climbing onto his back.

I disagree. This is impossibly weird. I am sitting on a living, breathing creature. Why? Who was the first person who climbed on a horse? What did the first horse think? It couldn't have gone well. Why keep doing it? Just so generations of horses and people could lead us down to this moment, where I'm staring down Shani's shirt while Otis stands here ruining the mood with his farts?

"You're shivering," Shani says, finally handing me the reins. I don't tell her that it's only half from the temperature, and the rest from fear, as she pulls off her jacket.

"I can't take that," I say, noticing the way her nipples have gone hard in the cold, peeking out beneath her barely-there silk shell. "You need it more than me."

"Put the coat on, Molly," she says, her voice warm but firm. I think about protesting again, but her face warns me not to. Damn, I love dominant Shani.

I slide the jacket on, immediately enveloped by its warmth and the scent of her body wash and cologne. A little spark spreads out from my belly, warming me from the inside out and I try not to think too much about what it means when my butterflies turn into floating hearts instead.

"Do you trust me?" Shani asks.

"Yes," I say, surprised to realize that I mean it.

Shani nods and then makes a weird clicking sound that Otis seems to translate as "let's go" because he immediately starts a slow walk around the paddock. I laugh, almost losing my balance. I use the reins to pull myself up, which makes Otis sigh and shake his head, but luckily, he's only looking at Shani. I think we both know she's the one in charge.

Riding a horse is . . . odd. The ride is bumpier than I expected, and my tailbone hurts a little—but Otis is slow and gentle, and I don't mind the way Shani is walking beside me, looking both proud and anxious, in her fanciest clothes. She has to be chilly in her skimpy tank top on this cool almost-autumn night, but she's looking at me like this is the best thing that's ever happened.

"What?" I ask when I catch her staring at me again.

"I'm just taking it in," she says, biting her lip.

"You never thought I'd get on a horse, did you?"

"Like I said, I keep being wrong about you." She grins, keeping us going at the same slow, steady pace.

"We could go a little faster you know," I say. "I'm not a baby."

"No," she says, meeting my eyes. "We'll go slow. I want to do it right."

"Okay, let's do it right," I say softly, because I hear her, and I get it, and I know neither of us are talking about horses right now.

Chapter Twenty-Five

I wake up early the next morning with a smile—and not just because I'm finally in the bedroom upstairs, curled under blankets that I know Shani once used. No, I'm smiling because after Otis had enough of our late-night ride, Shani walked me to my door and gave me the sweetest, gentlest good-night kiss I've ever had. It made me melt an entirely different way than her tongue did the night before. Yeah, I know we're doing everything a little upside down and backward, but I don't care.

Her insistence that we take our time, that we learn to really know and trust each other, that if we're doing this, we're doing it right, and giving ourselves the best shot we possibly can at this working . . . It's so different than what I'm used to.

I mean, it's not that my past relationships have all been whirlwind moments of impulsiveness . . . it's just that, okay, yes, all my past relationships *have* formed out of moments of impulsiveness. A swipe right that leapfrogs into living together before I've even decided if I like them. A Tinder date that never leaves. A hundred tears shed on my childhood bed after it never works out.

Shani's insistence that we start over now that I know that she's just as into me as I'm into her, feels both novel and important.

Knowing that she doesn't hate me, and hasn't this whole time, has me almost giddy, but knowing she wants to slow down and do this right has me thinking long-term.

I *want* to be the person that she believes in and trusts. I want to be a person deserving of this. Of her.

I admit I was disappointed that Shani politely turned me down last night when I invited her inside in every way possible, and I'm still frustrated in a way that has my hands drifting between my legs during my extra-long morning shower—but that can't really be helped. Because Shani is hot. Unbearably hot. And thoughtful. A perfect, chivalrous partner, which is honestly something I never knew I'd be into.

A loud bang outside shakes the house as I'm making my morning coffee. I barely have time to set my cup down before I'm racing outside shoeless, scared that something bad happened with the horses. I run off the porch only to find Shani standing sheepishly next to my ladder. The ladder seems to have fallen against the house, leaving a giant gash in one of the few pieces of siding that are still hanging on that side of the house.

I crinkle my forehead. "What are you doing?"

She looks nervous. Again. "I'm sorry. I'll replace that bit of siding."

"It's fine. I'm working on this part next anyway but—"

"I know," she sighs. "I was trying to be all romantic or whatever. I figured I'd let you sleep in, and when you woke up, I'd have this all started and maybe you would make us breakfast?" She winces. "And then we could work on it together all day and . . . I should really stop talking."

"Shani," I practically coo, not even caring about the broken siding.

She rubs a hand over her forehead and drags it down her face. "Well, this is mildly mortifying. I was trying to be all cool and instead, the ladder slipped, and I smashed a hole in the side of your house. Not really conducive to convincing you to stay or at least agree to another date with me, now is it?"

I look up at the gash and then back at her. "No, not really," I tease. "But it is very, very sweet. Well, not the cooking you breakfast part. Why do I have to do the cooking?"

"A girl can dream," she sighs, visibly relaxing. "Now that we aren't fighting, the apology muffins seem to have dried up. I've been craving them."

"They weren't *all* apology muffins," I yelp, but she looks at me like she doesn't believe me, and I have to work hard not to laugh.

I hold up my pointer finger and thumb, leaving the tiniest space between them. "Okay fine, maybe they were just a tiny bit apology muffins but still. There were also chocolate chip cookies, by the way."

She steps into my space—crowding me until I can smell her signature scent of leather and body wash. "They were delicious," she says, in a low husky voice. "And I want more." The way her eyes dance as she says it makes me think maybe we aren't just talking about muffins anymore. I look down, trying to keep my mind from running away.

She tips my head back and kisses me long and hard enough to let me know I was right. I try to calculate the odds that she'll let me drag her inside and have my way with her. Low, I realize, as she steps back to look at the gash in my siding with a sigh.

"Guess I owe *you* muffins now," she says, and glances over me.

"I could think of other ways you could make it up to me."

She pulls her hat off and smacks it against my thigh like she's chasing me away. "I'm trying to behave," she says, "and you're not making it easy."

"That's because I don't want you to behave." I smile.

* * *

THE NEXT FEW days pass in similar fashion. She's taken an interest in helping me tackle the list whenever she's got some free time—it's become increasingly clear that she's hoping I'm going to stay, and increasingly muddy how I feel about it.

Lochlin haunts the grounds while she's at work, getting more antsy as he heals, so I try to give him odd jobs here and there to keep him busy. He seems happy about Shani and me—and even happier about how much better he's feeling. I manage to con all three of them—Shani, Lochlin, *and* Tyler—to help me fix up all the gardens (Ashley has been on me about curb appeal now that we're for sure going to concentrate on a private buyer).

I pay them with a dinner of burgers on the grill and my mom's famous mac salad recipe, and we sit on an old picnic table I found in the middle of one of the seldom used paddocks I was cleaning up the other day.

"This is delicious," Lochlin says, shoving food into his mouth.

"If I knew all I had to do to get you all to work was feed you, I could have gotten through my list a lot faster," I tease. "Maybe tomorrow you two can come help me hang the window shutters in exchange for some muffins."

"If you even make muffins when I'm stuck with a full day of clients, I swear to god!" Shani laughs.

Tyler clears his throat. "About tomorrow, actually," he says, glancing at Lochlin. "As much as I would love to help, it's about time I get back on the circuit, now that Lochlin's doing so well."

I freeze as Shani's face goes serious, and then I flick my eyes to her brother—I can see the longing on his face already. I wonder how much of that is because he doesn't want Tyler to leave and how much of that is because he wants to get back on the circuit too.

"Well, thanks for all your help around here, Ty," I say, when I realize no one else is going to break the awkward silence. "It's been great having you around lately. I hope I see you again soon."

Tyler smiles at me, seemingly grateful, before turning to look back at Lochlin, who is aggressively chewing his dinner while staring down at his plate.

"A little notice would have been nice, Tyler," Shani says, and I can tell she's upset.

I blow out a heavy breath, focusing on eating and feeling very much like I'm intruding on this conversation. Lochlin leans forward on the table, bringing his hands up to rest his chin on them as if he's ready for a show.

"Shani, I love you, and I will always be there when you call me, but you can't get mad at me for going back to work," Tyler says, gently. "I know you hate what Loch and I do, but I stayed as long as I could, and if Loch's okay with me heading back, you need to be too. I've got bills to pay and people counting on me, and, yes, broncos to ride. I can't just stay here forever because you're scared Loch'll follow me when I leave."

I glance at Lochlin then, who's looking at Tyler kind of proudly, as if Tyler is saying things he wished he could.

"Well fuck you too, Tyler." Shani lets out a laugh that sounds like it's been punched out of her. "You know you can't go with him, right, Lochlin?"

Lochlin sighs and picks up his burger. "I'm not leaving quite yet."

"But soon?" she snaps, worry lacing her voice.

"The doctor's cleared me for riding, Shan, but I'm gonna be a good boy and finish up my last two weeks of scheduled PT." He smiles at Tyler when he says that, and I get the feeling that this was an argument they already had.

"Two weeks? Great," she says. "Perfect." She grabs her plate and marches inside.

I rub my face—so much for a nice family dinner—and then stand up. "I'm gonna go talk to her, but thanks again for your help. Just leave everything when you're done, I'll clean up, and Tyler? Be safe."

"You too," he says, and it takes me a second to realize he's warning me about Shani.

* * *

I find her frantically scrubbing her dish in my kitchen sink. I quietly scrape my plate and set it on the counter beside her, trying to catch her eye. She just keeps cleaning the same plate, staring off like she doesn't even see me.

"Shani," I say, turning off the water. She sets the plate on the drying rack and turns to me, her eyes wet from unshed tears. I pull her into a tight hug and she buries her face in my neck. Her hot tears finally falling, staining my skin.

"Baby," I say, leading her over to the couch, never letting go of her hand as we sit down. "It's okay. It's okay."

"It's not," she says, curling up into me as she wipes at her eyes, looking more distraught than I've ever seen her. "Every time he goes out in those arenas, I know he might not leave it. Do you know what it's like to just always be waiting for the call that he's hurt or he's dead?"

"Shani . . ."

"You see what kind of luck I have. Nothing lasts for me, ever. Not my mom, not my dad, not Christina, not . . ." I wince as she trails off, wondering what was next on the list. *The barn? Me?* "I don't get to keep anything. I don't. The next time Lochlin gets thrown, what if he doesn't get back up? What if he doesn't? And then I'm all alone. I'll have nothing left." Her words give way to sobs as I pull her back against me, kissing the top of her head and holding her close.

I realize in that moment, her head on my chest, my fingers in her hair, how much I *want* to stay. I don't want to be another thing that lets her down and leaves. Suddenly my life back home, if you can even call it that, seems far away. I could be happy here, I think. I imagine hanging out with my new friends, making Shani muffins while she gives horses manicures, and turning Otis out so I can clean the stalls. It seems so peaceful. I could be so content.

Who even am I?

* * *

"WHO EVEN ARE YOU?" Mom all but shouts into my ear. I texted her that I might stay a bit longer, maybe a lot longer, and rather than responding with a text she called me on the house phone. I should have seen that coming. Telling her via text was the coward's way out.

"Hi, Mom," I say, guilt crowding my throat and making it hard to speak.

"You're seriously thinking of staying? Molly, you don't know the first thing about horses, let alone running an entire stable of them."

She's not wrong, I think.

"You're not wrong," I say. "But I've been learning a ton. I think Aunt Christina wanted me to try. Why would she have left it to me?"

"I don't know! Maybe because you're the one person I have left, and she wanted to take that from me too."

"Why won't you tell me what happened between you?" I ask, my voice pleading. "Maybe then I'll understand why I'm here."

"You really want to know? Fine," she seethes. "I didn't want to speak ill of the dead but the truth is I asked her for help when your father left, and she refused. I told her exactly what I thought of her, and we never spoke again. My own sister. Now will you come home and let this go!"

"That doesn't sound like Christina," I say, thinking of everything I've come to know about her since staying here.

"How would you know?"

"I . . . I mean I live here. I hear a lot of stories and—"

"Oh I bet," she says. "I'm sure that's exactly what she was hoping would happen when she left you that place."

"Mom, just, is there any more to the story? I believe you, I do, and I love you, but it just sounds so out of character for her to turn you away when she's helped everyone else."

"Oh yeah, she always had time for everyone else."

"Mom!"

"There isn't more! I asked her to borrow some money, but she had already given all hers away. Yes, she offered us to share a room there, but I couldn't leave my job, could I? Do you know what she said? She said I should just leave you there. Leave you there! The most important thing I had, my daughter, and she wanted to just take you from me, like you were another one of her rescues. You weren't though. You had me. I loved you more than anything and I was not about to let you go live with her and forget all about me!"

"So she did try to help, then, she just didn't have money?"

"I knew this would happen when you moved there," she says, her hurt resonating through the phone. "Christina had this pathological need to always be the hero, ever since we were kids. She thrived off the attention—it didn't matter if she was rehabbing a baby bird or offering to adopt her down-on-her-luck niece, as long as people applauded her for it. It was hard enough to ask her for help, but I wasn't going to let her use you like that."

"Mom, I love you," I say, my voice going softer at the pain in her voice. "But this sounds . . ." I sigh. "I don't think she left me a barn to get back at you or anything like that. I've been going through all her things, and I've found so many pictures of you. I think she missed you and maybe giving me this place has something to do with that. Maybe it's not even really a gift for me, but an apology to you. This place has been making me so happy, and I wish you could be happy for me too. If you even knew how great everyone was here—"

My mother cuts me off with the biggest sigh. "Jesus, Molly. Have you met someone?"

"I—"

"Molly, not again."

"Not you too." I roll my eyes.

"You know you have a bad habit of picking up the interests of whoever you're dating. My therapist says it's 'mirroring.' I used to do it to your father all the time and look where it got me. Learn from my mistakes."

"This wouldn't be a mistake!"

"Yes, it—"

"I have to go, Mom. I'll . . . I'll call you soon, promise. I love you."

"Molly—"

"Sorry, a horse got loose, bye!" I say, hanging up.

I'm about to call Nat, praying that she's forgiven me so I can cry to her about everything I just learned, but when I turn around, I catch Shani standing in the doorway, my favorite iced coffee in her hand.

"Is there a horse somewhere you need me to catch, or did you just lie to your mother?"

"I lied," I sigh. "What are you doing here? I thought you had work."

"My two P.M. canceled, so I have a bit of a break. I thought maybe you could use a coffee while you're poring over the books."

"Thanks," I say, taking the cup from her and tilting my head up for a kiss. She brushes her lips against mine but then crouches down and wraps her arms around me—it's a warm, reassuring hug, exactly what I needed. "How much did you hear?"

"Nothing."

I look at her, narrowing my eyes.

"Fine, probably more than you wanted me to hear, but your mom is a loud talker. I was going to sneak back out before you saw me, but you looked upset, so I thought I'd stick around."

I lean my head back in the chair. "I don't know if my mom is more upset that I'm questioning her interpretation of what happened with Christina, or because she found out about you, and thinks I'm going to ruin my life. She said I 'mirror' whoever I date. Like what the hell?"

"Hmm," Shani says, considering. "A lot of times when someone says something that *really* pisses me off, it's because on some level I'm worried they're right."

I twist my lips to the side, not wanting to admit anything.

"If it helps," Shani says, "when I dated my last girlfriend, I got really into craft beer because she was. I even bought a little distillery kit. I don't even like beer if I'm being honest. IPAs are nasty, for the record. They aren't flavorful or full-bodied. They're just gross."

I laugh and lean forward in my chair to kiss her again.

"I was so caught up in her enthusiasm for it all, and that's what I loved. Not the beer, the fact that the beer was something that made her happy. You get what I'm saying?"

"Yeah, I mean, but is that really bad? Isn't it good to take an interest in your partner's stuff?"

"Yeah, sure, as long as you aren't losing sight of yourself or doing something you don't want to." She licks her lips and looks away with a sigh. "The question is, *are* you losing yourself here? You did have all these big plans before this place and I interrupted them."

"You didn't interrupt my plans, Shani. You just added to them."

She looks back at me. "Molly, I don't want to be your IPA."

I bury my head in my hands as she stands. "I just want to see where things go with us." She tips my chin up, meeting my eyes with a gentle smile. "Fine, yes, I guess there is always a possibility that I'm all caught up in this. I don't know! It's not like being bequeathed a stable and falling for its tenant is something they teach you how to deal with in college. I'm kind of winging it here, taking it day by day."

Shani is disappointed by my answer. I can tell, even though she's trying not to show it. "You'll figure it out," she says when the silence drags on too long.

"What do we do in the meantime?" I ask. "I don't want you to . . ."

She waits for me to find the words, so steady I could cry.

"I don't want you to walk away from me because I'm not a sure thing." I bite my lip. "I really want to see it through."

Shani rubs my shoulder and kisses the top of my head. "I'm not going anywhere," she says, but then glances at the clock with a frown and puts her hand on the door.

"You're literally leaving right now," I point out.

She walks back over, crouching down to give me another kiss. "I have another appointment, baby, but we both know that's not what you're talking about."

I sigh. "What are we going to do?"

"I'm going to go shoe a horse. You're going to go over the books and maybe hang some more siding after that. *We* will keep taking things slow. That way, we can make sure that you don't get lost, and I don't get lost. We keep fixing up the house and barn because you need to do that either way, and we keep making out every chance we get." She kisses my forehead with a gentleness that makes me want to melt. "Does that all sound good to you?"

"Yes," I say trailing a finger over her lips. "It sounds very good, especially that last part."

She catches my finger between her teeth and grins. "Second thought, maybe I can be a little late."

Chapter Twenty-Six

The first week of officially taking things slowly made me want to die. While we kept up the movie nights and snuggling, and dinners, and making out in a very PG-13 kind of way, that was it. Any energy she had left after work was sunk into helping me restore this place, and I think we both worked out our *frustration* with lots of hammers and nails.

The second week, I had three different meltdowns trying to untangle the various bank accounts and the books—super not helped by the constant low-level sexual frustration I was experiencing because my girlfriend—no, not my girlfriend, not officially, not yet, no matter how I think about her in my own head, because "taking it frustratingly slow" or whatever—and I have given each other the queer-girl equivalent of blue balls.

Two weeks of glorified edging, and the memories of our one night of *actual* edging, and I was basically living for my vibrator. Even though Shani said that was semi-cheating. I reminded her that we agreed to take things slow with each other, but me and my hands and my toys were already in a committed long-term relationship when she met me, so that was none of her business.

It wasn't until this week though, that I finally felt like I had a real understanding of how much I'd need to pull in to make the place profitable—spoiler alert: a lot—which is, of course, when Lita walks in.

"That bad?" she asks.

"Worse," I grumble, leaning back in my chair. "I'm trying to figure out if there is any universe where I can make this business profitable again."

She narrows her eyes. "I thought you were looking for a private seller."

"I am, in theory," I say. "But hypothetically, if I decided to stay, I would hypothetically need to figure out how to make this place profitable. Hypothetically."

"Right," she laughs. "*Hypothetically*, if you're just short some boarders to turn things around, I can probably find you a few. I know a really good trainer that's looking for a new space to lease for holding lessons and boarding all the lesson horses."

"Seriously?" I sit up in my seat. "If I got a rental fee on the paddock *and* boarding fees, that would be a huge help. Can you get me their number?"

"No," she says, and she sighs. "Not yet. It's extremely stressful to move a horse to a new facility, let alone several of them at once. I'm not going to vouch for you just to have them displaced when you change your mind. It can't be hypothetical when you talk to them." She must see how panicky I feel over the idea of committing right now, so she adds, "Run some numbers, think it over, and let me know. I have no doubt you can make this happen, Molly, if you really want to. You just have to decide if you do."

"Yeah," I say, staring back down at the ledger in front of me. If only I could figure *that* part out.

* * *

Of course, the day Lochlin leaves—when Shani has already headed off to work in a horrible mood, and mine is no better—Ashley stops in to talk to me about officially listing the barn. She'd driven by and was surprised to see how much work I had gotten done.

I don't bother telling her that I've officially moved my bedroom from the couch to the room upstairs—even my clothes are back in a closet. I also don't tell her I'm thinking about staying. I just thank her for stopping by and invite her in for a cup of coffee, trying to lean into the friendly small-town vibe, and not wanting to burn any bridges with someone I might be seeing a lot of if I stay. Shani pulls in right as Ashley is pulling out, but she doesn't say anything. She just gets out of her truck and heads right out to fix the fence we had talked about over breakfast.

I had assumed she would come in after, but she doesn't. That night, for the first time, Shani doesn't come over for a movie, nor does she invite me over to her place. I know we're supposed to be taking it slow, and a night off is fair, but it hurts. It hurts especially bad, knowing how upset she was about Lochlin leaving today. I should be there, curled around her, doing my best to cheer her up.

She ignores my texts, and I try to take the hint, the anxiety over being away from her welling up inside of me.

It's even worse in the morning, though, when Shani texts me about taking a little space this weekend. I tell her I don't need it, but she doesn't budge. She says she's going to go out and visit her brother, make sure he remembers that he's freshly rehabbed and not yet 100 percent before his show this weekend, and she'll be back late Sunday, but it feels like an excuse. Like seeing Ashley here put Shani's walls back up and now she's pulling away again.

I hate it, and I double down on the spreadsheet I started with some "hypothetical" numbers that Lita said I could expect if I decided to stay. Giving this place up would suck, I see that now, but losing Shani because of it feels unbearable.

Sunday, I call Nat, taking advantage of the "space" I have. She surprises me by asking if I can meet her in the city, even offering to treat me to dinner at The Greens, a place I used to love. I'm about to say no when I realize I have no excuse not to other than gas money, and besides, I definitely owe her some bonding time after that disastrous trip to the bar.

The drive down is nice, but it takes me forever to find parking, and then I end up still rushing to walk the few blocks to the restaurant. The Greens isn't a fancy place by any means, but it is trendy, with brightly painted walls, live plants covering every square inch of its windows, and a menu consisting solely of salad bowls.

I'm pleasantly surprised to see Nat smiling as she waves me over to the table. I wasn't sure how mad she still was—she's barely been texting me back lately—but the answer is, shockingly, not at all? Instead, she acts like nothing happened. She catches me up on the latest with her auditions, what's coming up, and how things are going at the coffee shop. I barely have a chance to get a word in for the first half hour, but I don't care. It's so nice to hear her talk.

Still, I can't help but notice as the night goes on that she hasn't asked a thing about me, the barn, or Shani. Maybe she *is* harboring some bad feelings about everything after all.

"Nat, I know I haven't been the best friend lately," I say, working up the nerve when our salads come, and there is finally a lull in the conversation. "I want to apologize again for what happened, and for how busy I've been. I've really missed you."

"Don't worry about it," she says, stabbing her lettuce with her fork. "I overreacted about the bar thing."

I scrunch up my eyebrows because *no, she did not*, and this doesn't sound like the Nat I know at all. "I left you at a bar. You were right to be angry. That could have been dangerous."

"It worked out. I'm over it," she says. "Which, speaking of over it, I think Randy is getting sick of paying me overtime. We can't wait to have you back."

She catches me staring at her as I try to puzzle out what's really going on.

"What?" She shrugs.

"Nothing, just, I don't know. I thought you might want to talk about what happened. We didn't exactly leave things on the best note, and you haven't been texting as—"

"Do you want to rehash the past or focus on the future? Because I know which one I would rather do." She smiles. "By the way, there's a really cool studio opening up soon in my building. I thought after we ate, we could go to check it out. My neighbor was fine with it."

"Why would you want a studio when you have a one-bedroom?"

"Not for me, for you!" She laughs. "Unless you plan on moving back in with your mom, we need to start looking."

"Right," I say slowly, realizing what this is now.

She didn't invite me out as my best friend. She invited me out to fix what she feels I'm doing wrong; to get me "back on track" and maybe even missing the city.

We finish our meal and I apologetically beg off apartment hunting, telling her I have to get back to feed the horses, which *is* actually true. Nat is disappointed, but she understands, saying she can't wait to have me back in town, and "wasn't this just like old times?" I hug her hard, because I know this all comes from a place of love, but the truth is: no, it wasn't. Old times was me busting my ass at two jobs and still not being able to afford rent. Old times was daydreaming about a future I couldn't afford, while slinging coffee for people who could.

I think long and hard my entire drive home about what exactly I want. I try to picture my life with Shani and without her, staying at Christina's or moving back home. I convince and unconvince myself a dozen times, but it finally becomes clear when I pull into the driveway, past the rickety old Christina's Corrals sign, and I'm so happy to get back to Shani, to get back *home*, that I can't imagine ever leaving.

* * *

I DON'T SLEEP at all that night. In fact, I spend it baking. I wait until the closest thing to a decent hour I can stand, and then march across the pasture—the still bright moonlight guiding my way.

"I'm going to stay," I say, as I shove a plate of apology muffins in front of Shani. She blinks against the glow of her porch light and pulls the door wider, letting me in even though it's barely five A.M. and my knocking obviously woke her up.

She takes the plate from me as I kick off my boots—muddy from walking across the field—and then follow her inside. Shani gestures for me to sit on the couch, then fishes out a giant fleece blanket from her closet.

"You're shivering," she says, wrapping me up tightly, and then making quick work of lighting a fire to chase out the morning cold.

"It's freezing out," I say. "But I couldn't wait to tell you."

She studies my face like she's not sure if she should believe me. I suppose that's fair. I've taken a lot of time to figure this out, more than she probably expected. Definitely more than I did.

"Have you slept at all?" she asks, running her thumb over the dark circles beneath my eyes. I noticed them while I was grabbing a sweatshirt for the walk. I also noticed that my hair was a disaster and that I looked just this side of melting down, but I didn't want to take the time to change anything.

I wanted Shani to know, right away, that she could stop worrying; stop looking so sad all the time like she had since she ran into Ashley the other day. I wanted her to know that it will be okay. *We* will be okay.

"Lita knows someone who's trying to find a place to teach lessons. That would put us firmly into the black, finally. We could start making real repairs around here and upgrading things. This place could be amazing because of us, you know?"

"Us?" she asks, biting her lip. I can see she's still nervous. Not trusting.

I grab her face and smile. "Us," I say, loving the ring to it. "I'm staying for real, and you better get used to it."

"How are you suddenly so sure?" she asks, her voice low.

My heart pounds in my chest, a steady thump that reassures me that this is the only place I want to be. The only place I should be. I wish she could hear it. I bet it would chase away all her doubts.

"I just am," I say, and then she kisses me, really kisses me— bending me back until I'm lying on her couch, her mouth on my neck, her hands skimming the bottom of my sweatshirt, teasing the cold skin just above my hip.

I let out a gasp as she slides her hand up higher and discovers I didn't bother with a bra or even a camisole. She sighs into my neck as her fingers skim over my nipples, drawing them to attention as I arch against her.

I've been missing this; her sense of confidence and purpose. A swagger that could rival anyone's. Shani slides my sweatshirt off and throws it on the ground, like she's annoyed it's in the way. Her mouth nips at one of my breasts while her free hand squeezes the other one and I let out a whimper before I can catch it. She's been hell-bent on taking it slow, and I'm going to relish the sight of her finally losing control.

I push her back and pull off her pajama bottoms and her tight white sleep tank. I struggle, slightly, with her cotton sports bra, which is worth a laugh or two, even if it is embarrassing. She reaches for the tie on my pajama pants, but I stop her, wait for her eyes to meet mine, until I can see that she's sure, that she's not half-asleep or overexcited and then, because I need to be sure, I say, "We don't have to, if you're not ready."

"You're staying," she says, so quiet the words almost get swallowed up by the hum of her fridge and the crackling of the fire in her living room.

"I am."

Shani smiles and kisses me again, and when her hands go back to the tie, this time I let them. She makes quick work of divesting me of the rest of my clothes, and then crawls up the oversized sofa to wrap herself around me under the blanket. Her skin is warm and soft, in contrast to her rough, strong hands, and I trace lazy circles on her hip with the pads of my fingers. She trembles slightly as we look into each other's eyes, and I tuck the blanket tighter to her.

"I'm not cold," she says, and my hand stops at the realization that I'm the one making her shiver. She presses herself harder against me, like she's trying to trap me, or keep me, or swallow me whole, her teeth marking up my neck as I let my hands wander again. My gentle massage turns more urgent as my fingers trail from her hips to her thigh. I watch her eyes widen and then go soft as I finally press my fingers inside of her. Our eyes locked on each other in the quiet darkness of the unrisen sun.

I swallow her gasps with my kisses, while my hand chases the softness between her legs, searching for just the right spot. She smiles into my mouth, her hips bucking when I do, but I don't stop kissing her, not even for a second. I want her to feel how much this means to me, how much she means to me, how I've grown roots because of her, grown strong because she made me think this—*here, us, home*—was an option.

I want to make her feel as good, as important, as *loved* as she's made me feel. Her fingers drift along my body and then press inside, both of us giving, and taking, and kissing, a tangle of lips and bodies and bursts of light that make my toes curl.

I gently press her to her back, climbing on top as I pepper kisses on her lips, her chin, her neck, her breasts, her belly. I push on her hips, and she slides up eagerly, grabbing a pillow and shoving it beneath her at the perfect angle. A practiced move that I try not to think too much about. It doesn't matter if I'm not the first person who's enjoyed the warmth of this fire and the softness of her skin. What came before me doesn't matter and neither does anyone who came before her.

Because when I taste her again, finally, when she presses against my mouth, my tongue, my body, it feels like home.

This time she spreads her legs wider and begs. This time she lets me lick, suck, nip, touch, taste anything I want—urging me on with whimpers of "so close" and "don't stop" and "fuck, Molly" as her body goes rigid with release. I don't stop, I don't want to stop, not even when she bolts up and grabs my hips, spinning my lower half on top of her with her strong, capable arms. I gasp as she lays back down and pulls me onto her face, arching my back and pressing against her, forgetting just for a second the way she's splayed out under me.

Just for a second though.

And then I'm back on her, with eager fingers and an even more eager tongue, wanting to make her feel as good as she's making me feel. And when she comes a second time, I follow right after, spent and exhausted, both of us smiling and panting against each other's thighs.

It could be the orgasms, or the relief of having finally made a decision, or the satisfaction of seeing our path forward—or some glorious combination of all three—but when I crawl back around so we can curl up together, our warm bodies pressed beneath the blanket that I will never look at the same, it hits me.

I love her.

Chapter Twenty-Seven

*E*verything is perfect, exactly how I want it.

Which means, of course, the next morning everything immediately goes to shit.

Well, not immediately. Waking up next to Shani is incredible. Even watching her drive off to tend to a horse with a hoof infection was kind of nice—a little taste of domesticity and a quick snapshot of what life will be like. She said she would be back in about an hour, so I decide to go to the coffee shop in town and grab some drinks and pastries to surprise her.

That is when it all goes to shit.

Ashley is sitting at the table closest to the cashier and she eagerly waves me over to join her after I place my order. I feel a little awkward about it all, knowing now that I'm not going to sell and all the work that she's done taking pictures and talking about staging has ended up being a waste of time for both of us.

"Hi, Ashley," I say, as cheerfully as I can muster. "I only have a minute. I have to go meet Shani—"

"I was going to stop by this morning actually," she says, talking over me. "I was pulling some information on the property last night in anticipation of updating the listing," Ashley says, her real estate agent voice on full display. I'm about to interrupt her to confess, but the concerned look on her face stops me in my tracks. "It seems there are several liens on the property. I'm not sure why they weren't closed out in probate. You need to set up an appointment with Michael right away and make sure everything is buttoned up legally. I've had to pause the listing."

"Liens?"

"Yes, several. It seems your aunt may have had a problem with running up debt. There are multiple judgments attached to the property. We won't be able to sell it until they're either paid off in advance or arrangements are made for them to be paid at closing from the proceeds of the sale."

"Oh," I say, relieved. "I think I'm staying anyway, so it's fine. We don't have to sell."

Ashley pushes her glasses up on her nose. "Molly, you misunderstand me. These creditors have the ability to force this sale, especially once they find out that the property has already changed hands. I don't know all the ins and outs of estate planning, but as far as I know, they have a claim that this should have been liquidated during probate to pay her debts. It's not a matter of if you stay or sell; it's just a matter of who gets the profits when it happens."

"They can make me sell?"

"Are you sure Michael never mentioned anything to you about this? He's usually so good."

"No," I say, leaving out the fact that as far as he knows, I *was* selling this place immediately. "How likely is it these people would ever find out though? If they haven't yet, maybe—"

"Pretty likely, with all this movement on the property," she says. "I've sent in requests to check property lines; I've done a title search . . . I'm sure they'll find out. Especially since one of the creditors seems to be someone fairly local who let your aunt run up a ridiculous feed bill with him. Almost ten thousand dollars to that vendor alone! From where I'm sitting, it seems like she owes about fifty thousand. I don't know what she was doing out there."

Dying while drowning in medical bills, probably.

"How is this just coming up now?" I ask, feeling my happily ever after slipping away. How will I ever explain this to Shani? *Hi honey, how was work? Do you happen to have fifty thousand dollars lying around so I can pay off some old bills?*

"I'm sorry." She sighs. "You're going to have to take that up with Michael, unless you have the money to pay these off yourself?" The hopeful glint in her eyes fades away as I shake my head no.

"Are you telling me I seriously might lose the property? Right when I've decided to keep it?"

"Unless you can come up with the money somehow, that's unfortunately how it looks." She flips through some of the papers in the folder labeled with the barn's address. "Unless," she says, studying something on one of the papers, "you may be able to look into refinancing options. There is *some* equity in this land. If you took out a new mortgage on it, I bet we could get enough to . . ."

Hope swells up inside of me and is just as quickly dashed. There's no way I would ever be approved. With my mid-tier credit rating and my always-looming student loan debt—not to mention the fact that I'm technically unemployed.

"I doubt I'd be approved." I wince. "No one is going to loan me fifty dollars, let alone fifty thousand."

I take a deep breath. Even saying it aloud is too much. It's an impossible number. I don't even have a tenth of that left after my last trip to Tractor Supply. This isn't fair. This isn't fair! I was just supposed to be getting coffee. I was supposed to be having a good day. *We* were supposed to be having a good day. Now here I am, having it all ripped away.

"I wish I had better news for you," Ashley says. "I would call Michael right away and see what can be done. Maybe this can be salvaged, somehow. Or maybe we can get creative and sell off a portion of the property, I don't know. Michael would know better about all of this. I'm honestly shocked that he didn't catch this sooner. I know you probably think we're small-town people, but we're usually incredibly good at our jobs."

"I don't think that," I say, as the barista calls my name, holding out my two coffees.

"Call Michael," Ashley says. "In the meantime, I'll see what I can do on my end."

"Right, yeah, thanks, I'll do that," I say, numb as I nod to her and head out toward my car.

I'm tempted to drive right back to the barn and pretend Ashley didn't tell me any of that.

I had planned a blissful morning of sitting on the fence beside Shani—just watching her work on some horses, letting her explain what she's doing in that excited way she does whenever I ask her about balancing a hoof or the latest treatments of abscesses or misalignment.

Shani caught me watching farrier TikToks the other night,

and was equal parts elated that I was taking an interest in her work and horrified that I would trust a farrier on social media. Then she laughed and set to work picking apart every farrier I followed. "I prefer to avoid that type of hot shoeing." "I don't care how dry that hoof is, he does not need a torch! Have them stand on a wet mat the night before." "I know it's a donkey, but they deserve better care than that. Would you want me doing Edward Cullen's hooves with a glorified guillotine?" "Oh my god, Molly. Molly! Leave a comment asking if that hurts, farriers love that." "Shit, I wasn't being serious! You know we don't actually love that, right?"

It was so easy, so fun—like today was supposed to be.

I set the coffee cups in the center console and then tap my hands on the steering wheel.

I could go right, and go home, pretend nothing happened, have the exact day that I was hoping for . . . while burying my head in the sand. Technically, Ashley said it was *likely* the creditors will find out, not definite. A one percent chance of it not happening is still a chance.

Or I could go left, to Michael's office. He told me to stop in anytime I needed something, and this feels like a hell of a need. I waver, my fingers tightening on the wheel, and then I turn on my car and pull out of the parking lot.

I go left.

* * *

IT'S ONLY A short drive to Michael's office, and luckily there's a spot open right up in front, like it was waiting for me. I leave the iced coffees in the car to melt, like my whole life feels right now—a cracker crumbling in my mouth.

Michael's receptionist greets me with a cheerful "morning, hon," and I smile weakly. She offers me a coffee and tells me he'll be right with me. I don't want his nasty old legal office coffee. I want the perfectly made iced one in my car. I want the happiness in my car. I want—

"Molly," Michael says, stepping out of his office to greet me with a friendly smile and a firm handshake. "What brings you to my corner of town?"

I stand up and follow him into his office, trying to choose my words carefully. One part of me wants to explode on him for not doing due diligence, but the other side of me wants to beg him for his help to get me out of this mess. I land somewhere in the middle.

"I ran into Ashley at the coffee shop, and she told me that I needed to check in with you right away."

"Did she?" he says, looking amused as he takes his seat behind the desk. At least one of us is having a good morning. "Does she need me to look over some closing documents for you two? Which developers did you go with in the end? She said there were two offers?" He pulls out some papers from his desk like he was expecting this.

"No, I'm here because I don't want to sell anymore. Ashley said there were multiple judgments against the house, but you never mentioned a thing about liens or needing to settle debts. I need your help figuring this out. If there's any way I can keep the property, I want to."

Michael leans back in his chair, looking concerned. "You don't want to sell?"

"If we can get the liens figured out, Shani and I were—"

"Molly, I'm sorry I didn't explain things more clearly. I thought we were on the same page when you signed the forms."

"What do you mean?"

"The property is the only asset that your aunt had when she passed, which is why I discussed selling it with you immediately. Ashley is correct that there are several creditors with vested interest in the land. Probate hasn't closed. It won't close until you sell."

"You said she left it to me."

"She did, but her estate needs to cover the debts first. Think of it like this: if someone dies with—for the sake of ease—let's say a hundred dollars, but they owe a creditor ninety-nine dollars, even if they will that hundred dollars to a descendant, all that descendant is legally entitled to is the single remaining dollar after the debts are clear. You were named as the trustee of the house, but she never intended for you to keep it. Your aunt understood that her debts would come out of the proceeds of the sale."

"No, she wouldn't do that. She wouldn't give me the house if she just wanted me to sell it."

"Molly, Christina wasn't just a client, she was a close friend. We had many conversations about this. She loved keeping up with you from a distance. Her gift to you was seed money. You *are* trying to get some event planning thing up and running, right?"

"Yes, but—"

"She expected you to sell the house, I promise you. I'm not sure how much your mother has told you about your family history, but there was a time that you needed money and Christina had none to give. She never forgave herself for that, and this was her way of making it up to you."

I guess guilt gifts run in the family.

"What about Shani?" I blurt out.

"She knew Shani might expect it, but she also knew Shani would be okay. She has a great career, and a wonderful support system at the barn, meanwhile you . . ."

My mind starts spinning out, his words blurring together. This wasn't fate bringing me here. It was regret. She left me this place out of regret over what happened with my mother. Not because she thought I would fall in love with it, or rise to the occasion, or any of that. She left me seed money, just like Nat found me an apartment, and my mother expects me to live in my childhood bedroom forever, and everyone, *everyone*, thinks they know what's best for me.

I take a deep breath, trying to focus on what Michael is saying, trying to pull it together.

". . . which means, yes, Ashley is correct. The house must be sold. Those debts are owed, and the clock is ticking to pay them off."

"You had me sign papers! I thought it was mine to do with as I please!"

"I'm sorry if you feel like we glossed over that part of things, Molly. That truly is a failing on my part. You were clear that you intended to sell as soon as possible, so perhaps I wasn't as detailed as I could have been about what would happen if you didn't.

"I've already sent death notices, and some of the creditors have reached out to me either with settlement amounts or to reaffirm their full claims against the estate. If you choose not to sell, you will essentially need to repurchase the property from the estate in the amount of its outstanding debts."

"How is this happening?"

"The agreement that I made with the creditors was that you were fixing it up with intent to list within ninety days. The proceeds of the sale would reimburse them and in turn they would remove the claims as you proceed to close with the new buyer. At closing, I would be cutting a check for each creditor and you would get any remaining balance.

"If you choose to seek funding to pay off the creditors, then the house is yours free and clear. They won't care who pays them, as long as they're paid. I can contact them with the update as soon as you secure financing."

"How am I supposed to do that? I left both my jobs to move here!"

"Molly, I wish you had come to me sooner. I apologize again, but I didn't realize your plans had changed. Ashley and I had dinner a couple weeks ago and she told me about the developers. I've already notified creditors of offers, so we can't really go back and make a case for keeping their accounts open longer without reimbursement."

"Wait, you told them about the developers?"

He has the good sense to look chagrined at this. "I was under the impression that you were leaving as soon as you could. I didn't think there was any reason not to."

"So I *have* to sell it to the developer?" I ask, horrified. "I don't even have the option to wait for a real buyer? I told Ashley to tell them no!"

"I'm sorry, Molly," he says, looking genuinely upset about it. "Unless there's another offer in the original time frame for an equal or greater amount, then yes. You *will* need to go with the highest bidding developer."

"You're my lawyer! Can't you help me?"

"I was Christina's lawyer," he says gently, "and executor of her estate. My role isn't to choose sides, it's to ethically get us through probate and close everything out. Believe me, I would love for you to find a way to stay in that house—I'm sure it would have made your aunt so happy."

"Right." I nod, wiping my eyes, because I have to go tell this to Shani. I have to go ruin her day the way mine is ruined. And I have to lose my home—our home—just when I found it.

Chapter Twenty-Eight

I lose my nerve, and call Nat instead.

I tell her everything I didn't at dinner the other night—how I want to stay, how much Shani means to me, and then, about what happened today. I'm hiccupping and sobbing through the call, so upset I can barely breathe. She sighs, but she doesn't argue. Instead, she promises that she'll make the drive up as soon as she's out of work.

I relax a little. Nat will have a plan. Nat *always* has a plan. So I sit at the table, surrounded by old, cold coffees, and wait, while Shani is still none the wiser.

She stopped over to see me between appointments, and while she could tell I was upset, she didn't pry. She just gave me a kiss and went off to her next client, saying she'd be back when she was done. If she noticed the two coffee cups sitting on the table, she didn't ask.

Meanwhile, I've spent the entire afternoon hunched over my laptop, researching mortgages and home equity loans (which as I said, I'm not even sure would be a viable option) and personal loans (which I'm positive I won't be eligible for).

The idea of going back, not just on my decision to stay, but also on my word about not selling to a developer, has me in a full-blown panic by the time Nat appears a few hours later. Instead of comforting me or insisting it will be okay, or worse, arguing with me about wanting to keep this barn in the first place, she just says "well, shit," and wraps me in the hug I've needed all day.

We take a couple shots of whiskey, courtesy of the giant bottle she carried in with her overnight bag. It was supposed to be a celebratory bottle; I bought it myself when she got a callback a few months ago that I was sure would turn into a role, but I guess this is as good a time as any. I have a good cry, get more than a little buzzed, and explain how bleak things look after a full day of research.

"I have to tell Shani," I say, when I finish sniffling out the story. "She's going to think I'm just another person who leaves."

"This isn't the same thing," Nat insists. "This isn't your fault, none of it. You didn't do this. As much as I'm not *at all* behind the idea of you staying, it was your decision to make. Your hand is being forced now, and that sucks. Shani's going to understand. And if she doesn't then it's really none of her business anyway. Maybe this is for the best."

"Don't say that," I cry. "I have to find a way to make this work."

"Why?"

"Because this is my home!"

"Molly," she says, but a knock on the kitchen door ends the conversation.

Shani walks in right after, not bothering to wait for an invitation. We're long past that. She looks between me and Nat a few times, as if she's trying to get her bearings. "Am I interrupting?" Her eyes flick to the whiskey bottle on the table between us.

"No," I say at the same time Nat says, "Yes."

Shani locks her eyes on mine. "Molly, would you like me to stay or go?"

And the thing is, I know she'd listen either way. Shani's easy like that. She doesn't push. She gives me as much space and time as I need, just like I try to do for her.

There's nothing I want more than for her to be here right now—even though this conversation is going to suck.

"Stay, please," I say, frowning at the way her shoulders drop in relief.

Somehow that makes this all worse.

"What's everybody up to?" she asks, taking a seat at the table. "Besides the whiskey, I mean?"

Nat kicks my shin under the table. I don't know if she's telling me to go for it or telling me not to, but I don't care anymore.

"Trying to save this place," I say, my buzz making my words looser than I mean them to be. More flippant sounding. The way Shani's face falls, concern etching lines in her perfect features, makes me flush hot with shame.

"What do you mean?" she asks quietly. Nat shifts in her seat, but Shani's stare doesn't waver from my eyes.

"Basically, we're fucked." I look away. "I bumped into Ashley when I went to get us coffee this morning. She found all these liens on the property that have to be paid off imminently or shit will start hitting the fan. Did you know about any of these debts?"

"No. Your aunt was very proud. If I knew she was having trouble, I would have helped, or at least tried to. We'll call Michael. He can fix this. He always does," she says, standing up to pull her phone out of her impossibly tight jeans. In another timeline, I would be admiring that. In this one, I just start crying again.

"Michael knows. Michael is the one who set them up to be paid off by the sale of the house," I sniff, pouring myself another shot. "He assumed since I was selling the place, we didn't really need to get into the nitty-gritty of the liens and what it means to keep probate open. I guess I didn't really look at what I was signing. Oops," I hiccup. "So now I need to sell or come up with tons of money."

Shani sits back down, her eyes worried. "You're very drunk."

"Yes." I smile.

She runs her hand over her face and shakes her head. "You've known all day? Why didn't you tell me? I was right outside!"

I realize immediately how colossally I've screwed this up. The hurt that stains her eyes is there because I put it there. I've made this situation even worse, which I didn't think was possible. This was about our home and our life, and I let it linger the entire day without telling her.

Not only that, but I told Nat first. *Fuck.*

"Shani," I say, but she just sighs and shakes her head.

"I should go," she says, heading back to the door. "I'll let you two finish up here."

"Don't," I say, grabbing her arm a little harder than I mean to, but she shakes me off.

"We'll talk when you sober up. Okay?"

"I'm not that drunk," I insist, even though we both know I'm lying. "And look," I spin my laptop toward her. "I've been trying to find a way out of this," I slur. "It's just so much money."

"We'll figure it out *later*," she says again, irritated.

"I'm not leaving you," I say, and her face softens.

"I know." She leans down and kisses my temple. "But we'll talk about that tomorrow. It was good seeing you, Nat."

"Good seeing you too," Nat says, her arms crossed. "Bye!" I don't know why she's acting mad at Shani, but I hate it.

"What is your problem?" I shout at her, and my tone of voice makes Shani hang back a little. She doesn't full-on rejoin the conversation, but she doesn't leave either. She just stays by the door, watching. There, if I need her.

"Nothing," Nat says.

"It's not nothing," I say. "Why are you being rude to Shani right now? She didn't do anything."

"I don't like that she's making you feel bad for not running to tell her about the situation with the house."

Behind her, Shani scoffs.

"She lives here!" I remind Nat.

"As your tenant," Nat snaps, turning around to face Shani. "This isn't your problem! She doesn't owe you anything and I'm not going to sit here and watch you guilt-trip her in real time with your little 'I should go' wounded puppy act! It's—"

"That's not what she was doing! She doesn't like to be around people who are drinking. That's all! It's . . . I made it worse."

"It's okay," Shani says, crossing the room back to me. "I'm sorry if saying I was going to leave upset you."

I take her hand. "It didn't! I get it."

Nat lets out a giant dramatic sigh that sounds more like a groan. "She has you so brainwashed, Molly. God, since you two started fucking, it's like I don't even know you! You're so swept up in this fantasy where you fall for a goddamn farrier," she says. "A farrier! This isn't who you are! I thought you'd realize that when I took you to dinner, but—"

"What the hell is wrong with being a farrier?" Shani asks, her voice going hard. "Sorry we can't all pour coffee while pretending we're gonna get an Oscar for being an extra in a diarrhea commercial."

And oh, shit, I can't believe Shani just said that.

"It's a fucking stepping stone!"

"Is it though?" Shani asks, and I wince. "From what Molly says, you two both spent a lot of time dreaming and no time making it a reality. At least I'm out here making an honest living. Now that Molly is too, I think you're jealous."

I should be mad that they're talking about me like I'm not here, except that what Shani just said is stuck in my head.

Making an honest living.

"Wait, wait, wait," I say, putting my hands between the two of them to get their attention. "I think I just figured it out."

"That your best friend is a colossal asshole?" Shani asks.

"That your tenant is a piece of shit?" Nat snaps right back.

"No, the house thing," I mumble, grabbing my laptop. "I've got it. You have the steady job, Shani. I have a little bit of cash and, based on what I read today, my credit score's not like, strictly unloanable if I had a cosigner, and I think if I defer my student loans even longer, they might not count them."

"What are you talking about?" Nat asks, clearly frustrated.

"Shani, we could both be on the loan," I say, ignoring Nat. "Split the property rights fifty-fifty and share it. Pay off the debts and turn it all around. You know how to run this place;

you grew up here! Lita has that trainer lead that will give us a little breathing room. We can make this work."

Shani looks at me with big wide eyes, a half smile crooking up on the left side of her face. "You'd want to do that with me?"

"Yeah, I think we—"

Another one of Nat's very loud, very pissed-off groans, cuts me off and we both turn to look at her. "Molly," she says. "Please listen to yourself. You're going to throw away half your interest in this property for some woman you practically just met? Think! This! Through! If you sell to the developer alone, you're in a much better position! I know there are debts, but I think Michael is really underestimating what you're going to get for this place. Please, think clearly for *once* in your life."

"This is what I want, Nat. This is where I want to be." I squeeze Shani's hand. "I love her."

And okay, maybe that's the whiskey pulling those three little words out of my mouth long before I planned to, and maybe Shani looks just as surprised as I am, but it's fine. It's fine!

Is it though?

"You love me?" she asks.

"I'm trying to buy you this barn, aren't I?" It's meant to be a joke, but Shani looks worried, glancing at Nat and then back at me.

"I don't want you to buy this place because of me," she says, looking increasingly concerned. "I want you to stay because you want to be here."

"I do," I say, feeling like there's a miscommunication somewhere—I just can't put my finger on it with my muddy, whiskey brain. "I love Otis and Eddie . . ." I trail off weakly, feeling so tired and so, so, buzzed.

"Craft beers," Nat yells, doing another shot herself. "I thought you didn't want to be her IPA, Shani."

"You told her about that?" Shani asks, looking upset.

"It was a great analogy." I shrug.

"She tells me everything, or at least she used to," Nat says. "And *you* are *definitely* her craft beer. Are you really going to let her do this to her life?"

"Oh my god, you're not craft beer, Shani," I laugh, because the whiskey has me feeling lighter and gigglier than I should right now.

"You said you cared about her," Nat says, glaring at Shani. "She's gonna throw away her life for you. I told you this would happen."

"What do you mean you told her?" I ask, looking between them. Shani looks away but I lean to stay in her line of vision. "What does she mean she told you?"

"Nothing," Shani says, looking guilty.

"I stopped by her place before I left that weekend you ditched me at a bar," Nat sneers. "I told her how you rush into everything, and I always have to clean up the mess. She said—"

"What the hell, Nat!" I shout.

Shani grabs my hand and tries to comfort me. "It's okay. It's . . . It didn't change anything, Molly. I wanted to take things slow and be sure anyway."

I drop back in my seat. "*That's* why we slowed things to a crawl?"

"Not just that," Shani says, but she doesn't meet my eyes.

"I *am* sure," I plead. "I thought you were too."

"Molly, I can't have you cosigning on this place because of how you feel about *me*."

"I'm not," I say, annoyed. "Will you two stop acting like I'm some irresponsible child! I'm a grown woman. I'm capable of—"

"You just said you were buying me a barn. You just said it," Shani cries, running her fingers through her hair. "You made it sound like it was proof that you loved me. I don't . . . that's not how this is supposed to be. I want you to stay because you love it here, not because you have a crush on me."

"A crush," I say, gutted. "I just told you I loved you and you call it a crush?"

"She's not wrong," Nat unhelpfully supplies, preening that Shani is finally on her side.

"That's not what I meant. I just . . . I need a minute. We'll talk privately, okay," she says, shooting Nat a look, and then crouching down to meet my eyes. "When you're sober. I need to think, and you do too."

"Shani," I say, because why does it feel like I'm losing her right now, losing her and my home, all at once. "Shani, wait."

I get up to follow her outside. I make it as far as the porch before she turns and stops me. "Molly, please just stay here tonight."

"Are you mad at me?"

"I'm not mad at you. I'm not," she says, coming back and wrapping me up tight in her arms. "But you kind of just put everything in a blender. Last night you were staying, then tonight you say you legally can't, and now suddenly you want to split it fifty-fifty? This is a huge commitment, Moll, and you're all over the place with it. I think you should sleep on this; see how you feel in the morning when you're not drunk."

"You don't think what we have is real, do you?"

"I want it to be real," she says, leaning back, her eyes a little glassy in the yellow glow of the porch light. "I really, really want it to be real."

"That's not an answer," I say, feeling the panic setting in, fueled by a blood alcohol content that passed "reasonable" long before Shani even got here. "Answer my question, Shani. You don't believe that I love you. You don't believe in us. Do you?"

"*We* are not the point." She chews on her cheek, looking at me for way too long. "Molly, let's just take a night, sleep on it."

"You know what?" I say, full-on sobbing now, more out of frustration than sadness. I feel out of control, like my body is made of bees, all of them ready to sting. "If you need a night before you can answer that, maybe you should just take all of them. If you don't already know if you want to do this with me, let's just not do it at all."

"Molly, you don't mean that."

"No," I say. "I probably don't, but what the fuck am I supposed to do?"

"We'll talk tomorrow," she says, pleading now. "I promise, we—"

"Maybe we shouldn't." I huff out a breath, trying desperately to pull my head together.

"What do you want?" she asks quietly, her voice coming out like a plea. "What do you *really* want! Because one second, it's Immaculate Events and the next it's this place and—"

"You, I thought. This place, I thought," I say, wiping at my eyes. "But Nat is so sure this is a mistake, and it sounds like you're starting to think so too. What am I supposed to do with that? If my two most important people don't have any fucking faith in me then—"

"Molly."

"Just go, Shani. Maybe I *am* the one who needs some time to think."

She doesn't say anything after that. Just nods once and then slowly turns to make the lonely trek back across the pasture.

Chapter Twenty-Nine

L ast night was unnecessary," I say, stomping into the kitchen to take some ibuprofen.

"Do you even remember it?"

"Enough. I remember being very pissed at you, Nat, and I remember you being obnoxious to Shani."

I rub my temples and swallow down the pills, chasing them with a glass of water. I have a raging headache. The only reason I came out in the first place was because I smelled coffee.

Discovering now that Nat apparently both made a pot and finished it off herself is not helping my mood. I open the cabinet only to find my coffee bag equally as empty as the pot. I sigh and snag the plastic tub of Folgers Choice that has been living in this cabinet since long before I ever got here.

Nat leans against the counter, still sipping what is no doubt the last of the *good* coffee, and studies me. "You basically proposed marriage to that woman. No, worse than marriage, you proposed a business partnership. May I remind you that you barely know her?"

"You know, it's not really your problem," I snap, pulling the filters out of the cupboard and getting ready to make a fresh pot.

Well, as fresh as probably-multiple-years-old coffee grounds can be.

I glance at the clock to see if I have time to make some apology muffins and get them delivered to Shani before she heads off to work, but it seems unlikely. I scoop some extra coffee into the filter. Stale apology coffee it is, then. Nat's right, I don't remember everything I said to Shani last night, but I know I didn't pull my punches. I was hurt, and drunk, and lovesick: the worst possible combination.

I grab my phone to see if Shani has texted me her usual good morning, but she hasn't. *That* worries me.

It takes me a second to realize that Nat hasn't responded. I look up, startled to realize that she's not even in the room. Instead, she's by the air mattress shoving her blanket and pajamas in a duffle bag. Great, now everyone's pissed at me, I guess.

"Nat, I'm sorry I snapped at you, okay? I just wish you could be supportive of me, of this!" I say, sweeping my hand around the room.

"You don't need my support, Molly. It's not my problem, right? I'm just the person who puts their life on hold to pick up the pieces for you every five seconds." She shakes her head. "But what do I know? It's fine."

"No, it's not. I don't want us to fight over this anymore," I say, trying not to get frustrated. "I know you're worried but give me the chance to prove that I can do this. Just have a little faith in me, please. This is different. I . . . I'm so happy here. In a way that I haven't been anywhere except maybe that stupid internship like five years ago."

She stops packing then and turns to look at me. I can tell my words have resonated with her, whether she wants them to or not. "Molly," she sighs.

"What?"

"I'm trying to be all tough love on you and you're making me feel horrible about it."

"Personally, I think you *are* being horrible about it, but I'm willing to admit that I might be a little biased right now. What are you so worried about?" I ask. "For real, maybe if we talk about it, you'll see that—"

"That you're making a huge mistake when there's a real opportunity right in front of you?" She crosses her arms with a shrug. "If you let this deal slip away, you might not get another chance like this. If I got a major audition, would you want me to give it up for KiKi?"

"No, but if you told me that you didn't think that was the life you wanted anymore, I wouldn't tell you it was a mistake to fall in love with a new opportunity."

"Molly . . ."

"This isn't like before. I swear to you, it's not. I truly love it here. And yeah, I don't know anything about horses, but I'm learning and it's been so nice to feel needed. I'm actually contributing here! I have a community! I know they just seem like barn weirdos to you, and they are." I smile. "But they're also becoming like a second family. I know it doesn't make any sense, and it feels fast. Yes, I'm going all cheesy romance movie on you, but the people in those movies are happy, Nat. And I want to be happy too!"

"They're happy because they're not real!"

"You and KiKi are happy and you're very real!"

"Except KiKi and I joined our lives; we didn't *give them up*. That's the issue here, Molly. You're giving your life up for hers."

"What! Life!?" I ask, raising my arms in frustration. "I wasn't exactly on a fast track to success. I was working in a coffee shop and living with my mom!"

"Oh, so you're too good to be a barista now?" she snorts. Oof, I struck a nerve without meaning to.

"No," I huff. "Either you're not listening or you're being deliberately obtuse. Yes, we both work there, but it isn't the same. You go on auditions all the time. You're working toward something! Plus KiKi moved in, and I'm sure you'll probably even get married someday! You have a *real life* there. It might not be perfect because you don't have that first Oscar yet—" she laughs and I smile—finally, a breakthrough. "But you're happy, right?"

"Yeah, and you could be too, if you sell this place!"

"I already *am* though," I say. "That's what I'm trying to tell you."

"What about your mother?"

I wince. "We're . . . kind of going through something right now, but I'll figure it out. I don't know, maybe she can just move here when she retires or something."

"Bethany? On a horse farm?" She shakes her head.

"Yeah, probably not. But I really think she'll understand once emotions calm down. It might even be better for her. I've been her stand-in partner since Dad left. Maybe this will encourage her to find her own happily ever after."

Nat bites her lip, shaking her head. "And what about me? What am I supposed to do without you?"

"What?" I ask, caught off guard by the emotion in her voice.

She wipes at her eyes. "What am I supposed to do without my best friend around?"

I hadn't realized that was a part of this. I've been so caught up in my own feelings. I close the distance between us and hug her like I mean it. "We survived my internship in Boston and aside from when we worked the same shift at Randy's, I've seen you *way* more here than I do at home. The hangs are higher quality too."

"Yeah, but that's because I thought this was temporary the whole time. You're talking about something permanent."

"Like you and KiKi are?" I ask, and she nods, finally getting it. Things change. Plans change. People change. Nowhere on those long FaceTimes we had when I was living in Boston did our plans include her having a live-in girlfriend.

"Yeah," she says, quietly.

"Look, I'm not that far away, and I'm not going to blow you off, I promise. I'll even let you film here if you ever book a western," I tease.

She laughs and wipes at her eyes, finally setting her duffle bag back down. "Are you sure about all this?"

"No," I laugh. "But I want to try anyway. What's the worst thing that happens? I fall on my face? I've been floundering since we graduated, and I happen to know my mother will *gladly* take me back in a pinch."

She narrows her eyes and nods. "You swear you'll let me film a movie here someday?"

"Naturally," I laugh. "And when the time comes, you and KiKi can have an authentic barn wedding right in the . . ." I trail off, because *oh my god, the answer has been right in front of me this whole time.*

"Molly?"

"What?"

"In the . . . what?" she teases.

"Nat," I say, my eyes going wide. "Nat!"

"Yeah? You're freaking me out!"

"This could be an event space!" I practically shriek. "I *could* still do wedding planning, except instead of being a general planner, it would be just for this specific location." I spin around. "I could fix up this house and make it a rental space for the night before the nuptials, and then move into Shani's or get an apartment, I don't know, I'll figure that out later. I could combine everything though! Maybe I could even get a small business loan to cover the liens!"

"That's actually a really good idea," Nat admits.

"Yeah, and Lita was just complaining about how there's not many spaces left for local horse shows. I could host shows when I didn't have weddings, and maybe even turn the house into a bed-and-breakfast or something. I'd still be using my event planning skills for all of it. This could be really good! Like really fucking good!"

"It could be amazing. This is the first time you've sounded like a logical businesswoman and not just a lovesick fool," she laughs. "Even I could get on board for this one."

"I can't believe I didn't think of this before!" I say, excitement and hope rushing through me. "I have to go. I have to tell Shani!

Well, first I have to apologize for what I said last night, but *then* I have to tell her. This could be perfect!"

"Wait, Molly—"

But I don't. I can't. Instead, I grab the second cup of coffee and race across the pasture toward Shani's house, feeling lighter than I have in forever. I'm practically jogging, my hands being scalded by coffee with every step. The cups will be more than half-empty by the time I get there, but I don't care.

I have a plan to fix everything now. It might take some time to work out the details, but it wouldn't be like co-buying a house together, it would be an investment in the business. A *real* business, with serious potential. It could work, and it's completely separate from how I feel about her, so she can't even use that as an excuse to worry.

It must have rained hard last night after I passed out—all the dirt turned to slippery mud—but I don't care. I'm giddy as I step out of the pasture, wet shoes, and a stupid grin on my face— which falls immediately as I realize her truck is gone.

Shit. Did she leave early for work?

Maybe I should call her, see if she can turn around if she didn't get very far, but then it registers. My sneakers have cut sloppy paths in the mud, but there's no fresh tire tracks here. Her parking spot is just as smooth as any other part of the driveway. She didn't leave recently; she's been gone a long time.

I peek in her windows, but everything looks the same; it's not like she packed up in the middle of the night or anything.

It's okay. It's fine. She probably just . . . left . . . for the night? Where though?

I reach for my phone to call her, but realize I left it back at the house. Without wasting any more time, I run back across the pasture, hoping somehow her truck will magically be parked at my barn. It's possible. She came straight from work yesterday, and she did leave my house on foot last night. She might even be asleep in her house right now. I should have knocked.

But the truck isn't there. Of course it isn't.

I race inside the barn, hoping against hope I'm wrong about what I think I'll find, but knowing I won't be. I see it as soon as I step inside, but I walk all the way down the aisle anyway, setting down the coffee cups so I can rest a hand on Otis—wishing he could make this all better, but knowing he can't. Because the stall beside him is empty.

Somehow in the night, while I was sleeping off all that anger and hurt and whiskey, Shani took her horse and left again.

She's coming back. She has to come back. She did last time, I tell myself. *Her stuff is still here too.* But that doesn't mean anything. For all I know, Tyler and Lochlin could show up later with a moving truck.

I take a shaky breath and then wrap my arms around Otis as I whimper into his mane. He leans his old head against mine, hugging me as best he can, as I cry over the empty stall where my future used to be.

Chapter Thirty

*N*at finds me in the barn a little while later and presses a crumpled envelope into my hand. My name is written on it in Shani's familiar handwriting.

"That's what I was trying to tell you when you were rushing out," Nat says, wrapping her arm around me. "Shani came by while you were asleep. She asked me to give you this."

"Why didn't you tell me as soon as I got up?"

Nat frowns. "I don't know. We jumped right into fighting and then you had your idea. There wasn't exactly time to get into it."

We're walking back to the house now, her arm still around me as I clutch the envelope like a lifeline. Maybe there's a note inside that will explain everything, make it all better somehow.

"I need to go lay down for a little while," I say, my head pounding from tears and the hangover and this roller coaster of a morning.

Nat nods, and if she's surprised when I go upstairs and lock myself inside Shani's old room, curling up under her blankets before sliding the envelope open, she doesn't say anything. I take a deep breath, hoping against hope for a note—an explanation— but it's empty except for her key.

I tell myself we've been here before, and I jumped to conclusions that time too. But this feels different, more final somehow. Vague memories of telling her to go, and then trying to take it back flash through my mind, and I roll over, hugging the envelope to my chest, and wish for sleep to come.

* * *

"So what are you going to do?"

Nat has to go home today, no way around it. She works the afternoon shift. I can tell she's nervous about leaving. She doesn't need to be.

I've been staring at Shani's key since I crawled downstairs at four a.m., sixteen hours after I went to bed. Not that I slept. I spent most of the night poring over everything I could remember about my fight with Shani in my head. I debated calling her a thousand times but decided not to. Calling her feels pathetic in a way I haven't in a long time, like I'm begging her to love me back.

I want to believe that what we had was real; that she's running and hurting just as hard as I am. But there's always a chance she's not or that I scared her off. I assume she went off with Lochlin, wherever he is, but there's no way to know. I don't have his number, and even if I did try to check up on her through him, I doubt he'd tell me anything.

During the dark hours before sunrise, while Nat slept on the air mattress and I paced the floor in the kitchen, I rapid-cycled through most of the stages of grief. Anger was a big one, alternating between "screw her, I'm going to sell to a developer just to watch it burn" to "maybe if I keep this place she'll come back" to "I deserve this chance at making my dreams come true on my own terms."

Somewhere around dawn, I reach acceptance.

Shani left. She took her horse and left her key. She didn't believe in us, and she left. It's as simple as that. She would have stayed if she wanted to. We could have talked it out the next morning if she wanted to. She would have said *I love you* back if she wanted to.

She could have done anything to show me we mattered, that I mattered, besides grabbing her horse and running away in the middle of the night. She wasn't my craft beer, but it looks like maybe I was hers. As much as I want to spend another twenty-four hours or so dying in bed, I can't. I have to decide what comes next, what it means for me, and what work needs to be done either way.

"I'm still going to keep this place," I say. "I think the wedding venue and event planning idea I have is a good one. I want to see it through, if I can." I wait for Nat to tell me what a mistake I'm making or how I need to get on with it; to take the money and run. But instead, she wraps me in a big hug—a proud and unexpected smile on her face.

"I'm really impressed by you, right now," she says, squeezing me tightly. "You're going to make this place awesome. I know it."

"Yeah?"

She leans back to look at me. "Yeah. And I'm sorry for being so dramatic about things this weekend. I'm happy for you. I'm excited for you."

"Thanks. It's going to be a lot of work, but if there's any way to figure it out, I'm determined to." I don't bother pointing out that Nat wasn't saying *any* of this kind of stuff while Shani was still here. It doesn't matter anymore anyway.

That's the kind of clarity you get after twelve hours of crying and four cups of coffee. If Shani wanted to be here, she would be here. Nat couldn't have scared her off if Shani wasn't already prone to running.

"You're being weirdly logical and calm about this. I love it."

I sigh. "I don't have a choice. If I want a shot at saving this place, I can't fall apart right now. I owe it to everyone still here to make this happen, and to do it right. With Shani gone, things just got a hundred times harder."

"I know, but you've got this," Nat says, and then, with one final hug, heads out the door.

* * *

THE FIRST THING I do is call Michael and notify him of my renewed intent to keep the place. I explain that I understand the deal and ask him if he can buy me a little more time before I have to accept the developer's offer. He's hesitant about it, until I explain my plan for the place, and how I have an idea to fulfill Christina's apparent dream for me to kick off my business *with* the ability to keep the place. He's excited then, but still realistic. He reiterates it can only happen if—big if—I can figure out my financing pronto. He says he *might* be able to buy me another thirty days, but that would be it. I tell him his grandkids can have free trail rides for life once the place is up and running, and he promises to hold me to it.

Next, I call Ashley and ask her if she has any leads on financing, specifically on the business side. I know it's a long shot given that I'm not employed right now, but my credit is okay. Plus, this place was in the black for a while before everyone took off and Christina had to spend all her feed money on medical bills. Ashley says she'll get right on it, and while she doesn't exactly sound hopeful, she sounds less down than she did before. She says that's the kind of business the town is trying to attract here, and there might even be some grants I can apply for.

Maybe that means that other people in town will be happy too, and willing to help me get this off the ground.

I spend the next few days looking over the books in the office, only coming out to turn out horses or give Otis his medicine. Otis is annoyed with me—he's getting much less attention without Shani around, and I'm sure he misses his buddy Gideon, but we manage and eventually start to fall into a new routine. When you're a horse as old as Otis, with the history he has, I guess you get used to people coming and going.

Shani doesn't call, and I don't call her. No one has showed up to take her things, and I do my best to pretend her house doesn't even exist right now. Still, her shiny key glares at me from my kitchen counter, until I throw it in the junk drawer and vow to never look at it again.

I double down on the books, calculating down as close to the dollar as I can the profit and loss and how to get us seriously and significantly into the black. I'm frustrated that I spent all my time here scraping paint instead of working on the business. I didn't realize what I had before, and now I'm playing catch-up just under the wire.

At least it doesn't leave me much time to cry over Shani.

When I finally get my numbers sorted a few days later, I approach Lita. She puts me in touch with her trainer friend, Macy.

Macy and I hit it off right away. Over coffee that same week, I explain my situation and she explains hers. By the time the coffee shop in town closes, she's made a decent deposit—refundable if I can't pull this off, of course—and signed a contract whereby, pending successful removal of the liens on the property, she's committing to moving her training space to my facility, as well as boarding five horses.

That should bump us up enough to look profitable to banks, I hope. I'd have to work as the barn manager myself and barely take a salary, but I can make it work. I'll be living off ramen with the heat set at fifty-eight all winter, pouring every spare dollar into fixing up the place enough to launch the real event side of things, but it'll be worth it.

A few days later, Aiyana spills the beans that this trainer I just brought on is actually Lita's girlfriend—the same one she ditched out on a date with after Lochlin was hurt. Lita laughs and claims the only reason she kept it a secret was because Macy didn't want to be a nepotism hire, but I suspect the truth is that she didn't want me to feel obligated if we didn't hit it off.

The whole barn crew insists on helping when they get word of what I'm trying to do, despite my inability to pay them and my insistence that they *really* don't have to. I wake up one morning to find that Lita and JJ have organized a team for a day of fixing up the paddocks and putting a fresh coat of paint on things. It's more lipstick on a pig, but it will do for now.

Aiyana even finds two friends willing to sign on as boarders, once everything is settled. I get all the contracts together and bring it to the loan officer that Ashley set me up with, but it's still looking a little dicey. She submits everything and we cross our fingers.

Twenty days until deadline and the rejections start pouring in. Even the ones that approved us initially are canceling during underwriting because of my student loan debt, or because I didn't plan enough of my own salary into my numbers, and they're too worried I'm going to be pulling money out of the business that I shouldn't be. No matter how much I try to convince them otherwise, they say the numbers don't lie.

The developers send a second, better offer, through Michael this time. This pisses Ashley off, and she puts me in touch with someone who will help me find a private investor willing to give me a short-term loan for a small fee. We just need a little luck.

I'm hunched over my laptop in the office, staring at the accounts on a cold afternoon, and trying to figure out how to appeal the town's ruling that I can't subdivide the land and sell off a couple acres for quick cash. (Spoiler alert: that's actually a months-long process that would have probably had to have been started before Christina died if I wanted a prayer of doing it before I hit deadline.) I don't even realize Lita and Aiyana have walked in until they're right in front of me.

"We have a proposition for you," Lita says, dropping onto the couch across from me.

"What?"

"We found a private investor, but you might not like it," Aiyana says.

"Why wouldn't I like it?"

Both women look at each other. "Because it's Lochlin," Aiyana says, wincing.

"He's got the money. I know he would give it to you for this." Lita agrees.

"No way," I say, going back to glaring at the angry Excel sheet in front of me.

"He's not Shani," Aiyana says. "You let him stay here rent free to recover, and he's wanted to repay you somehow. He's mentioned it to me like twenty times."

"You've told him about this?" I sigh. The last thing I want is for Shani to hear how badly I'm messing things up without her. "Can you please not broadcast my problems to that family?"

"I didn't call him specifically to tell him, if that's what you're asking, but he texted me and I mentioned it," Aiyana says. "I can't cut them out just because—"

"Don't finish that sentence please. So, what, you told him and *his sister*," I say because I can't bear to say her name, "all about my little sob story and now he wants to come save poor pathetic Molly? No thanks."

Lita crosses her arms. "Your stubbornness is going to get this place shut down."

I lean back in my chair, frustrated. "Really, you think he's just going to hand me the money? No strings?"

"No, but he'll give you a loan with good terms and let you pay him back once you're on your feet, I bet. He invests in all kinds of places like this. Remember that rodeo we took you to?" Aiyana asks. "How do you think his friend got that off the ground? With a loan from Lochlin."

"Why didn't he offer this before? Shit, why didn't he just help Shani buy the place outright from me in the beginning then?"

"If you think Shani would *ever* accept his rodeo money, you don't know her as well as you think you do."

"I don't know her at all, clearly," I say, getting up to look out the dingy window.

"Look, I'm not sure what happened between you two, but whatever it was, I know that Shani cares about you a great deal and—"

"That's right, you don't know," I say, turning back around to cut Lita off. "And I don't want Lochlin's money or his pity. I'll figure it out."

Lita shakes her head, muttering something that sounds suspiciously like, "You're just as stubborn as she is," before going to tack up her horse. Aiyana stays a beat longer, probably hoping I might still change my mind. She puts a slip of paper on my desk—Lochlin's phone number—but I don't pick it up.

I stare at my laptop until she finally gives up and goes.

* * *

THERE ARE SEVENTEEN days left until the deadline, and Michael has proceeded to start drawing up the contract with the developer. "Just in case," he says, but I can see the resignation in his eyes. Ashley and everyone she's put me in touch with reluctantly admit one by one that they've exhausted every lead they could find, and I still don't have a drop of financing.

I sit in my kitchen, alone with cup after cup of old Folgers Choice, and wallow. I think about Lita saying my stubbornness would shut this place down. I think about how incredible it would feel to combine all my event planning dreams with my love of this place. I think about how all the banks laughed me out of their lobbies. I think about how much easier it would be to sell this place and move on.

And then, eventually, I pick up the phone and call Lochlin.

* * *

LOCHLIN IS SURPRISED to hear from me. I guess Aiyana told him it was a no-go already, but he happens to be only a couple hours away, back at his friend's ranch for another event, and agrees to meet me the next afternoon to discuss a possible business agreement.

I try not to think about how that means Shani is probably also close by. I don't know where else she could have gone if not the circuit. I suggest we meet somewhere in the middle, playing it off like it's for convenience, but really it's just so I don't have to risk running into Shani. He agrees readily, and offers to come all the way here, which makes me think this isn't just a setup . . . and also that he *definitely* is taking pity on me.

At least someone is. I take him up on his offer; at least it saves me the gas money and heartache of looking at my dwindling bank account.

* * *

"MOLLY!" LOCHLIN SAYS, wrapping me in a too-tight hug before we take our seats. He orders a caramel frappe, laughing when I make a face.

"Cowboys like sweet things too." He winks—actually winks. Same old Lochlin.

"You look great," I say, noticing his cast is off and he's walking with ease.

"I feel great." He fiddles with his coffee. "Look, there's no delicate way to ask this, and I'm on the slate tonight to ride, so I don't have a ton of time. I'll just come out with it. How much do you need and how fast do you need me to get it?"

There's something about his tone that rubs me the wrong way. This feels less like business and more like a handout, and I bristle proudly even though I shouldn't. For not the first time, I wonder if Shani has maybe put him up to this. I bring her guilt muffins, she brings me a guilt investor. *Thanks, I hate it.*

"I'm not looking for charity, or a handout, Lochlin," I say. "I'm looking for an investor."

"Right, well Shani doesn't—"

I groan. "I knew she was behind this. Forget it. I'm not doing this. I don't need Shani sending her brother to give me a guilt-loan or whatever this is, so she can sleep at night. If she wanted to help, then she shouldn't have left, and you can tell her I said that."

"Wait, wait, wait, what?" Lochlin rears his head back, scrunching up his face.

"Your sister, Shani? You can tell her I'm fine without her and I don't want to be with someone who'd rather run away than figure shit out. You can—"

"Run away? Where is she? She's not with you?"

That shuts me right up. "Um . . . She's with you, I thought. On the circuit? I just assumed. Where else would she go?"

"Shani's not with us. What are you talking about? What happened?"

"She left, she . . . haven't you talked to her? It's been a couple weeks."

"Yeah, I talked to her this morning and asked if she was coming to the coffee shop with you. She said she was tied up with work. She hasn't said a word to me about any of this. I thought things were good with you two!"

I stare at him dumbfounded. How does he not know? "She left. We got in a fight, and she took Gideon and dropped off her key without a word," I say, starting to panic. *What if something happened to her and no one knew because I never called?* "Wait, you talked to her today? She's okay, right? She . . ."

Lochlin sighs and shakes his head. "Fucking martyrs, man. I knew she would pull something like this. Yeah, I talked to her. She sounded fine. No, she's not with me, but I bet I know where she is. I'm gonna kill Tyler."

"Tyler?"

"He bought some land the next town over from here. He calls it our retirement place. It's a little shack on a ton of acreage. She's crashed there before, and if she told him not to tell me, he wouldn't." He huffs. "I'm gonna kill them both, but first, I'm gonna drink this coffee and you're gonna tell me what's going on. You're not going to be like my fucking sister and climb up on a crucifix you don't need to be on. Let me help with this, please. You helped me when I was in a bad way, and I'd like to return the favor. Does that sound okay with you?"

"I don't want your—"

"Charity, pity, whatever you're gonna say, this isn't that. Lucky for you, I'm an asshole. I'm not doing anything for you that's not mutually beneficial, got it? I'm gonna charge you enough interest to make my financial planners very happy, but I'm gonna trust you know what you're doing with it the way your bank must not. Now can we talk business? I have friends to beat up before I ride now, so I'd like to make this brief."

"Y . . . yes?" I say, confused.

Over the course of one caramel frappe and two giant chocolate chip cookies, Lochlin explains that he's always looking for new event spaces. He reiterates what Lita said about them being few and far between.

He says he's also looking for a training facility as he starts inching toward retirement—although quickly adds it's not imminent. He wants to teach people how to ride broncs and bulls as safely as possible. He'll need space to do it, and a place to board the animals he doesn't travel with. My place isn't set up for bull riding, not that I would let him do that anyway, but he says it's perfect for other western shows—barrel racing, roping, that kind of thing—and we can figure out the rest later.

I tell him bucking-anything is a firm no, unless he's rehabbing them for new homes, and he calls me a bleeding heart, but eventually agrees, saying he can set all that stuff up at Tyler's place, which is apparently close enough to mine that it won't matter.

I pretend it doesn't hurt to know that Shani has been practically around the corner this whole time.

As if he senses it, he distracts me by telling me that a couple of the other riders are looking to get into the organizer side of things. He shows me some figures on his phone of what his friend's place is bringing in hosting monthly rodeos in the summer and how much he's making off his original investment, to prove it's not charity. I'm actually impressed; I've never seen this side of Lochlin. He's a savvier businessman than I gave him credit for.

Eventually, he gives me two options. He can loan the money to me at a nasty 15 percent interest rate, or he's willing to use my space as his home base, personally hosting two small shows a year, and sign a multiyear contract to board his off-circuit animals—minus the working broncos—at my facility. The contract would include some funds for fixing it up to his specifications, in exchange for only an eight percent stake in the land.

And he's willing to pay off the liens immediately as a credit toward his rental fees, along with his down payment for the buy-in for the property.

It's clearly the better option; a 15 percent interest rate would kill my cash flow, which I need to get the events side up and running. There's just one catch. He wants to try before he buys.

"What does that mean?"

"It means I want to see how you host events before I commit. I want to make sure we can pull this off before I pony up this cash, because, no offense, I like you a lot, but I'm not in the habit of making bad business decisions, and I'm not about to start now."

"We only have two weeks before the deadline."

"Then you better get started."

"What do you even want me to do?"

"You're not set up for much yet, but I think you could pull off some barrels."

"Barrels? Seriously?"

He shakes his head. "Yeah, it would be much easier if my sister was around to help. Unfortunately, you fell in love with a total jackass." He snorts. "So here we are. I'm gonna go talk to her, see if you two can—"

"No." I set my coffee down. "Deal's off if you talk to her."

"I've been listening to you all day say you want this *not* because of her, but for you."

"And?"

"And my sister is an expert at barrels. *You* need an expert."

"No."

"Molly, come on." He studies my eyes and lets out a sigh, like he's finally accepting that I'm not backing down on this. "Fine, suit yourself. You have ten days. Pull it off, you get your contract. Don't and, well, we tried, right?" He holds out his hand and I stare at it before reluctantly shaking it.

What have I gotten myself into?

Chapter Thirty-One

Ten days is not much time to do anything, let alone pull off a barrel racing competition from scratch, but still, my new community rallies.

Nat and KiKi come up to help, and Lita and Macy, along with Aiyana and JJ and a bunch of their horse friends, excited about the possibility of not having to move their horses, but also of having a new local showing space.

I even called my mom to try to patch things up, but it's going to take time. Any fantasy I had of her showing up here to pitch in for a fresh start was dashed when she told me she "hopes I'm very happy at the barn" and then immediately got off the phone. It's . . . fine. I know we'll get there in the end, it's just going to take a little effort. Right or wrong, her hurts about this place, about my aunt, run deep.

Besides, the only thing I can do is try to shake it off for the moment. There's too much to get done.

Lochlin gave us a list of things to sort out: mostly stuff that needed to be fixed up around the facility to make it safer, and a list of equipment and other things we'll need. I spend every night watching YouTube videos of rodeos, specifically barrels—carefully avoiding Shani's old ones—to get a feel for things.

The event planner in me notices right away that Lochlin has left some things off his list. I wonder if it's a test at first, but he's forgotten things like porta-potties and refreshments, which, while they are going to be tricky to procure on this short notice, are nonetheless *extremely* important.

I have to admit, it feels good to be in the groove of event planning. Maybe I don't know what kind of barrels horses like to jog around or proper prep for temporary stalls, but I for sure know how to make my human guests comfortable and happy, and I can google everything else.

I put a rush order in for fresh flowers, since I can't afford silk yet; even though Lochlin says it isn't necessary, I disagree. I want the barns and main house to have a welcoming, joyful feel to them. This place isn't in the best shape, and I want to show potential vendors, renters, and attendees that we're really trying over here.

I manage to scrounge up a portable bathroom vendor who is willing to drop off four on short notice for a stupid price. I run the math; you want one for every fifty people for a four-hour event. I think that should be plenty.

Ah yes, crippling student loans just so I can accurately calculate how much people will have to pee on average. Look Ma, I made it!

Once the basics are set up, I start tackling vendors. The local coffee place in town doesn't have the staff to do events, so in desperation I call Randy. He's hours away, but I know he's done a bunch of festivals and coffee conferences. While he doesn't think it's wise to cart his coffee two hours just to have it sit for another four, he does give me some tips and offers to let me borrow his portable coffeemakers. I go back to the local place and negotiate a way for them to provide the actual coffee at a reasonable price, as long as they don't have to be the ones to serve it, and miraculously they agree. Nat offers to man the booth, and I'm so grateful I could cry.

Next, I reach out to the bakery and deli, and put in a mega order to sell on the side. They even cut me some wholesale prices because the owner knew Christina and liked her. I try and fail to get a couple food trucks to come in (not that I was expecting much on such short notice), but the pizza place in town agrees to keep me stocked with pizza throughout the day—largely, thanks to the fact that JJ's boyfriend works there. JJ is thrilled about the prospect of selling them with him, saying that his horse career robbed him of the crucial life experience of working in food service, but I think he's just excited to have his boyfriend hanging around all day.

I try to pay everyone for helping me—Lochlin did give me an advance to set this up—but they refuse, swearing they're volunteers. I cry for real then, and everyone gets uncomfortable until Lita gives me an awkward half hug. It's kind of perfect.

Every night I fall asleep worrying that I won't be able to pull this off, but every day I wake up and keep chipping away at it. It feels pretty great. This is mine, just for me. Win or lose or fall on my face, it's on me and *for* me.

And in those moments where it does creep in—that feeling that something, no, *someone*, should be here too—I desperately try to shove it away. Shani left *me*. I didn't want her to, and I can't change it anyway. I need to keep moving.

Lochlin checks in regularly to make sure I kept up my end of the bargain and to sign some initial contracts. He'll be at our event signing autographs, and hopefully announcing his partnership with me if all goes well. That alone should be enough to draw a crowd both locally and from the wider area. People love him, based on the sheer number of calls and emails I get once I start advertising the event as his pop-up barrel racing show.

I realize we're the buzz of the town when I head in to do final meetings with the coffee shop and bakery. People even stop me on the street to say how much they're looking forward to it. Every inch of me is smiling for the first time in what feels like ages.

So, of course, that's when Shani reappears like a knife to the heart.

She's standing outside the coffee shop after my meeting, like she's been waiting for me. I realize too late that maybe she was.

"I saw your car," she says sheepishly, leaning against her truck.

"Yeah? You've seen it lots of times, so what's the difference now?" I ask. I clutch my papers close to my chest and walk past her with my head held high. *She doesn't get to do this.* She doesn't get to reappear right before one of the biggest events in my life, acting all cute and nonchalant, like she didn't blow us all up right when we were getting good.

Her boots tap loudly on the concrete as she follows me, but I pretend I don't hear her. I toss my papers in the passenger door and then cross over to the driver's side to get in. I can't look at her. If I do, I'm not going to be able to keep up this façade of not caring.

"Molly," she says. And as much as I want to get in and drive away, to not give her the satisfaction of seeing how much she hurt me and how much I miss her, I can't.

This is Shani. Shani! As much as I lie to myself that I don't love her anymore, I do. I definitely do. And I hate that I'm not over it. I stop my escape, and stand back up, meeting her eyes from across the top of my car.

She fidgets like she didn't expect me to do that. "You're doing a horse show?" she asks, after a long stretch of silence.

"I specifically asked Lochlin not to discuss my business with you."

"He didn't. I mean I knew he was putting a show together, but I didn't realize it was yours until I saw the ads. That's amazing, Molly. That's really good. I'm proud of you."

"I didn't do it for you," I say.

"No, I know. I just . . ."

"What are you doing here, Shani?"

"I had a client that was worried about an abscess in her stallion's hoof. Asked me for an emergency appointment. I couldn't—"

"What are you really doing *here* though? Here, as in my car, my coffee shop, my town."

"They were mine first," she says, a small smile.

"Yeah, and they could have been both of ours except you took off instead."

"No, that's not—"

"Hi, Molly! Can't wait for the show!" Ashley waves, walking into the coffee shop with a client.

I wave back, smiling until she disappears and then glaring at Shani. "That's exactly what happened."

"Can we talk about this? Somewhere we won't get interrupted?"

"I don't think that's a good idea. I have a lot going on. The event's in two days and I—"

"After then? Do you think we could talk after?"

"I don't know, Shani," I say, shaking my head, my mind spinning a mile a minute at the idea that she's really standing here in front of me. "Maybe."

"Okay," she says, grinning at me, like I just said the best thing somehow.

"Why are you smiling like that?" I snap, getting back into my car.

"Because it's not a no."

* * *

I AM DETERMINED not to let Shani showing up derail anything. Even though my mind keeps slipping back to her little "It's not a no," I can't let myself get distracted. I manage to get through the rest of the day, buttoning up all the loose ends, and getting ready for tomorrow.

The day before any event tends to be a shitshow no matter how well you plan it, and I want to be rested. I *need* to be rested.

Of course, as soon as I get into bed—the bed Shani used to sleep on every night when she was taking care of Christina—my mind starts to wander. She didn't seem that sorry at all. She seemed sad, sure, but also cute and confident, like everything might work out somehow. Then she acted all proud of me even, which would seem so condescending, if it didn't feel so sincere.

I stare up at the ceiling and groan. I've taken to thinking of this as my room, permanently upgrading from the couch to make this place seem like home all over again. But now, after seeing her, I feel like it's back to being hers. Ours, if you squint.

I can't afford to squint.

I only make it until six A.M. before I grab my phone and pull up her number. She's up, I'm sure. But then I change my mind. I toss my phone under my bed for good measure and go pace in the kitchen until Lochlin shows up at nine A.M. for a walk-through.

He seems impressed, especially by the paddocks. I show him the sketches I did of the flowers and how the vendor area will look. He agrees they're nice, if a little girly. Tyler elbows him in the side for that, but Lochlin just shrugs and mumbles, "Well, they are."

Everything is snapping into place, and if all goes well, I'm really going to be able to pay off the liens this week, in plenty of time. The developer can fuck right off. Victory is so close I can taste it.

If only I could stop thinking of Shani.

I wait until Tyler goes off to make some phone calls and to help load in some of the horses and riders who are coming in early today. The contestants are staying overnight at a little hotel in town I worked out a bulk discount with, or in their trucks in the back of my property.

I find Lochlin alone by the main paddock. I know he and Tyler are spending the night in Shani's old house tonight, and I wonder if he knows she's been around. I wonder if she's staying there with them, now that she knows it's his show too.

"Shani came up to me in town yesterday," I say. The surprise on his face tells me he wasn't behind her visit.

"You two finally talk?" he asks cautiously, and while I'm tempted to tell him it's none of his business, he's been a friend to me, so I figure I at least owe him this.

"Not really, but I get the impression that she wants to."

"Do you want to?"

"Are you asking as my friend or her brother?"

"Can't I ask as both? I know she's been hurting since you—"

"She's the one who took off. Not me."

"That's definitely how it looks," he says staring off into the distance. "But I do wonder what her take is."

"What other take could there be? That's what happened," I say. "Why? Did she say—"

"I don't tell her any of your business, and I'm not gonna tell you hers, sorry," he says with a soft smile. "You don't have to talk to her, Molly, and you certainly don't have to forgive her, but just make sure that you're doing that because it's what you truly want and not because of hurt pride or bad feelings. Stubbornness isn't the same thing as being right."

"What's with people calling me stubborn lately?"

He gestures around us, to the porta-potties being delivered and the people bringing in their horses to prepare for tomorrow. "You say stubborn like it's a dirty word, but none of this would be happening if you weren't. Most people, if you tell them they're gonna lose this place or they can sell it to a developer, they roll over and take the money, but not you. Even when it seemed like it was game over you wouldn't listen. You're stubborn and you make things happen."

"That's . . . actually kind of sweet of you to say."

"Yeah, well, I can occasionally be sweet. Shocking, I know."

He laughs. "The point I'm trying to make is just make sure whatever *else* you set your mind to, you're doing it because you think it's the right call. Otherwise, you're just hurting yourself on principle and that's not the good kind of stubborn, it's just being foolish."

"Okay," I sigh, not ready to think too deeply about his words. "Thank you, seriously, but I think I just reached my limit for getting relationship advice from a guy who seems terrified of settling down with the man he clearly cares about."

"That might be a family affliction." He laughs and tips his hat. "On that note, I'll leave you to it. I've got registrations to check and horses to get settled. You've got my number if you need me for any of these other logistics, otherwise, I'll see you at show-time tomorrow."

"I'll see you," I say, smiling, and walk over to check on my vendors. Because I got this. I know I do. Just like I know staying here was the best decision I ever made.

Now if only this thing with Shani was half as clear.

Chapter Thirty-Two

It's busy.

It's busy from the second the sun comes up and I'm running around, setting up the coffee stand and managing the bakery deliveries all at once. It's a rush of adrenaline as I slide into event manager mode, easy as riding a bike.

There are a few hiccups and hang-ups, like when one of the ponies from the kids' show gets loose and runs away to steal a blueberry muffin off the bakery table, but other than that, it's been going pretty well.

Aiyana and Macy are directing people where to park on the large open grass beside the auxiliary barn, and while my grass is definitely ruined, at fifteen dollars per ticket and $150 per rider entry, I'll just throw some nice gravel down there after this and make it official Immaculate Events parking. Nat is behind the coffee stand tending to a long line of riders and attendees, and JJ is selling out the pizza as fast as his boyfriend can plate it.

Everything is running as smooth as can be, so I decide to sneak off to see how Otis is holding up with all this commotion. I turned him out earlier today with JJ's horse and while Marlowe has been trotting along the fence begging for scritches and treats, Otis has been sullenly hiding in the trees. I knew he wasn't going to like having so many people and strange horses around.

I head toward the trees with a sliced apple and a few of his special horse cookies stashed in my pocket, determined to cheer up my best boy.

I'm surprised to hear a muffled voice as I get to the clearing, and while it's not my proudest moment, I duck behind a tree and peek out until I can figure out what's going on. It only takes me a second to realize it's Shani—her face buried in Otis's neck. Her arms are wrapped around him like a lifeline as she murmurs into his scratchy mane. Otis sees me, but like the good boy he is, doesn't do anything more than flick his ears in my direction.

I should leave. I should turn around and head straight back to the barn. This isn't my business or my problem to solve. Instead, I stand there, mesmerized, watching her. I've missed her so much, and while part of me wants to storm up to her and tell her to get out—if I wasn't enough for her to stay before, then she doesn't get to come back now—I don't. I stand there transfixed, and yeah, maybe I'm wishing she were hugging me instead.

I can't help it; I creep closer, trying to make out what she's saying.

"... right thing to do. I thought she'd read the note and get it. Maybe I deserve it. You play stupid games, you win stupid prizes, right?"

Otis whinnies softly, like he agrees, and I would almost giggle at his timing, if it wasn't all so goddamn sad. Then I register what else she just said. *What note?* I got a key in an envelope and nothing else.

Shani's talking more quietly now, and I move even closer, trying to still hear. Of course, I'm so distracted trying to make out words, that I don't notice I'm about to step on a giant rock until I trip over it completely. I go flying, facedown into the mud, just a few feet away from them.

Goddammit.

"Molly?" Shani asks, looking genuinely shocked.

I push myself up, wipe the mud off my face, and try to play it off like falling was all part of the plan. "Hi!" I say, giving her a little muddy wave.

"What are you doing out here?"

"Uh . . . gardening?" I pull out a couple weeds with a pained smile, just trying to lighten the mood, but it doesn't work. I sigh, lowering my head for a second before meeting her eyes. "I was coming to check on Otis."

She raises an eyebrow like she still doesn't believe me. "Seriously," I say, standing up and pulling out the slices of apple. He immediately ditches Shani to investigate my offering, and then noses against my hip for the cookies instead. I laugh and give him an ear rub. "Apple first," I say, trying to sound like a good mom.

Shani has a tight smile on her face.

"See? I told you," I say, as he nibbles on his apple. "I know he doesn't like crowds, so I put him out here with Marlowe this morning—who sucks as an emotional support horse by the way. I wanted to make sure that he was doing well and not stressing out or anything since it got busy."

Otis wipes some drool on my side, discarding half the apple to the mud and searching out the cookies. "Okay, okay," I say, "you win." I feed him a couple cookies and rub his nose just how he likes.

"You're really good with him," Shani says. "You're a lot more comfortable."

"Yeah, well, I had to get it together pretty quick after you left. He needs his routine and his attention, and so do all the other horses I'm responsible for. I couldn't just dip like you did . . . or, well, I guess I could have, but I didn't."

She looks down. "I deserve that."

"Yeah, and more. So, what are you doing here on my farm, petting my horse, Shani?" She winces at that, but to her credit she doesn't make any smart remarks or any effort to hide her emotions. It's plain to see how much she's hurting.

"I miss you," she says, and I frown.

"You're the one who left."

"Yeah, well, I didn't think you'd just move on like that!" she says. "I thought you'd come see me or at least call."

Frustration burns up my veins and makes my tongue thick with anger. "Was this some kind of test? Break my heart to make me prove how much I care about you? That's sick, Shani, that's . . . I thought you were better than that."

"That is *not* what I was doing! I just . . . you were talking about really big things. You said you loved—" She cuts herself off, squeezing her eyes shut for a moment. "You were drunk though, Molly."

"You don't get to—"

"No, I do," she says, wringing her hands as her eyes search mine. "Because my father used to say beautiful things at night too once he'd had a few drinks, but he *never* remembered them in the morning." She looks away. "I couldn't risk that with us. I couldn't keep listening. If you woke up with regrets . . ." Her voice cracks. "I couldn't be here. I had to go. I had to go until you could say them in the sunlight, until you had a clear head. I prayed you'd show up the next day and we'd—"

"I did show up, Shani! I ran to your house! But. You. Weren't. There. I'm done being with people who play games, or who take off when things get hard. I want someone who shows up for me. For us."

"I want that too, Molly! I don't screw around, okay? I get very attached when I fall, and I was very attached to you. I *am* very attached to you." She takes a shaky breath. "I just wanted to be sure that *you* were sure. I didn't want our first I love yous coming from alcohol or desperation." She runs tortured fingers through her hair. "A part of me wishes I stayed and fought for us, begged you to stay with me, but maybe this is better."

"How is this possibly better?"

Shani sniffs and rubs at her nose. "I need a level of reassurance that's a lot for people. I don't blame you for not buying in, for not coming to Tyler's. It's better that I know now where we stand." She gives me a sad smile. "Believe me though, no matter what happened between us, I'm so damn proud of you Molly." Her eyes tear up, and the urge to comfort her is so strong it almost doesn't register what she just said, but when she tries to push past me, I reach out my hand and place it gently against her chest.

"Wait, Shani," I say, and her eyes snap to mine. "I'm missing something here. None of this is making sense. What do you mean 'not coming to Tyler's'?" Otis jerks back nervously as I wave my hand around. "I didn't even know he had a place around here until Lochlin told me! And, I'm sorry, at what point in your whole leaving-in-the-middle-of-the-night thing was I supposed to understand that you wanted reassurance of my feelings? I wasn't the one who was unsure about anything. You abandoned us, not me."

"I didn't! I was waiting for you! I would've been back here in a heartbeat if you had asked. Is it so bad that I wanted to be invited instead of inherited?" She wipes at her eyes. "You didn't even call."

"You're not putting this on me. You slid a key into an envelope and took off to god knows where. I had to figure out how to hold myself together through that to keep this place going. I wasn't going to call you and beg. I told you I wanted to stay here, *with you*. That *was* your invitation, Shani, and I was *not* drunk the day that I said that."

Shani looks bewildered. "I didn't just slide you a key. I left you an embarrassingly honest letter explaining how much I loved you. Please don't minimize that . . . I know I'm not as good at expressing myself as you are, but it still happened. I sat on Tyler's porch every night for a week waiting for you, praying for you to turn down that driveway or pick up your phone. You chose not to."

I shake my head just as a commotion kicks up when the first rider takes off. The crowd's cheering across the pasture and I'm drowning, dying, trapped in this little oasis of confusion with

the woman I love. "What note?" My voice breaks. "What porch?
I don't know what you're talking about," I say, wiping my hands
on my jeans like I can wipe off how much this hurts.

Shani looks stricken, gutted in a way I've never seen. "You
didn't get my letter?" she breathes.

"No," I cry. "If it was so important why didn't you hand deliver
it, why didn't you—"

"I did hand deliver it!" she says, fiercely. "I gave it to Nat. She
said you had just fallen asleep and she wouldn't let me in. I asked
her to tell you I was taking Gideon to Tyler's."

"Why Tyler's?"

"I spent a lot of time riding in his woods toward the end with
Christina. It kind of became my hiding place—it's so peaceful
there," she says, taking a deep breath. "I wasn't hiding from you
though. I hoped in the morning, you'd come and we'd both ride
Gideon out. I'd show you how beautiful it was, and maybe you'd
say more of those things you were saying and I'd say them back,
and we . . ." She shakes her head. "This whole time, I thought you
changed your mind, and you thought I just left you?" She buries
her face in her hands. "I was so hurt and so mortified that you
read my note and didn't care. I thought staying away was the *right
thing*. I thought it was what you wanted."

"No," I say, falling a step back in my shock. "Why would I
want that?"

Shani hangs her head. "I was right down the road, waiting for
you."

I shake my head. "But you gave me back your key!"

"I *made* you a key. I didn't give it back . . . it was in the note,

Moll. I wanted us to be more official. I wanted you staying with me all the time. It was *in the note*."

"What the fuck," I say, taking another step back. "What the fuck?" My thoughts are swirling a million miles an hour. *Shani wanted me to move in with her; Shani didn't leave?*

"Molly, are you okay?" She looks concerned and starts to walk forward, but I hold my hand up, gesturing for her to stop.

"I need to get back," I say, my brain switching to autopilot as my emotions overwhelm me.

"Okay," she says quietly.

"I have to . . . to . . . to get changed," I stammer out, trying to process everything she just told me. "I have a horse show to run that decides, like, everything. I need to go. I don't . . . I can't." I meet her eyes once more and, before I can stop myself, I rush toward her, needing to feel her, needing to know she's really here. I bury myself against her, letting her hold me, my hot tears falling against her skin as my body swirls with relief and confusion. *She didn't leave.*

"It's all right. You're okay," she says, raising one of her hands to rub soothing circles into my neck. "I know you have to get back." She presses her forehead against mine, an almost kiss. "You got this, Molly."

Before I can say anything, the crowd cheers again, ripping us from this moment as we both turn in the direction of the noise. As much as I want to just stay with Shani and figure this all out, I know everyone is counting on me at the barn. Everyone. I owe it to them to pull this off, to give them the best version of myself, even though I feel like the entire universe just flipped upside down.

I nod, and give her one last tight squeeze, not sure what to say or what to think, but knowing that's a conversation for later. For now, I have to go.

But as I walk across the paddock, leaving her there whispering to Otis, there's one thing I can't stop thinking about:

She left me a letter. A letter that explained everything. *And she gave it to Nat.*

Chapter Thirty-Three

I find Lochlin watching the show once I'm back and changed. I'm still reeling from my talk with Shani, but I'm doing my best to tamp it down and focus on the task at hand. The show must go on, as they say. I can't afford to fall apart now. Literally.

"How's it going over here?" I ask, leaning against the rail beside him.

"Other than the pony escape earlier, smooth as butter," he says with a grin. "Tyler's keeping things in order in the barn, the judges are happy with the facility, the timer's running well for once. I agree, we're going to need to put gravel down in the parking area before next time, but otherwise it's going great."

"Next time?" I ask.

He holds out his hand. "I'm in if you are, partner."

I sag against the fence, emotions overtaking me. "I'm in," I say, shaking his hand like it's a lifeline. "That was cheesy, but I'm in."

Lochlin turns to watch Tyler leading a horse and rider out of the barn and toward the paddock in front of us, probably giving me a second to collect myself. The grin on his face spreads impossibly wider, and I nudge his boot with my foot and stand up a little straighter.

"You sure you don't want to make an honest man of him?" I ask, my emotions crossing wires and making me say things I probably shouldn't.

Lochlin looks down and shakes his head before meeting my eyes. "Am I really *that* obvious?"

"It's impossible to miss when you know what you're looking for," I say, thinking about the way Shani always used to look at me. The way she *still* looked at me today in the trees.

"And what's that?" he asks.

"Love."

Lochlin rolls his eyes. "Now who's the cheesy one?"

"I never said I wasn't runner-up," I say, and he laughs. "Full disclosure, I did ask your sister about you two once, and she semi-confirmed your endgame status."

"Meanwhile, I've been Mr. Confidentiality when it comes to you. Where is the loyalty? Where is the love?" he asks, clutching his heart dramatically.

"About Shani . . ."

"It's fine," he says, waving me off. "Well, it's not, you broke her heart, but I'm gonna try not to hold it against you. It's your life and I know she's not the easiest person to get along with. I didn't even stay with her that long and I wanted to kill her."

"The thing is, I had no idea I was the one who broke it until a few minutes ago."

His eyebrows pinch together, and he opens his mouth to say something, right as Tyler sends the next horses into the ring, racing around barrels at the speed of light and grabbing both of our attention.

"Did you know she was here?" I ask. In front of us, the horse twists like it's on tracks, and curves around for another lap.

"Here like in town? Yes, you mentioned it, remember?"

"Here like at the barn, right now."

He pinches his nose. "No, if I knew she was planning on showing up, I would have talked her out of it. I swear."

"She's in the pasture with Otis. It might be good for you to go check on her when you get a chance," I say, because if I can't be with her right now, maybe at least he can.

"Got it," he says, as the horse gallops toward us, full force. "You okay?"

"Not at all," I say as the rider makes her mare stop short right before hitting the fence, exactly as they do on YouTube. I'm in awe, my face somehow splitting into a smile. "I wish I could do that," I say quietly.

"You can," he says, tilting his head. "You got a lotta steps before you get there, but if that interests you, I wouldn't mind popping around when I'm in town to give you a lesson or two. You could be my inaugural student at our new training facility."

"I'd like that," I say, feeling like I'm gonna cry again, my emotions ping-ponging from one extreme to the next as I struggle to keep a grip on them.

"Molly," he says, watching my face. "You really kicked ass today. I'm excited to collaborate with you on this, no matter what goes down between you and my sister."

I hug him then, unable to resist. "Thank you," I say with a watery laugh. "Now, let's get back to work before I lose it."

* * *

I MAKE THE rounds as the crowd starts to thin out, the afternoon sun giving way to a dwindling autumn dusk much too early. I'm exhausted from spending the last few hours putting out fires, like when a rowdy group of teens tried to knock over the porta-potties and almost succeeded, or when the escapee pony made a second break from the little girl who was supposed to be holding him—at least this time he didn't get any blueberry muffins.

Then there was a woman who got thrown from her horse and needed a ride to the urgent care to check for a broken wrist. Not to mention the various horses who saw fit to nibble on my decorative flowers . . . luckily, I only chose horse-safe flowers, so technically that's less of a fire and more of a minor inconvenience.

Lochlin gets called up during the winner's ceremony to address the crowd, and I'm thrilled when he announces that this is going to be an annual event, along with several mini events he's planned for next spring and summer, *and* that this is going to be the home base for his event production company.

This is met with a bunch of cheers from the audience, and several local news reporters even stop by after the announcement to interview us both. It's wild. I think I see Shani here or there, but I could be imagining it. Wishful thinking and all that.

Once all the spectators are gone, leaving only a few vendors and the assorted rider or two still loading up their horses, I make my way over to where Nat is packing the travel coffee stuff to bring back to Randy tonight. She looks so cheerful, I almost don't want to say anything—it would be so nice to just linger here, in this good mood.

And it is a good mood. No matter what the truth is about Shani, I pulled off my first major event and it was a success. And Nat contributed to that. Tomorrow, Lochlin and I are going to get cashier's checks to pay off the remaining liens and sign contracts with Michael—who now is officially on retainer as my business lawyer. We really did it. We pulled it off.

But as much as I want to avoid any darkness to this excellent day, I have to know. I have to hear Nat's side before I can talk to Shani again. I can't be like my mother and Christina, lost among half-truths and misunderstandings. I need to drag it all out into the light, face what can be faced, while we're still all here to do it.

"Nat," I say, when she finishes hugging me.

"You crushed it today!" she says, smiling, but then she takes in the sight of my face. "Are you okay? Did something go wrong? Is Lochlin not—"

"No, he is. Everything's all set. It's been a great day."

"Yeah, it has!" She grins. "Guess what else?"

"What?"

"I booked that commercial! The diabetes one! Finally! I was getting scared out there."

"That's awesome," I say, trying to muster up a little enthusiasm.

She cocks an eyebrow. "Why do you look upset right now?"

"I saw Shani today."

"Wow, seriously?" Nat starts shoving the coffee warmers into the back of her car. "I can't believe she'd have the nerve to show up here."

"Yeah, the thing is . . ." I swallow hard. "She told me there was a note with the key."

Nat hesitates for a second and then goes back to fussing with things in her back seat. "Really?" The way that she refuses to meet my eyes hints at the truth.

"Nat."

She sighs and leans against the car. "Molly."

"Did you take it?"

"Why would I do that?" she asks, which is not a denial.

"I've been wondering that all day. Maybe you were . . . worried?"

"You're just going to automatically believe anything she says?"

"No. If you look me in the eye and tell me there was never a note, I'll believe you," I say, studying her face. "But if there was a note, I'd like you to be honest, because a lot of people got hurt and—"

"Would a note have made a difference?" she asks. "She gave you back the key! You didn't need to read any of her breakup bullshit when you were already hurting. I was just looking out for you, like I always do, Molly!"

I take a deep breath, trying to rein in the anger and hurt coursing through my veins. "She wasn't giving it back; she was giving me my own."

"What?" Nat asks, spinning to face me head-on. "No, she said that she was giving you space and—"

"What did you do, Nat?" I ask, my voice strained as I fight back the impending tears.

"Molly, I—"

"What did you do?!"

"Okay, I took the note! I wanted to give you a clean break, because a woman who leaves in the middle of the night is not the person for you! A woman who—"

"You don't get to decide that, Nat! What if I broke you and KiKi up for no reason! How would you feel then!"

"That's not the same."

"How isn't it the same!"

"Because KiKi and I are solid! We love each other, we're building a life together—"

"So was I! So was Shani!"

"You barely knew her! You always get so carried away so fast! Do you even know how many times I've skipped open calls because you needed me?! How many times you've called me crying and I've dropped everything to help you?"

"So, what? This was revenge? I never once asked you to do any of that! I would never *ever* want you to miss a casting call! Sometimes I feel like you focus so much on my mess, so you can feel better about yours?! 'Oh, at least I'm not as bad as Molly.' Is that it?"

"No. No! Of course not! I care about you. I'm genuinely happy to be there for you, I swear, but if I'm always left picking up your pieces, then you can't be surprised that when I saw a chance to make the inevitable breakup cleaner, I jumped on it."

"That was *not* your place! It wasn't the same old thing. I love her, Nat!"

"How do you know?"

"I just do!"

"You sound like a child!" she shouts. "Are you really taking her back? She dumped you in a note!"

"I don't think she did though," I say, honestly. "Why would she tell the truth about handing the note to you and then lie about what was in it? Give it to me. I want to read it for myself."

"I threw it away after I saw the key and the opening line about 'giving you space,'" she says, making air quotes. "It's long gone now, sorry."

"You really don't have any respect for me, do you?" I ask, my heart breaking for a totally different reason this time.

"Molly, you're my best friend."

"No, I'm like . . . your project or something. You don't even see me as an equal, so how can I be your friend?" I sneer. "This whole time, Nat, this whole time she thought I didn't want to be with her, *because of what you did.*"

Nat bites her lip. "I—"

"You need to go."

"Molly—"

"Please go. Thank you for your help today. I will cut you a check and put it in the mail tomorrow."

"You don't have to pay me. I was doing this as your friend."

"I do, actually," I say, taking a deep breath.

"Molly."

"She asked you to go," Shani says, walking up beside me. She looks nervous, like she's worried I'll send her away too. I give her a shaky smile—doing my best to reassure her.

Nat opens her mouth to say something to her, but then seems to think better of it. "Fine. I'll call you later." She's gone before I can reply, leaving me and Shani standing alone under the darkening sky.

"How long were you listening?" I ask quietly.

"Long enough," she says. "Sorry."

"Fair is fair, right? I eavesdropped on you and Otis." I try to sound light, but it doesn't really work.

"Molly," she says softly. "I—"

I hold my hand up gently. "Is it okay with you if I just take a second?" I ask quietly. "I'm glad you're here, and I definitely want to talk more, soon, *tonight*," I add, just in case she's thinking of taking off again. "Today was a lot of good and a little bad, and I need like some Tylenol and maybe to cry in the shower for a second before I'll be any use."

"Take all the time you need," Shani says, giving my hand a quick squeeze. "I'll head over to the staff house. If that's okay? Lochlin and Tyler will probably be hung up here for a couple more hours anyway."

"Yeah, I'll meet you over there," I say walking toward my porch.

"I'll be waiting," she says, a shy smile working its way across her face.

Chapter Thirty-Four

I give myself ten minutes in the shower to fall apart, head buried in my arms, as I sob against the tile wall.

Nat's the person I always called when I was upset; it's strange to be upset with *her*. It hurts to know what she did and hurts even more that she still thinks it was the right thing to do. I know that I'll call her in a few days, or she'll call me. There's too much history not to.

I hope she spends the ride home thinking it over and realizing that she was wrong, but who knows. If she doesn't, we can't stay friends, as much as that kills me to think about. I hope though, that we can set some boundaries and someday move on from this, but, like things with my mom, it's going to take time.

Time that I'm currently wasting crying instead of sorting things out with Shani.

What am I doing?

I turn off the water and rush through drying off and getting dressed. As I step out onto my porch, I hope she's there waiting for me, even though we said we'd meet at her place. That she somehow had read my mind and knew I was ready to talk.

But if we could read each other's minds, she would have known that I meant it when I told her that I loved her that day. And I would have understood that when she left, it wasn't forever.

"Shani?" I call out into the night, just in case, but there's no answer. Fear creeps up my spine. *What if she didn't believe me when I asked her to stay?*

I dart down my steps and make my way through the field. I forgot a flashlight, and of course there's barely any moon in the sky tonight. I stumble over nearly every rock and stick in the place, but I don't fall, and I never stop moving forward. By the time I make it to the other side of the pasture, I'm freezing from the cool summer night and my still wet hair, but all I can think about is how bad I want to get to her. How much she needs to know what she means to me.

I bolt to her front door, letting out a huge shivering breath but then hesitating before I knock. I hadn't planned out what I wanted to say to her, and now that I'm standing on her porch, I wish I had.

I pace around, my boots clacking on the wood planks, but I don't even care. I need to get this right. I have to. I should have written something down. I should have come ready. Maybe I should go back home, figure it out, and then come back. Yes, that's what I should do.

I'm definitely not procrastinating from nerves, definitely not.

I make it to the first step before she pulls her door open behind me.

"So that's it then?" Shani asks, and I turn around guiltily. "You're just going to pace around this porch and then leave without saying a word?"

"Sorry, I didn't mean to bother you."

"You're not," she says, tipping her head. "Missing you bothered me. Seeing you? Never."

I smile at how genuine she sounds and try to think of the perfect thing to say, but my mind has gone blank at the sight of her, reduced to longing and need.

"Why were you leaving, Molly?" she asks, her voice sad and strained.

Oh, does she think . . . ? *No.*

"I wanted to go get a piece of paper from my house to make some notes."

Shani licks her lips, her brows furrowing like she's trying and failing to understand what I'm talking about. I clear my throat and I try again.

"I was at my house, crying for lost time, and crying over not getting your letter and . . . I know you said you were going to wait here for me, but when I opened the door, I hoped you would be on my porch—like that you had figured it out before me how much I still love you. But you weren't there, so I—"

Shani rushes toward me. She takes my face in both of her hands and kisses me hard, cutting off my speech completely. My hand tangles in her hair as I pull her even closer, scared of ever letting go.

Shani is here. Shani is kissing me, even without any flowery speeches, and I get to kiss her back.

I pour every ounce of my feelings into chasing her lips, her tongue, her skin and pray she can feel how much I mean it. I've missed the way she tastes so much I can't stand it.

Home. I think. *Shani.* I think.

She pulls away and rests her forehead against mine but only for a moment, and then she steps back, blushing. God, I've missed the way she blushes. She pokes her tongue into her cheek and looks away before meeting my eyes again.

"I think we've had enough notes, Molly. I just want you."

I grin and grab onto the collar of her shirt, walking her back against the door the way she always loved to do to me. She hits it with a little thud and a laugh, and I kiss the corner of her lips because I've missed her laughter. I want to swallow it up and keep it inside of me forever.

"Say it again?" she asks, her voice rough and low.

"I love you," I say, nuzzling against the side of her neck. "I love you, and I'm so sorry for my part in what we've both been going through. I didn't know. I didn't know." My voice cracks, and Shani holds me tighter as I bury my face against her. "I'm so sorry, Shani."

"Shh, shh, shhh," she says. "I'm sorry too. This is all my fault, I should have—"

"No, we both—"

"Baby, you're freezing. Let's talk about this inside." She reaches behind her and pushes the door open, holding on to me with her other hand firmly, like she's worried I might disappear.

Her house looks just the same as she left it. The air feels a little stale, and a little cold, like she might have opened some windows for a moment when she came back inside. There's a fire lit already, and I walk over to stand in front of it as she bumps up the heat even more.

"Hang on, don't go anywhere," she says, and disappears into

her bedroom. She comes back a few seconds later with our giant fleece blanket. The one from our most perfect night. I want to cry at the sight of it, but we owe each other more than just falling apart.

Shani wraps me up in it and moves back like she wants to give me space, but I've had more than enough of that. I reach out my arms, holding the blanket open like wings, and wrap her up in it too. She's trapped now, pressed against me. She smiles, clearly happy about this turn of events.

"I missed you," she says, looking me in the eye. "I'm sorry I left and that I didn't call. I should have known right away that something was wrong. I guess I always felt like you were too good to be true. It was easy to believe you were done with me and it shouldn't have been."

I shake my head. "I should have known that you wouldn't just get up and leave me in the middle of the night without even a goodbye."

"And I should've realized that you don't just give up, ever, on anything." She laughs. "It's one of the best and worst things about you."

I wipe my nose, trying to get the tears to stop in earnest now. "I *am* pretty stubborn," I say, thinking about how Lochlin made me see the strength in that, but also the limits.

"Yeah, and smart, and funny, beautiful, tenacious," she says. "You thought I took off on you, and instead of falling apart, you pulled off one of the best barrel racing shows I've been to in a long time. Lochlin told me about your deal tonight. You get to keep this place. That's . . . that's amazing, Molly."

"He really didn't tell you before this?" I ask, arching my eyebrows.

"He really didn't tell me," she says. "Your deal with him has nothing to do with me. If anything, after I found out, I was kind of hoping you'd hit a snag and it would give me an excuse to get back here."

"Lochlin did suggest I call you for help setting it up, but . . ."

"So stubborn," she says, tapping her forehead against mine gently, with a smile.

I kiss her again and then lean back. "I couldn't have done this without your brother's help. He's an impressive businessman," I say.

Shani tilts her head. "Do you mind if we stop talking about my brother right now?"

I laugh. "Why's that?"

She trails kisses up my neck. "Because I'd like to take you to bed, if you'll have me, and I don't want you to be thinking about him when I do."

"I better have you," I tease, shivering when her lips meet the base of my jaw. "I walked all the way over here, didn't I?"

"Yeah, but then you tried to leave, so." She takes a deep breath.

"I'm not doing that ever again and you better quit doing it too." I smile, leaning away just enough for our eyes to meet. "You're stuck with me now."

"Promise?" she asks.

"Yes," I say, my freezing fingers trailing under the bottom of her shirt until she sucks in a breath. I peel it up over her head, chasing away the cold with my mouth.

She sighs, letting me take control, but just for a moment. And then she's walking me back, swallowing my giggles as my calves hit the couch. She makes quick work of undressing me, peppering my body with kisses and whispers of "I love you" and promises of forever, as she slips down between my legs.

And yes, I think, *yes. Who says you can never go home again?*

Acknowledgments

Creating this book has been such a fun ride, but I could not do it alone!

My deepest thanks to:

My agent, Sara Crowe, who constantly blows me away with her dedication, knowledge, and business instincts; along with my editors, Sylvan Creekmore, who helped make this book shine, and Madelyn Blaney, who enthusiastically took us over the finish line.

And to my copyeditor, Nancy Fischer, and proofreader, Heather Bosch.

To Tess Day, Kalie Barnes-Young, and DJ DeSmyter for all of your efforts behind the scenes to make this book a success! To Monika Roe and Diahann Sturge-Campbell for creating a truly gorgeous cover and interior. And to the entire Avon team, for giving this book such a great home.

To all of my friends who have cheered me on and been there for me, especially Gina Vendetti, who helped me fact check all things horse and riding related, the XC and soccer moms who have stepped up for my family whenever I had work trips or a tight deadline, Erik J Brown, who always has good game and movie recs (except for that one time) and didn't make fun of me too badly when he realized I accidentally played the majority of RE8 without knowing I had a map. (Turns out, it is not an exceptionally slow-paced and difficult game at all!) And to Rory, Kelsey, Charlie, Dahlia, and The Coven, for being absolute rockstars. I would be utterly lost without all of you!

And to my ever-supportive family who has been there for me for all the ups and downs that come with being an author . . . and regularly reminds me there is a whole world outside of my Microsoft word docs, even if it doesn't always feel like it.

And last but certainly not least, a sincerely massive thank you to my readers, along with all of the booksellers, bloggers, booktokkers, and bookstagrammers. I wouldn't be here without you. Thank you. Thank you. Thank you.

About the Author

Jennifer Dugan is the author of the young adult novels *Melt with You, Some Girls Do, Verona Comics, Hot Dog Girl,* and the adult romance *Love at First Set.* She is also the author of the YA graphic novel *Coven.* She lives in upstate New York with her family.

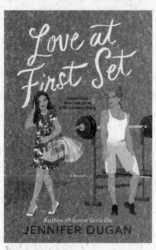